# The Cornish Village School –
## Second Chances

KITTY WILSON

# The Cornish Village School

SECOND CHANCES

CANELO

First published in the United Kingdom in 2018 by Canelo

This edition published in the United Kingdom in 2019 by

Canelo Digital Publishing Limited
57 Shepherds Lane
Beaconsfield, Bucks HP9 2DU
United Kingdom

Print ISBN 978 1 78863 576 9
Ebook ISBN 978 1 78863 117 4

Look for more great books at www.canelo.co

Printed and bound in Great Britain by Clays Ltd, Elcograf S.p.A.

*Namdi* ♥

# Chapter One

Sylvie felt Sam's little hand grasp hers even tighter as they rounded the corner by the pub and turned down past the butcher's. The sand was spilling out onto the pavement as they approached the beach, the golden grains signalling their arrival long before they set foot on the beach proper. She knew, if she glanced at him, his little teeth would be clenched with excitement.

They had been here every sunny day throughout summer and most of spring, and if truth be told they'd been here on the odd rainy one too. Sylvie had a feeling they could come every day for ever and neither she nor Sam would ever get bored. In fact, that was her plan.

The beach opened up wide in front of them, and as they reached the bit where pavement ended and beach began, they kicked off their flip-flops in a tradition they had built ever since Sam could walk. A quickly embedded ritual meant that the two of them bent over at the same time to pick their shoes up and glanced at each other and smiled. It was a shared signal that their beach day had started and that the next couple of hours would be nothing but heavenly.

The two of them had developed the perfect day over the last couple of months. Chores in the morning, when Sylvie would help her uncle out with the day-to-day running of the farm and Sam would be expected to get on with his work too. Work that largely involved his action figures and a city he would construct out of blocks, carefully colour coding each bit. And then as the sun began to fade from its midday high the two of them would grab their beach stuff, piled by the door next to the wellies and walking sticks, and make their way into the village.

Sylvie knew the sting of sunburn – as a child she merely had had to look out of the window and she'd fry. With Sam sharing her freckles, red (really red) hair and the pale skin that came with it she made sure that there was no way her child would experience blisters raised on his ears as her uncle used to out on the farm all day, or toss and turn at night – too burnt to sleep.

The spades, body-boards and buckets would be grabbed, the swim shoes and the rash vest dried out by the Aga from the day before, and the two of them would slather each other in factor fifty, with special attention paid to the neck and the ears. Fruit and water would be thrown into a bag along with a book each and then the two would race to the car, spades dropped to the floor as they put seat belts on and turned the music up loud, singing all of Sam's favourite songs on the short journey from Lovage Farm into Penmenna. Sometimes as they belted it out together she thought she might love 'Wheels on the Bus' more now than she ever did at four. Other times she suspected she might hit saturation point Very Soon Indeed.

Back on the beach now, they felt the sand squidge between their toes as they headed to their favourite spot, getting damper and squidgier the closer they came to the water. She raised a hand to a group of mums from the village who were just leaving, and again to Alice, who was sitting at the foot of the cliff, engrossed in her book. Her heart melted as Sam saw their little spot – tucked away next to a natural stream running from the cliff straight down to the sea, perfect for keeping their water cool in the sun – and ran towards it. He was more confident here than anywhere else, the shadow recently cast over the farm still failing to shift completely.

Happy to let go of her hand to shake his towel out and claim his spot, he stopped short as she watched and turned back around to face her, perplexion written all across his little freckled face.

For the whole of summer that spot had been theirs. At no point, even at the peak of Regatta week, had they turned up to find the crime of all crimes committed – someone else's towel. But today there was. Two to be precise. One great big luxurious one that looked like it should be rolled into a glamorous curl on some chichi hotel bed and one covered with little foxes' faces, next to a small matching bag. Cute. But not theirs.

Sam looked at her for answers, and she was tempted to pick them up and place them just over there, a couple of feet away. Or perhaps she could chuck them behind the cluster of boulders piled up near the entrance to the cave. Or, if she could persuade Sam to close his eyes, she could peg it down to the shoreline super-fast, throw them out to sea and then come back and pretend she didn't know what had happened. Although, of course, she would not do either. Instead she would use it as time to educate Sam about public spaces and the need to share them, no matter how personal they felt, how much you saw them as yours.

'It's OK, Mum. We can just go the other side of the stream.'

'Plan, Sam. Like the way you're thinking.' OK, so the four-year-old didn't need the lesson, that would just be her.

The two tiptoed through the little stream, their mouths opening as the cold of the water hit their toes and made them dance through, making high-pitched ow-ing noises, before laying their towels down in the not-quite-as-nice-but-really-not-remarkably-different spot.

Sam immediately started stripping down to his trunks and gently lowered himself onto his own towel, pulled on his beach shoes carefully and then jumped to attention.

'OK, I'll go find some stones.' He looked longingly at the slate patches on the beach, nestling next to the boulders. The other side of the strange towels. 'Do you think they'd mind?'

'I'm sure they wouldn't? Go on, I'll keep my eyes peeled. And anyway, you know the rule – grab the moment!'

Sam liked to build a couple of slate towers once he had got himself changed. He was a funny little thing, fond of routine and order, set in his ways. He would start with the tower, then they'd go down for a paddle, starting in the stream and heading to the shoreline, where they'd jump waves and slowly-slowly get a little deeper each time. He was happy past his knees now but Sylvie was hoping to get him in a little further. He had swimming lessons at the leisure centre in Roscarrock but the difference between the safety of a pool and the wildness of the waves, even on a millpond-smooth day, was great. The swimming pool wasn't salty brine, riddled with seaweed and probable sea monsters.

As she watched him collect his first slate, she saw a man approach. Tall, imposing even from a distance, his dark head bowed as he chatted away to a girl who looked about Sam's age, and was leaping gazelle-like at his side. They were coming around the cave mouth and heading towards the towels.

She quickly diverted her gaze as he looked up, but she felt his eyes sweep across and dismiss her. Good. The last thing she wanted was interaction. This was her and Sam's special bit of the day. The time when she didn't worry about money, or next steps, or moving out from the farm and letting Tom move his girlfriend in, which she was fairly sure was his plan.

Sam, seeing the arrival of the towel-owners, had thrown his usual caution to the winds and instead of carefully bringing back one or two slates, was clasping three bits to his chest, with one more tucked under his chin. His eyes were wide open as he made his getaway, beach shoes saving him from freezing toes in the stream as he headed purposefully back to his mother. Looking at the panic on his face, she was fairly sure he didn't have a career in burglary in his future.

'Phew.' He clattered the slates at her feet as he let out an over-expressive sigh of relief. 'That should do for a minute.' He flicked a quick look over his shoulder as the two approached.

'Good job. We can get more in a minute, if you want?'

'Hmm, let's see how we go.'

As the man reached his towel she experienced a jolt of familiarity that made no sense, but was there all the same –

quiet and determined and very present. She couldn't place where she could possibly know him from; he certainly wasn't from the village, she would have definitely noticed him before. Everyone would have noticed him before!

He exuded an animal magnetism, sleek and dangerous like a jungle cat, and yet she didn't feel in the slightest bit fearful, just intrigued and certain that she was meant to meet him, here and today. She felt her tummy flip a little with lust. Wow! She had forgotten what instantaneous attraction felt like – the last time her tummy had flipped was after an ex-boyfriend had drunkenly cooked some shellfish in a kind of (failed) rapprochement.

The man pushed his floppy jet hair out of his eyes as the small girl tried to stop him from sitting by divebombing onto the swish towel, her cornrows waving as she did so. Next she starfished out and smiled up at him with a real ner-ner-ner-watcha-gonna-do look on her face, before flipping her own foxy towel out of the way so he had no options left but sand and slate.

Sylvie couldn't help but smile at her mischief, whereas when she flicked a look over to her son he looked entranced – half horrified by the girl's behaviour and half enchanted. It would appear that both strangers were capable of weaving a spell.

The man cast a quick glance at Sylvie, a smile teasing the corners of his mouth, a see-what-I-have-to-contend-with look, conspiratorial. Bugger, that made her tingle all the way to her toes, and she had been fairly sure that side of her had died shortly before childbirth, and very definitely after!

For goodness' sake, she didn't even feel fizz when Idris Elba was on TV any more. And now she was virtually squirming around in the sand because a stranger to the village had stood within twenty feet of her. Please God, don't let him speak – Lord knows what she'd do then. Present responses indicated there was a strong chance it would involve forgetting her son was present and hurling her bikini top to the four winds.

She felt herself flush at the mere thought of it. Gah, she had a habit of blushing at the most inopportune moments – she really hoped her body wasn't about to start this nonsense again. Please don't look over here again, she mentally begged, forcing on her jolliest tone in an attempt at self-distraction.

'Let's build these then, shall we?' She smiled across at Sam, willing him to collude so she could get her head back into motherhood rather than unexpected lustful thoughts over strange, and presumably married, men.

Sam, apparently unaware that his mother was under-going some kind of freaky sexual transformation, dragged his eyes from the girl and back to her as he silently nodded.

The minute Sylvie leant forward and watched Sam carefully stack the second slate upon the first one, the girl started shuffling forward on her bottom towards the stream, bringing the towel with her.

'Whoa, now you need to get up, you'll soak that. Come on, up you get, and give me the towel back.' Sylvie didn't look around when the man spoke, but there was something familiar, again only just, about his voice as well. His tone might have been gentle but it had an underlying steel to it which made Sylvie want to obey immediately. She was intrigued to know if it had as much power on the little girl as it seemed to on her. But there was no way she was going to turn and look.

She didn't need to – she heard a high-pitched giggle and the sound of a thwack as the towel, she guessed, was hurled into the air and landed.

Sam broke out into a delighted guffaw and despite her best intentions Sylvie felt her head spin around, and there, slightly less imposing now, sat the most tempting man Sylvie had seen in years with a luxury towel draped across his head and shoulders and a shocked expression on his face, whilst two small children stood nearby with tears streaming down their cheeks.

He shrugged and smiled as he removed the towel, catching Sylvie's eye and sharing a what-can-you-do moment with her as she found herself smiling back.

'I'm Ellie.' The girl had taken advantage of the shared mirth to get through the stream and move closer to Sam. 'What you doing?' She had a musical lilt to her voice that spoke of another country, perhaps more than one, that Sylvie couldn't quite identify. Possibly a French accent, maybe a hint of an African dialect, she couldn't pinpoint it.

'You can help if you like. I'm just building a tower here. See how many you can build up before it topples.'

'But you don't have many.'

'I do.'

'No, you don't.'

'I do. I've got one, two… um, lots, haven't I, Mum?'

'You've got one, two, three, four.' Sylvie counted them out. 'Four is lots, you're four. But you could get more if you wanted. Maybe Ellie—' she smiled at the girl, including her in their circle '—could help you get some.'

'I could. I'm nearly five. I can count a lot more.' She nodded violently, about twenty nods, all in quick succession.

'Hmm.' Sam didn't sound particularly impressed. Sylvie wished she could shake off the spell cast quite as easily.

'Come on. We can do it over there, and then we can build lots, lots and lots, like maybe even…' She cast around for her biggest number. '…maybe even twelveteen.' She held her hand out, with the openness of the truly confident. 'Come on.'

Sam looked at her with big eyes as she gave him an even bigger smile, and then checked what his mum thought. Sylvie gave him an encouraging nod and he crossed the stream and allowed himself to be led to the cave mouth where the two of them started to round up slates and build them into towers.

The man smiled across at Sylvie as the children played.

'Hi, I'm Alex. It's good for her to have someone her own age to play with.'

'Hi, Alex. Sylvie. It is. Sam is usually quite shy, so it's nice to see.'

'Ha! Ellie is about the absolute opposite of shy. She's a whirling dervish of a child. I think this is the most I've seen her concentrate in ages.' He couldn't help but smile as he glanced across at his daughter, her little pink tongue poked just out of her mouth as she piled another slate on top of an already teetering pile.

His indulgent parental smile was contagious, spreading to Sylvie's lips as well.

'She's certainly got a cracking aim.'

'She has. That towel hit its mark perfectly.'

'It suited you.'

'You think I suit the draped-towel look?' His eyebrows were raised pretty high.

'I think you could probably get away with it.' Mind you, she thought, he could probably get away with anything and still look pretty damn hot. Oh God, she realized how sexual that all sounded. He was going to think she was trying to pick him up on the beach in front of their children. Worse still was the fact that if he had made her feel a bit of a twinkle before, now super-close up and talking to him, that was making her feel downright combustible. If she thought a mild blush was embarrassing, imagine what it would be like just to suddenly burst into flames – that would be so much worse. He'd have to fill the children's plastic buckets up with seawater, maybe make a line down to the shore, and come and douse her.

She quickly checked out his hands, just to see how many primary-coloured buckets he could manage at a time – quite a lot, she decided, they were large hands, with something very masculine about them, hands of experience – and felt herself flush even more. Great. She might have escaped bursting into fire but there was a definite flame creeping across her face, down her neck and probably – she didn't dare look – all across her chest as well. A bright red blush always looked so attractive juxtaposed against her very ginger hair. And now she was worrying about looking attractive. This was mortifying! What had happened to her in the last twenty minutes? Come back, vaguely asexual Sylvie, I was much more comfortable with you, she pleaded silently, whilst reminding herself to tear her glance away from his hands before he had her arrested for overtly predatory behaviour.

This was absolutely ridiculous. Why was this happening? Admittedly the quota of dishy men around here was shockingly low. Most of them smelt of cow or three hours in the pub, but surely she could trust her hormones not to go into mad overdrive the minute a vaguely civilized man wandered into her eyeline.

Actually, the vicar was gorgeous, far better looking than a man of God had the right to be, but he didn't make her fluttery inside, and the butcher was quite dishy but she had felt mildly repulsed when he asked her out for a drink the other month, so it couldn't just be a good-looking-man thing. It must run deeper than that. Whatever it was she really needed to get back to reality – who was this new woman and what had she done with her mind?

As she looked up it would appear Alex might be asking the same question, his eyebrows raised quizzically at her. What had she done now? What if he was familiar because he was like that bloke off the telly and could read her mind? Maybe the sand could just open up now and swallow her, or a nicely timed tsunami could just swing on by.

Glancing at the sea, there was no sign of a massive, life-threatening wave on the horizon, which she was supposed was a good thing. Oh shit, he was still smiling, and waiting.

'Sorry, I didn't catch that?' Surely the safest response.

'I was just saying that the towel look might not catch on at work.'

'No, very true, employers are funny about that sort of thing. Expect you to be fully and appropriately dressed. Madness.' What was she saying? At least if she carried on burbling nonsense he'd eventually edge his towel to a safer part of the beach, the bit this madwoman and her child didn't occupy.

'Yup, I have to admit it is lovely not having to rush from pillar to post all day long. I can't remember feeling this relaxed in a long time.'

Sylvie looked up at the seagulls swooping overhead and breathed the salty air in deep. He was right. This was a whole different life from her old one, and a damn sight more relaxing – it was just a shame it might not be sustainable. However, worrying about that now wasn't a sensible option either. She'd shelve that for tonight when she could gaze out at the moon wishing sleep would hurry up and flicker its fingers over her, just for a couple of hours.

'It's magical here. It slows you right down. Are you here on holiday?' She was itching to ask about his wife but knew that dropping it casually into conversation would alert him to her curiosity. And that was not a path she wanted to wander down.

'Yeah, we thought we'd come down for a week, catch up with a friend that moved down last year. It's been lovely. I can see why he decided to stay.'

'Cornwall's a funny place, it's said it will either welcome you with open arms or spit you back out fairly quickly. You'd be amazed at the people who come down here thinking it's perfect but find that once the holiday vibe has worn off they just aren't suited to it at all, and then for others it's instant. Like this is the place they should be and they've been waiting all their lives for it.'

'Ha! And I'm guessing you're the latter?'

'Oh no, I'm born and bred. Eighth generation, I think, if not more. But I did escape for a short bit. I think everyone should. It can be quite insular down here. But then, well, you know, I wanted to raise Sam as I had been, on the beach, buckets and spades, the only threat being pasty-stealing seagulls rather than gang culture and knife crime.'

'I've only been here a couple of days, but you're right, those things do seem to be distinctly lacking from Penmenna. It seems as if nothing could disturb the peace here, and that's coming from someone who has...' He paused. '...well, never mind.'

Before Sylvie could decode what he was possibly alluding to, or indeed press him on it, the peace of Penmenna was very much disturbed.

'Cheese an' Chrise!' Ellie stood, hands on her hips next to a large pile of tumbled slates. Her stance very much suited to a fishwife of old, with her hands on her hips and fury writ across her face. A scarf tied in a knot and perched upon her head would have completed the look perfectly. Whilst Sam stood next to her with that slightly amazed look that he seemed to have adopted since meeting her and Sylvie was beginning to worry might become permanent. She hoped that the wind didn't change quickly.

'Ellie!' Alex leapt to his feet and headed straight over to his daughter.

'Did you see that? We worked so hard, didn't we, Sam?'

'We did.' Sam nodded intently. He was clearly going to be #TeamEllie on this one.

'I'm sure you did, but that's not really the point, the point is that...'

Sylvie tried to cover up her smile. She knew she'd have to be #TeamAlex, simply because of the Parent Code, but secretly she was with Ellie all the way. It was healthy to express frustration, but the truth was she was glad it wasn't Sam being so terribly healthy.

'We worked really hard and then the buggering thing fell over! What's a girl supposed to do with that, huh?' Her arms uncrossed as she spread them wide, palms upturned in a universal what's-a-girl-supposed-to-do-with-that shrug.

That was it! Sylvie broke the code and dissolved into a giggle – only a very short one – but a noticeably obvious giggle all the same. She liked Ellie.

Alex threw her a desperate look over his shoulder, to which she did a mini shrug of her own, and then waited to see what he'd do next. She was clearly failing at the parents-stick-together thing, but she was as intrigued as Sam as to who would win this particular battle. And her money wasn't on the six-foot-two man in front of her.

'Ellie, I see that your tower fell, and I know you worked hard at it, but you just said some very naughty words…'

'Very naughty.' Sam decided to chime in and Ellie shot him an amused look, whereas Sylvie winced a bit.

'And no matter how upset you are, you can't use words like that.'

'Which ones?' The young girl managed the perfect combination of confusion and challenge.

Sylvie no longer liked Ellie, she thought she might just love her a little bit instead.

'I'm not going to repeat them. I'm sure you know which ones were naughty.'

'Does it mean I don't get an ice cream if I don't know which ones are naughty? 'Cause I do really want ice cream and you did promise.'

'Um…'

'And I don't think I could say anything *that* naughty. Although if I did then I didn't mean to so I still get ice cream, right? I bet you love ice cream too, don't you?' Ellie turned to Sam to back her up. He nodded frantically. Alex looked as if wasn't quite sure what to do next and had a horrid feeling this whole discussion was going to end with both children being rewarded with a double cornet whilst he apologized. 'See, Sam loves ice cream and he didn't say any naughty words, did you? Did he?'

Sure enough, fifteen minutes later the four of them were sitting together, on the cave side of the stream, eating ice cream whilst Sylvie tried to reassure Alex that Cheese, regardless of intent, wasn't actually a swear word and that at four they were largely mimicking. From what it sounded like – they had been subjected to a long, largely nonsensical monologue on the way to the kiosk as to why none of this was Ellie's fault and it was something to do with a show called *Real Housewives of Something or Other* that someone called Angileeena liked – Ellie wasn't really swearing, merely copying expressive behaviour which demonstrated that she was terribly bright.

Alex had responded with a look of complete disbelief before turning back to his ice cream, whilst Sylvie had sat there, sun beating down on her face and legs, with a tub of mint choc chip and a feeling of smug relief that Sam was far too shy to do anything embarrassing.

The rest of the afternoon was heavenly, as long as Sylvie didn't allow herself to look at Alex for more than five seconds. This made answering questions whilst appearing to be a normal person fairly difficult, but she thought she might be pulling it off.

Sam had broken from routine and ran, yes, ran, down to the beach with Ellie and played the jumping-the-wave game with her instead of doing it clutching Sylvie's hand, whilst the two grown-ups sat at the tideline and talked about the things parenting manuals never tell you. By the end of it she had learnt lots of things about Alex – that he had never realized that the trauma of buying shoes for small children was worse than having a root canal in a third-world nation; that he still didn't understand why clothes manufacturers made crop tops with glitter lips on for three-year-olds, noisy three-year-olds who apparently had to have glitter-lips clothing or they would fall to the floor screaming as if they had recently been beaten with a metal pole; and that he was genuinely worried that if he heard the theme tune to *Peppa Pig* one more time his ears would bleed, largely because he'd be tempted to hack them off himself – but still she didn't know what he did for a living, where he lived and what his relationship status was. Not that she was interested – she had more than enough to contend with at the moment without introducing a man into her life – but it was always worth knowing these things.

He on the other hand had learnt all sorts about her – more than once she had cursed her all-too-ready tongue as personal detail tripped over personal detail whilst they spoke. She didn't know how he did it but he seemed to have a skill for getting her to impart information that she was not normally prepared to share with anybody – let alone a complete stranger on the beach, wearing nothing but his shorts, and who she was never going to see again. Although perhaps that was why. There was a catharsis about pouring out stories to a complete stranger, especially when you had been living in a small community for a while. Small communities meant very few secrets – usually the person you were talking to had already heard a lavishly embroidered version of the tale you were trying to impart and much preferred their garnished version to your unvarnished one.

People began to move from the beach, families gathering up their beach clutter as they started to head home. Teenagers with disposable barbecues and bags that clinked with cheap wine and even cheaper cider drifted onto the sands and started walking to the furthest corners. It had been a lovely day, and though she wasn't working tonight, Sylvie knew she needed to head home and get Sam fed and to bed. Although the whole summer had been made of beach days, today had been different, like a holiday.

She slowly started to pack up and gave Sam a five-minute warning. He developed a slightly mutinous look, which she quelled with an eyebrow.

'Wow. That's impressive. I need to learn that.'

'A little bit of practice and I'm sure you'll be fine. Thank you for a lovely day, it's been a pleasure to meet the both of you.'

'You too, and lovely to meet you, Sam.'

Alex stretched out his hand to shake Sam's, only to have the small boy – hat askew and looking like he wished he had the guts to be more defiant, more like his new friend – drop his bucket and spade, ignore Alex's hand and cling instead to his leg, turning his face up to Alex's as a flower does to the sun.

With his eyes as wide as they could go, his very best puppy-dog eyes that had never failed him before, he pleaded with Alex non-verbally. Which unfortunately meant neither adult could actually work out what he was pleading for. But he did look like he was building up to a whimper.

Sylvie took control of the situation with her mummiest tone.

'Come on, Sam.'

It didn't seem to work.

What next? If she tried to pry his fingers off Alex that would involve touching the man's leg, and as enjoyable as his company had been, she felt that was a little too intimate for a first meeting.

'Sam!' She tried her fiercest tone next.

He clung harder.

'Hey, little man. It's been great meeting you, but you will need to let me go at some point.'

'Come home with us,' Sam entreated, but very quietly.

'What was that?' Alex bent down to see if he could hear clearer.

'Come home with us. You can be my new daddy, and Ellie can be my sister, and you can be Mummy's boyfriend, she really needs one of those. She's never had one, you know, never, never ever.' Sam had made his voice louder this time, and several people on the beach turned around to see what this was about. Some gave reassuring smiles, some just smirked. Sylvie hated them. This would be all around the village by teatime.

However, if she thought she had blushed earlier that was nothing compared to the scarlet hue that was currently overwhelming her, whilst directing her best 'kill' looks at the smirkers. From the tips of her hair to the ends of the toes she could feel the heat.

She knew that had it been anyone else she would have struggled not to laugh herself so she couldn't really bear the other beachgoers any ill will. But to have been outed in front of this man, and the whole beach, as a desperate, sex-starved, and probably shrivelled and dried-up, old prude was more embarrassment than she could take in a day. Especially one so unattractive and inept that she needed an infant to find her dates. Intimate or not, she was unfurling those bloody fingers, no matter how cute (and getting less so by the minute) the boy attached to them was and getting him in the sodding car before he could say anything else!

'That's a great idea! Oh, can we, Daddy, can we? Can we?'

The only positive to this was that Alex was looking as uncomfortable as she was.

'Um… that's a lovely idea, Sam, Ellie, but not um…' He exchanged a look with Sylvie as the whole of her insides curled up in mortification. His look said that he couldn't answer that question without being insulting so was completely stuck for an acceptable answer. She was half tempted to stick around and see how he dealt with it but her own embarrassment was too strong.

Trying not to pull at the hairs on his legs as she unwrapped the suddenly remarkably strong and uncharacteristically difficult four-year-old boy off this full-grown man's body was quite tricky. She would have been proud of herself for managing it had she not been too busy clasping Sam's form to her, gathering all the bags with her one remaining hand and racing off the beach, merely shouting, 'Enjoy the rest of your holiday,' at the man and the little girl left standing, staring after her. Thank goodness she would never, *ever* have to see them again.

# Chapter Two

'Daddy met a mummy, Daddy met a mummy!' sang Ellie as she raced through the big front door, left ajar for her, and through to the sleek kitchen where Chase was doing something clever with vegetables as Angelina poured them both a drink.

'Never know what's going to wash up onshore here, but even in my book, that's pretty quick work! Here, I'm guessing you may want one of these.' Angelina smiled, and as an automatic reaction to having an attractive man in the vicinity flipped her perfectly groomed blonde hair over her shoulder and twinkled as she passed a glass to Alex who, a couple of beats behind his daughter, had entered the kitchen looking a bit frazzled.

'Tell them, Daddy, tell them!'

'Hmm, that's not all Angelina and I have to discuss, Ellie, if you remember?'

Ellie looked blank and then sidled up to Angelina, trying to worm the glass out of her grown-up friend's hands. 'Can I have some? Is it gin? I like that, don't I?'

'No, not in front of Daddy!'

'Are you joking? You'd better not have been giving her alcohol!'

'Relax, it was just a little taste on my finger. We do grown-up-girl things, don't we, Ellie, when we're together. It's not all drink-based. I was going to teach her how to shave her legs later – it's never too early to perfect these skills. And she's very bright, she much prefers Hendrick's to Gordon's and has quite grown-up taste in television, you know?'

Angelina took an appraising glance at Ellie, winked at her and turned back to Alex. 'I expect there's nothing this girl couldn't do. I had a phone call from my agent this morning about a new circus-based reality show, look at her...' Angelina pinched Ellie's cheek in an affectionate, not a hurty, way, '...she'd look great coming out of a cannon. Neat little braids flying and sequinny spangled leotards.'

'You and I need to talk.'

'I always find talking is desperately overrated.'

'Stop winding him up, Ange, he's been known to take men out with a Vulcan death grip in times of high stress, and I think this might turn into one of these times if you don't stop!' Chase grinned good-naturedly at his girlfriend. They had been together a few months now and Chase had confided to Alex that he was never sure when she was teasing or whether she was as extreme as her words implied. He chose to believe it was the former – otherwise there was a chance he was dating a narcissistic, delusional psychopath – a chance that her brother Matt had assured him, and anyone else who would listen, was a strong possibility.

'What's a death grip, Daddy, huh? Teach me, teach me!'

'A death grip is something that happens to little girls who don't put away their beach stuff the minute they get home.'

'Well, then, why didn't I get one yesterday? I want one!' Her voice took on a whiny tone.

'Hey, hey, you don't really. Daddy is just teasing. Here, have this and then you can go for a bath.' Chase slid a cheese-and-tomato omelette he appeared to have just whisked up whilst they had been talking onto her plate, and then fetched a bowl of chop-chop salad and placed it to the side. 'And I know how much you like this. I even put pomegranate in, just how you like. Can you see it?'

Ellie grinned up at him and wrinkled her nose. She loved it here. It was the most settled she had been since the adoption, and they had only been here a few days. Alex was discovering that parenting was a darn sight easier with your friends involved. There was a Nigerian proverb that said it took a village to raise a child, and if this was the difference two friends (well, one friend and his rather alarming new girlfriend) made then he could see that with a whole village it would be a breeze. He knew also that he was going to have to make a decision soon, find somewhere to settle. The nomadic nature of his professional life might have been what brought him into Ellie's life but he was fairly sure it was unsuited for keeping her there. Her night terrors were lessening all the time and considerably so since they had arrived at Chase's, thus he imagined a settled life and routine would be the quickest path to recovery.

Ellie didn't look particularly traumatized now, although her face did wrinkle as she tasted the odd bit of celery snuck into her chop-chop salad, but it wasn't stopping her from wolfing her supper down as if she hadn't seen food for three weeks.

'Can Angileeena give me my bath tonight? I'll be extra good and won't even make a mess or nothin'?'

'That depends largely on whether Angileeena will be using gin or razorblades anywhere near the tub tonight?'

Angelina looked at him and grinned. He still hadn't quite got her measure yet, and he was particularly good at reading people and situations. He had to be.

'No, not tonight. I'll be saving them for the next time Chase tries to take me fishing.'

'Are you happy to give her a bath?' Alex mouthed this over Ellie's head. Angelina didn't look the mumsy type, in fact she looked about as opposite as one could get, but for some reason Ellie had taken to her and spent far too much of her day chanting 'Angileeena says...' which was usually followed up with something so heinous that he expected Dr Barnardo's to pound through the door the second she stopped speaking. They hadn't yet, but it could still happen. Angelina nodded back.

'She'll have to hurry up with that food though. I reckon I only have about ten minutes of nice left in me today, and that's drawing on tomorrow's reserves.'

Ellie walloped the last bit of omelette into her mouth and jumped up, then quickly stuck her finger in the salad bowl and scooped out a bit more.

'Come on then. Let's go!' She jumped around on the kitchen floor, hopping from foot to foot.

'Angelina, is that top silk? It could get a bit splashy.' Chase had been on bath duty the day before and Alex knew that 'a bit splashy' was characteristically understated.

'Well, I'm hardly going to be wearing polyester, am I? God, you ask some daft questions sometimes.'

'I told you not to call me that!' Chase shouted after her as she left the kitchen, Ellie hoppity-skipping in her wake, and gleefully imitating the harrumph that Angelina responded to Chase with, all the way down the hallway.

Alex watched as Chase tidied up the omelette mess and then gathered a stack of ingredients from the super-sized American fridge that dominated the kitchen with its cherry-red door and began washing and chopping.

'You weren't this skilled when we were at school and we had to live off oranges and toast stolen from the sixth form. It always amazes me how good you are in the kitchen.'

'I know. An all-round renaissance man, who would have thought it? Especially as, let's face it, our school was all about churning out entitled Neanderthals who could run a country but not wash a dish.'

'You've let the side down by being such a thoroughly decent human being.'

'I figured someone needed to balance out Hector!'

'Ha! I haven't seen him for years, are you still in touch?'

'Of course, he's in Morocco at the moment. Actually he's coming to stay next month.'

'Really? For all his evil, I'd like to catch up.'

'Well do, then.'

'I won't be here next month.'

'Interestingly, I wanted to talk to you about that. Maybe you could be. More importantly, maybe you should be.'

'Eh?'

'You surprised us all when you adopted Ellie. None of us saw that coming.'

Alex grimaced. Neither had he, truth be told, but life threw curveballs and that day, the day he had set eyes on Ellie, turned out to be one of those times.

He had been covering a story in South Sudan, about the civil war that had been raging through the country and the ceasefire that had just been agreed. It turned out to be the first of many. As Central African correspondent for a British news organization, Alex was used to being in dangerous situations, very dangerous situations, and relying upon his instincts to keep him and his team safe.

However, as he was getting older, he was beginning to wonder how much longer he could, or should, keep doing the things that had won him the reputation for cutting-edge journalism. And that regularly involved him putting himself in situations that could go badly wrong. He wasn't sure if it was maturity or experience that was making him slightly more trepidatious in his line of work, or if he was just developing a bit of a cowardly streak – he really hoped it wasn't that. But finding Ellie as he had, that seemed to embed these concerns even deeper, and he knew the time had come for some serious reassessment.

'It was a shocker for me as well, mate. But you know the situation, I had no choice in the moment. Then afterwards, well, you know how it turned out, that little madam got her hooks into me, the minute she bunched my jacket in her little hand and stared up at me. It was like falling in love as I never had before. I fought a good fight, but I didn't have a chance. It certainly wasn't part of my life plan.' Alex answered his friend honestly, although he knew Chase knew the ins and out of the story already, how he had lain awake thinking of the little girl for months, literally months, before he made the decision he had. And the wrangling to ensure that he made this adoption happen, and with no loopholes, that had taken years.

'Ha! No, I imagine it wasn't! And you're a man that likes to plan, have every eventuality covered. Even when we used to have midnight raids on the tuck shop, do you remember? You'd insist we had a Plan A through to at least a Plan D, leaving nothing to chance.'

'It saved both our arses more than once. And it helped me later. Always know your exits… it's a good motto. For all parts of life.'

They heard some very loud squealing coming from the bathroom, which really was too far away to hear easily.

'What the hell?'

'Leave her, I reckon both of them have met their match in each other. It's kinda cute. You would not believe the amount of people that think it's OK to warn me off of Angelina, but they don't see this side to her.'

'The side that sounds like it's trying to drown my daughter?'

'Oh no, they see that side. The side that will at least make sure she looks pretty if she does end up killing her. But you know what, having met your daughter, it looks like a fairly even fight to me. Anyway, don't try and distract me with talk about Angelina.'

'Oh, I won't. But we were talking exit plans and I was wondering if you had one. She's a handful.'

'Hey! I don't have an exit strategy for Angelina because I don't want an exit. I think this could work.'

'I think that's very noble but a little short-sighted.'

'And not wanting to get too personal, Alex, an exit strategy has saved your bacon more times than I know,

I should imagine. But a healthy relationship it does not make. Commitment doesn't start by finding the best way out. You may be doing a grand job of distracting me, but no longer. I want to talk to you about something specific, something serious, whilst those two are no doubt waterlogging that entire side of the house.'

'Do we have to?'

'No, of course not. But we're going to. Or rather, I'm going to speak and you can choose whether to listen.'

'You've always been a silver-tongued bastard. I don't suppose I stand a chance.'

'Yeah, 'cause you're such a weak specimen of a man.' The two exchanged fond looks, looks that only a lifetime of knowing each other can bring.

'I do hope you're not defining me based on outdated stereotypes, Chase Cooper. Go on then, seeing as me and my child are staying in your house, I guess I should hear you out. Plus, the way you're slicing that fish, I don't think I want to tangle with you.'

Chase smiled and waved the knife around whilst making faux martial arts moves, and even stranger noises, before he continued to speak.

'Excellent, it's nothing to worry about, buddy. It's just I think it would be good for you to take a bit of time out from work at the moment.'

'Don't disagree, that's what I'm doing.'

'Yeah, I know, but I'm thinking a bit longer than a couple of weeks. Put down some roots, not for-ever roots, but maybe just commit to a short amount of time and see what happens. Ellie has to be ready for school soon, if not already, and I wondered if you'd thought about what to do?'

'Well, yeah, obviously. I thought I could send her to board.' Chase's eyes went wide and Alex couldn't believe he had taken him seriously. 'Obviously that was a joke, no boarding school would have her, not just yet anyway!' He pushed both hands in a downward motion, the international gesture for calm down. 'No, seriously, I appreciate your concern, but I had looked at a couple of great schools in London. I've talked to the team and they're happy to give me an anchor job. If I got a nanny to help out, then if I do need to shoot off for a story, I'd have cover.'

'Your tone sounds like you know that's not ideal.'

'You know me way too well. Truth is, the school stuff is sorted, but professionally, I don't know so much. What I love about my job is that on-the-ground, in-the-moment feeling. I'm a bit ambivalent about working from a studio full-time. A small team on the ground, great, the politics of working in central London, being more presenter-y and less investigative-y – I mean, don't get me wrong, I respect what those guys do, and it's just as adrenaline fuelled – but I'm just not sure it's for me. If I'm going to be deskbound, and I'm happy to do that for Ellie, then I'd rather be deskbound and getting my teeth into something I'm passionate about. Focus in on one issue, really get stuck into it, you know?' Alex paused, waiting for his friend to respond, but Chase merely nodded wisely and carried on slicing fish. Alex knew the technique, he used it himself, silently waiting for the other person to fill in the gap. He guessed if Chase wanted him to continue he could do so.

'So, I think where I am at the moment is stay in London, pop Ellie in a good school there, still get a nanny just to help a bit so I don't go stir crazy, and find something, a project I can really get my teeth into. I'm juggling a couple of ideas at the moment. Maybe a book. Um… that's an awful lot of fish you're doing weird shit to.'

'Preparing, I'm preparing. Not really weird shit. But OK, I've heard you. Sounds like a plan. A pretty good one. Now, Mr Ten Plans at a time, how do you feel about another one? An alternative to consider.'

'Go on.'

'OK, well, London's great, some good schools. Cultural melting pot, lots of like-minded people, can always be busy. Or you could go the other way.' Chase looked up from his prep. 'And I've got another way that you might like.'

It was Alex's turn to stay silent and let Chase fill the gap. His friend smiled at him – they knew each other inside out.

'Stay here. Now before you react, think. I mean it. Stay here. It's not London, not by a long shot, but it's damn heavenly. Ellie may not grow up going to violin lessons and freaky Japanese maths classes, she could just chill on the beach. When she's not on the beach she can build dens in Penmenna woods, learn to surf, kayak, sail, and if that's not her thing there's the moors, vast open space to get lost in, horse riding.'

'I don't think getting lost is going win me over.' Alex said, the teasing clear in his tone.

'And I'll tell you what else – if you were to stay here, we've got an amazing village school, you've got a network of… oh, hang on, that's the door.'

'Are you expecting someone?'

'Well, I don't want you to feel bombarded, but you have options, and to make sure everything is covered I've invited some friends over to answer any questions you may have. You're going love them. One I think you may already know.' Chase grinned so wide that it looked like his ears might fall off as he headed to answer the door. And Alex, for all his death-defying, alpha-male, action-hero ways, felt a teeny bit scared.

He was right to be. For only a minute later a hazy memory from years gone by tripped through the door. She was accompanied by a smaller, dark-haired woman with a face that spoke of apple pie who, in turn, was followed by a man with curly dark hair and a great big smile on his face.

'Darling, so good to see you again, it really has been years.' Marion – he thought that was her name – enfolded him into an embrace and he was struck by the cloying nature of her scent. Ugh, that could really do with being taken down a notch. She was more heavily made up than he remembered, much blonder and very thin, her skin taut across her cheekbones, her clothes a little too tight. And with a lot of pattern.

'It certainly has, how lovely to see you again.' He avoided using her name, just in case. 'Fancy you being here as well, I had no idea.'

'Yes, we were so happy when Chase bought a house down here. Absolutely fabulous. Richard would love to see you again as well, Alex, but he's away with work at the moment.' She laughed a tinkly, slightly insincere laugh and it took him right back to university days, when he had visited Chase at Oxford and met his closest new friend, Richard, who had, if he recalled correctly, only just started dating this woman; she had been in her final year then whilst they were just freshmen and the age gap had seemed huge. At some point they had all gone away together, holidaying as a large gang at one of Hector's many houses. It was a long time ago and the memories were very hazy but he knew he had found the laugh as off-putting then and couldn't quite believe she and Richard were still together.

The man accompanying them stretched out his hand.

'Pleased to meet you, I'm Matt. I believe you already know my sister, Angelina. And this is Rosy, my partner.' He said the last bit with pride, as those in the first flush of romance do, as if he couldn't quite believe his luck. Alex couldn't help but smile, it was nice. It also reminded him that it was something that he did not have. However, that passed in a millisecond – he had Ellie and that was more than enough for now. Way more than enough. He was fairly sure two females in his life would be beyond his capabilities at the moment.

'Hello.' Rosy leant forward and kissed him on the cheek in greeting.

'Hi, nice to meet you both. Angelina is your sister, huh?'

'Oh yeah.' Matt grinned. 'In fact, it's very quiet around here. Is she not in?'

'She's taken bath duty. She's bathing my daughter right now.' Both Matt and Rosy looked startled at his words. 'Whoa, don't look like that! Chase assures me she isn't going to drown her.'

'Chase hasn't known her that long,' Matt replied without missing a beat, as Rosy punched him on the arm.

'Hey, you have to admit Chase has brought out a new side to your sister. You were saying you couldn't believe how good he was for her, only yesterday.'

'Yeah, tell all my secrets! I've told you before, you would make the rubbishest spy.'

'Nah, I'd be awesome. I can high-kick and everything. I was going to practise crawling across the roof later tonight.'

'And Chase has ninja skills with a fish knife – you two would make a crack team.' Alex joined in their teasing as Chase quirked an eyebrow comically and started peeling potatoes.

'Can I help at all?' Rosy queried.

'Nah, Ange should be here in a minute and if I need help I know that Alex is a bit of a whizz in the kitchen, for all his teasing. Why don't you four park yourselves at the table and you can tell him why Penmenna School is the best school in the world. Like, actually the best!'

'Oh, we can do that.' Rosy smiled and pulled out a chair. 'And I can assure you that I will be completely objective, Alex. Bias free. It's just fact, Penmenna School *is* the best in the world and the head teacher, well, she's a wonder. The head of the PTA, however – bit of a dragon, I'd avoid her at all costs.'

All of them laughed, the blonde woman a bit too loudly, which Alex interpreted to mean that she was probably the monster referred to.

'Hello, Matt, Marion… hmm.' Angelina bounded into the room and it was impossible not to notice the disparaging look she shot at Rosy. Interesting. Rosy, however, didn't appear to pay any attention to the blatant rudeness in Angelina's greeting and smiled a welcome at her anyway. 'Well, this is no fun. Let's get this party started, huh?' and she swung open the big fridge door, grabbed two bottles of fizz and whirled back around, holding them aloft as she did so.

'Not really a party, Ange...' her brother responded, pointedly adding, '...and you forgot to say hello to Rosy.'

'Matt, it's fine,' his girlfriend protested, placing her hand on his arm.

'No. No, it's not.'

'Hello, Rosy.' Angelina flashed her a fake smile, usually only found on catty teenage girls. 'And it's a dinner party, Matt, duh. Dinner *party*!'

'Where's Ellie?' Alex noticed that Angelina's top had been changed and, more importantly, that his daughter was nowhere to be seen.

'Oh, she's in bed. I told her she didn't need to come and say goodnight, she's all clean and in her pyjamas and I've logged her into Netflix.'

Wow! Why had he trusted her? Alex jumped from his chair, raced down the hallway and up the stairs to Ellie's bedroom. By now she'd probably be halfway through some documentary about girls in prison, or a serial-killer movie. He threw open the door and saw his daughter tucked up in bed, head laying in a little nest of pillows and staring at the screen.

'Daddy, look. *Peppa Pig!* Angileeena set up an account and everything for me. And she says after this I can watch *PAW Patrol*. Well, she pointed at it and said that thing there with those dumb animals, what she meant was *PAW Patrol*. How cool is this?'

'Yeah, that's pretty cool. Did you have a nice bath?'

'Angileeena squirted me with the ducks!'

'Great. Can I just have a quick look and then you can have it back?'

Alex had no intention of turning the TV off tonight, although he normally had very strict screen-time rules, but he just wanted to double-check. Sure enough, Angelina had set parental controls so there was no danger of Ellie watching anything she shouldn't.

'Now, just tonight, and tomorrow we'll go back to a story before bed, huh?'

'OK, Daddy. Oh, and Daddy, this is the best day. I love the beach and I love Sam, and I lovvve Angileeena. Night, night. Oh, I love you too!'

'Love you too, Ells.'

Alex wandered back down to the kitchen, mulling over what Chase had said and the group he had invited tonight. Maybe this was an idea worth considering. Maybe living by the beach with an inbuilt support network of friends, even if just for a short while, was exactly what he needed, and very probably exactly what Ellie needed. She certainly seemed happy here – there had been fewer tantrums and more sleeping over the last couple of nights.

If he was careful with his money he could afford to turn down the anchor job, let his flat out and rent somewhere down here for a bit, see how things panned out. Solutions started pulling together in his mind – this could work.

Heading back into the kitchen he could hear the fast-paced chatter between the group of friends, the laughter and Angelina's squeals. Maybe he should consider this after all.

## Chapter Three

Sylvie was awake before the dawn broke. Today was Sam's first day at school and she was veering from excitement to worry to disbelief and back again to celebration. She had been keeping a close eye as the day approached and he didn't seem to be displaying any of these emotions just yet, but then with Sam anything was possible. As long as she held it together and set a good example all she could do was hope it would be fine.

His only other first day had been at playgroup and that had been as far removed from fine as possible. He had burst into tears the minute he realized she was leaving and clung to her leg, rather as he had the man at the beach the other day. After a substantial period of trying to calm him as the other mothers looked on with sympathy, and some with an element of smugness, she ended up having to drag him to the front door, attached to said leg with the tenacity of limpets on the rocks scattered across Penmenna beach. The playgroup supervisor dragged him off and she made a hasty escape, tears welling in her eyes as she was unable to believe she had just abandoned her distraught son, despite her strict inner voice explaining all the reasons it was the best thing to do.

She had stood for a full five minutes with her ear against the old battered wooden door that was the entrance to Penmenna's playgroup, straining to hear if her son continued to cry. It was apparent after thirty seconds that he had stopped once she was out of sight, but her predilection for self-torture meant she had to stand there for another few minutes just in case he started again.

It was only the fact that she had needed, at that time, to get back to the farm to help care for her mother, who had been living with motor neurone disease for the past couple of years, that propelled her feet away from the little door.

Today there would be no burning rush to get back to the farm. Not any more.

But she did have to get out of bed, make a cup of tea and get on with some chores, before waking Sam up with her very best excited aren't-you-a-big-boy face on.

Thus, a couple of hours later, she stood over him, watching as his little eyes blearily opened and he shifted from asleep to awake. Her heart filled with pride and an intensity of love she would never have believed possible before motherhood.

'Hey, you. Wakey-wakey. How you doing?'

'Mmm, hey, you,' he snuffled back in his sleepiest tone. She sat next to him, perched on the side of his bed as his eyes flickered from closed to open, back to closed and then open once more.

'Come on then, I've got pancakes downstairs with our name on it.'

'Mmm.'

'Come on, up you get.'

He managed to drag himself into a sitting position, his red hair all mussed and his eyes now open, a slow smile creeping across his face. 'Pancakes? With strawbries?' His tone was still sleepy but a bit more engaged. If the old adage about men and their stomachs was true, it had started young in her son. Although to be fair, it might have little to do with gender and more with genes – she was a sucker for them too.

'Yes, pancakes and strawbries.' She deliberately echoed his mispronunciation. 'Tell you what, I'm going to sit and close my eyes and I bet if I count to ten to give you a head start, I can still beat you to the kitchen.'

'No chance.'

'Every chance'

'Go on then, close your eyes, and… ready for action!'

Sylvie closed her eyes, smiling at her son as he shouted his latest favourite catchphrase. She felt him jump out of the bed and race to the door.

'Hey, I hadn't started yet!'

He responded with a laugh and bounded down the stairs as she started to count.

–

Several pancakes and a short car journey later, Sylvie and Sam pulled up outside Penmenna School. Being the very first week the Reception Class started a little later in the day and was only lasting two and a half hours today, slowly inching the children in before they realized this was how they were expected to spend every day for the next fourteen years.

She felt a surge of comfort and familiarity as she returned to the school that she too had attended until she was eleven, happy that her son was carrying on the family tradition.

Sam clasped her hand as they headed through the big Victorian doors, the school itself having been there since the 1850s, tall, imposing and built from the granite that dominated the Cornish landscape. It was the central feature of the village that had sprung up around it. He looked so smart in his uniform, all of which he had insisted on putting on for himself. Sylvie knew for a fact his pants were on inside out.

They found their way to the Reception Class, and saw they were one of the earliest with only five or so other children there and a couple of mums lurking. Miss Winter, the Reception teacher and head, was there with her colleague, Lynne Rowe, the teacher who job-shared the responsibility for Class One. Sylvie raised her hand to the both of them – she knew Rosy from before, having taught her in a self-defence class a few years back – before going to find Sam's peg. Knowing Rosy Winter, as well as the school itself, made today so much easier; it meant she knew that Sam would be in the best hands. And thankfully, so far he had shown no sign of repeating the playgroup incident.

Sam grew excited as he recognized his name next to a peg with a spaceman on it. He was so clever. He hadn't needed a jacket this morning but hung his brand-new Lego-themed bag on the peg with pride. Then he remembered that his school bag had not just the book he had picked up on their introductory day the term before but also his PE bag inside. Carefully he unzipped the school bag and took the sports one out, also placing it on the peg.

'Good job, that boy!' Sylvie smiled down at him as he looked up at her. They headed back into the classroom just as his nemesis from playgroup came whirling in, a particularly rambunctious boy called Alfie who meant no real malice but was fond of dressing up as Batman and shouting in the other children's faces. Playgroup had never dealt with him particularly well, although Sylvie had sent him more than her fair share of withering looks in an attempt to warn him off. Sam's smile faded a little. Harry, Alfie's best friend and Spider-Man fan, came hurtling in next and the two boys high-fived boisterously. Sam looked at her for reassurance.

'Let's go and have a look at these jigsaws. You're always super-quick at them, I bet you can do these easily.' Sylvie led him to a table full of puzzles, one of his favourite things to do, logical tasks where he could create order. 'Hello, Alfie, Harry.' Sylvie made sure to address them in a friendly tone as they walked past.

'Hello, Sam.' Rosy joined them at the table. 'Are you excited now you're here at big school? I saw that you found your peg really quickly. That's pretty cool.'

'You gave me the spaceman badge.'

'I did. I remembered how much you enjoyed our space story when you came in before, so I thought you'd like it. I'll let you into a secret if you like.' Sam edged closer. 'I'm going to read it again later, I love it too!'

Sam beamed at her and showed her the jigsaw he had completed in super-quick time. She grinned back in response and said she had some terribly hard ones if he was up to the challenge. His little face took on its worried expression so Sylvie mouthed, 'Grab the moment,' at him, their little code to reassure each other that the time was now and they had each other's backs. He nodded and Rosy pointed to a drawer nearby and suggested he went and had a look.

'Hello, Sylvie, lovely to see you.' She quickly assessed Sylvie's face. 'It's going to be fine. It's always such a big day this, and I always think it's far worse for the mums and dads, but I promise Sam is going to have a fab time. You wait and see.'

'I'm sure he will, Miss Winter, he seems settled already. I'll just stay a minute or two and then slide on out.' She didn't understand why – she wasn't normally an overly emotional person – but seeing her son rootling through the classroom drawers, all grown up and in his uniform, was beginning to make her feel a bit tearful.

'You're welcome to stay as long as you feel necessary, but you're right, the quicker they adjust to being independent the better for them. How are you doing, anyway?' Rosy smiled sympathetically and touched her on the arm. Sylvie, determined not to let the tears well up any further, tightened her lips and nodded in movements she felt were a little too jerky. She remembered how Rosy had come to her mum's funeral, along with a huge number of people from the village, and how much she had appreciated it. She knew her mother would have been so touched and felt very humbled, the turnout being evidence of her popularity amongst all in the community.

'And are you still teaching?' Rosy changed the subject quickly.

'Yes, um… yeah. Still doing the adult self-defence twice a week at Roscarrock leisure centre. And a couple of ballet classes on a Saturday for little ones. Once I've got Sam settled though, now Mum is gone, I'm going to see if there's any way I can do some more, ideally set something up locally in the village, so it's less of a trek.'

'That's a great idea. I'd forgotten you were a professional ballet dancer. The parents here would bite your hand off if they had local access to your talent. If you want, I can hook you up with the head of our PTA. I'm sure she could help drum up some support. I loved doing self-defence with you, you were a natural. But you know, until then, if you do have a few hours spare we're always looking for parent helpers. Come in and read with the children once we're all in full-time and settled.'

'Really? I'd love to do…'

'Sam! Sam!' A whirling dervish of black braids and huge pink bags came hurling her way to the jigsaw table. 'Oh yeah, I knew I was going to like it here! Angileeena said school was boring but sometimes she's wrong. I'm so pleased you're here.' She spoke so rapidly, the words falling over themselves to get out before she threw her whole body into a hug, nearly knocking a beaming Sam to the floor.

No, surely not! She thought they had been on holiday? Whilst half of Sylvie was overjoyed at the look of sheer bliss on Sam's face, the thought of having to meet Alex again was too mortifying. Especially right this second and with no warning.

Talk of the devil.

'Oh, wow. Hi. Nice to see you again. Ellie hasn't stopped talking about Sam.' And yup, there he was, all six-foot-plus of him, looking absolutely freaking gorgeous, broad shoulders to match his grin. Oh, bloody hell, and – oh, great, yes – now she was blushing too.

'Oh, do you know each other?'

'Oh, hi, Rosy, thank you so much for the other night. I'm so glad you talked me around. I think this will be a great fit for Ellie. I can't thank you enough. And yeah, we met on the beach, didn't we, Sylvie? It was quite a day.' The amused lilt in his voice reminded her of Sam's suggestion.

'Uh… guh…' Great – blushing and speechless. Clearly an even better second impression than the first. And the great news was she'd be seeing him every day now, probably twice. Perhaps this afternoon she could tuck her skirt into her knickers and fall over in the playground and make a tit of herself that way – make it a full three strikes!

'Oh, wow, that's great. Ellie will have a friend straight away, oops, yes, she certainly has.' Rosy jumped in to spare her Sylvie's sudden inability to form words. They all looked over as Ellie was dragging Sam at speed to the water tray, having hurled her bags to the floor. Sylvie tried super-hard to control the strangled sounds that still seemed to be emitting from her throat.

Alex arched an eyebrow at her before he noticed his daughter's bags on the floor. She wasn't sure if it was his way of checking if she was all right, or if it was because he was a little freaked out.

'Oh, I'll just pick those up. Where should I put them?' he asked Rosy.

'Oh no, that's OK.' The teacher called across the room, 'Ellie, in school we put our things on their pegs before we play. Sam might be able to help you. You've got a dolphin by your peg.'

'Thanks, Rosy. Oh, I should call you, what was it? Miss Winter?' Alex smiled at Rosy and as she started to respond Sylvie looked over at Sam and decided now might be a good time to leave, whilst he was happily occupied with Ellie.

43

Raising her arm, she waved a high wave. 'Bye, Sam.' At least her voice was back. But would it work? Was it really going to be this easy?

Sam glanced up.

'Bye, Mum, see you in a bit.' It seemed it was.

She smiled briefly at Alex and Rosy, who were in full stream of chatter about reading levels, and nodded her goodbye.

She couldn't believe Sam had gone in so smoothly, this was fabulous. She had been dreading him becoming upset. He was so grown up. She gulped. Oh, for goodness' sake, what was happening to her? This was ridiculous.

She was nearly out the door, fighting for a bit of self-control and reminding herself that there was nothing wrong in being so proud of your son on his first day of school that you got a little choked, when she heard Alex's voice calling her.

'Hey, Sylvie. Wait up.'

She blinked her eyes, ready to turn, but something stopped her; she didn't think she could bear to embarrass herself again. Could she just keep walking and pretend she hadn't heard? She speeded up. There was only one way to find out.

# Chapter Four

Sylvie drove back to the farm whooshing quickly around the lanes, the last of the blackberries dotting the high hedgerows, and giving herself a loud talking-to all the way. Not only was she embarrassed about being a little tearful, she had also finished off with being deliberately rude to a man who had been nothing but pleasant. She could catch up with him after school. She *would* catch up with him after school and welcome him to the community rather than run away from him. If anyone knew what being an outsider felt like, it was her.

As she pulled into the drive, she realized that this new slightly blubby behaviour could be exactly what she had been wishing for. She hadn't been able to cry for months, not since the funeral. And she really wanted to. Not because she was some kind of masochist but because she was carrying her grief as a tight, heavy bundle; ever present and whispering that she was a bad daughter for not having sobbed and sobbed.

Maybe she should take these two hours to go and sit in her mother's room, find the strength to start packing some things up. Not everything, just make a start. Her tears over Sam's first day could be the catalyst for shifting a smidgen of this numbness.

As she entered the farmhouse through the kitchen she saw Tom sitting in the big old rocking chair near the range. The range was an absolute beast, cast iron, Victorian, black and bleak and somehow still working – it was probably the most modern thing in the kitchen. Or certainly felt like it at times. There was something about the farm, perfectly encapsulated by the cooker, that hung over this place, and as much as it was home Sylvie knew she needed to get some more work and look into moving her and Sam out for good.

Tom, her uncle, would not say anything directly, but he too had had his life put on hold, hanging, waiting, stopped from making the progress he had hoped for. And Sylvie knew that her presence in the farmhouse was unintentionally continuing that pattern. Both of them needed to move forward, Sylvie from this place and Tom fully into it, with the woman he had loved, to take his turn.

Tom and Sylvie had a good relationship, both wanting to cling to the last of family as they knew it. But they were poles apart in their world views. Sylvie knew Tom thought of her as flighty and could never understand why she would leave Cornwall for London to do something as capricious as dance. He had very firm views about a woman's role, and they seemed to centre largely around marriage and baking. Taking to the stage in a tutu and tights was not what he considered proper. But then he probably felt that the Corn Laws should never have been repealed and that her returning home pregnant and voluntarily single was the natural conclusion to such a career choice.

Despite this Sylvie couldn't help but smile when she saw him perched there basking in the warmth thrown out, all seasons, by the range. He might be a taciturn old bastard, but he was hers.

'Hey, Tom, Sam's first day at school started well. I have to go get him again in a couple of hours. I'm just going to put the kettle on, can I make you a cup as well?'

'Seems a bit daft, maid. Not much point 'im being there for that then, is there? Will cost you a fortune on petrol, should'a waited in the village.'

'Well, they like to start them off slow, get them used to it. I'm sure they know what they're doing, and it's only a couple of miles. Tea?'

'Aye, full day's wages for half a day's work. Bleddy get them used to it, society gone soft. Why, I was practically working a full day on the farm at his age.'

'Mmm-hmm. Tea?' Sylvie grinned wider but knew not to argue and was now highly skilled at non-committal noises. She was fairly sure one day he'd progress to telling her that he was working in the tin mines when he was two and a half.

'I'll make me own bleddy tea, maid. I'm not so old that I can't use a kettle.'

'I know, you moody old bugger, but I'm making one for myself so it's no harm to do you one too. Then I thought I'd go and look through some of Mum's things today, maybe start sorting them out.' Sylvie quite liked the way her accent became more pronounced Cornish whenever she was near her uncle; she certainly hadn't had that twang in London, where her voice matched her life, fast-paced and excitable.

'Good idea. 'Tis about time, maid. She wouldn't want us keeping it like that for ever. You know she liked things fresh.'

Sylvie took a look around the kitchen and knew Tom's idea of fresh was wildly different from hers, but it was true that as dark as the house might be, her mother did keep things as citrus sharp as possible. It was simply that Margaret preferred function and utility to frippery and would no more have thought of giving the heavy dark wood a lick of white paint than she would fly through the air, and Sylvie loved her for it. Why waste the money and time on paint when there were cows to milk and ballet shoes – her daughter's dancing her only indulgence – to buy? Margaret was very sure where she stood when it came to fuss or fripperies; indeed, Sylvie remembered her mother had a whole host of go-to sayings – *fussing makes a fool not a fighter* was one of them. Applied equally to child-rearing as it was to furniture.

There had been a solidity to her mother, as there was to Tom, that gave them and her roots – a security that allowed Sylvie to take the path she had, that freed her to take risks, knowing that she could explore the world as she wished and home would be always there and never changing.

Until it wasn't. Young and with her head only ever in the world of dance, Sylvie had forgotten to take note that no matter how solid and secure her mother might be, there was one thing no one could fight and win.

And now as she opened the door, the stale air hit her nostrils and the guilt welled up. She should have come in here sooner. Once the hospital had taken all their equipment back she had rested her hand on the door handle more than once, but never got any further. It had all seemed too final, too much. But Tom was right, it was time, and the very least she could do was give the room a good dusting now, air it out, make it sparkle and honour her mother that way.

She went back to the kitchen to grab cloths and sprays and the hoover, nodding at Tom as he left again, the dogs by his side. Knowing that in the dip of his head was approval, a gentle unspoken indicator that he thought she was doing right.

Scrubbing and brushing and dusting and shaking, making the room smell of lemons and finishing it by popping some blue hydrangeas from the garden by the side of her mum's bed was cathartic, and blew away the inanities of the morning. Getting worked up because her son had hit a milestone and embarrassed by the presence of a man she barely knew was senseless.

Sitting here on her mum's coverlet, breathing in and out, she looked at the things that had been ever present in her life – the silver-backed hairbrushes, the photos of her as a child next to them on the dresser. A bottle of Tweed, still half full, sat next to a large pot of Nivea and as Sylvie lifted the lid of the cream she could breathe her mother in and see her clear as day when she had been little and her mum would pop a splodge on her cheeks and rub it in for her. 'All grown up now, Sylvie-bear.'

She sat there for a couple of minutes letting memories of being a small child in the fields and on the beaches of Cornwall envelop her. Still no tears, but a feeling of warmth, of gratitude at how lucky she had been.

Moving over to the wardrobe door, a clunky dark wood affair that had been sitting in this farmhouse for probably long before her mother was, she pulled open the door. Yanked it as it stuck and saw her mother's clothes, not many for her mother didn't see the need, not when she could spend her pennies on gauzy ballet clothes and pretty silken slippers for her only child instead.

There were dresses, skirts and trousers hung neatly on a short forward-facing rail, and stacks of jumpers and some shoes in the little wooden shelves to the side. There were the heels she would wear whenever she had anywhere special to go to. Next to that was a little carved box that Sylvie remembered tracing her fingers over the top of as a child. It was a fanciful thing for her mother to own and Sylvie wasn't sure of how it had come into her mother's possession.

So many things she wished she had asked.

Sitting back on the bed she lifted the lid and saw all that her mother held dear in one small place: there was a sepia photograph of her and Tom's parents, stern faced and dressed in their Sunday best; a clutch of all of Sylvie's school reports from Penmenna, and then the Royal Ballet School from eleven on; a sheaf of photos of Sylvie dancing, from child to adult – many taken from the audience where Margaret would sit bursting with pride in her pleated skirts and best court shoes telling all who would listen that that was her daughter – as well as newspaper clippings of reviews of all the shows she had been in.

The tears fell full, warm and heavy, spreading into circles upon the yellowed paper.

# Chapter Five

Rosy looked up from her teaching activity to see Marion Marksharp bustling in through the doorway. She was head of the PTA and fearsome with it – there was a rumour circulating the playground that she was actively trying to get pregnant again so that when her youngest child, Rufus, left Penmenna School she could hooch another one in and maintain her crown. Rosy and Marion had grown close over the last few months, but even she accepted that it was a possibility.

Friendship or not, watching her enter the classroom with that terrier-after-a-rat expression on her face still sent a frisson of foreboding up Rosy's spine. It normally pre-warned of some ridiculous demand that Marion would insist was necessary for the sheer lifeblood of the school and she would, unfortunately, often be partially right and wholly successful. Rosy was tempted to close her eyes and hope she'd go away, but if she did that there was a strong chance that when she reopened them Marion would have organized all the children into ranks based on parental income, made them hold up posters about how Penmenna was the best school in the world *ever*, and uploaded the photos onto Instagram.

Marion marched her way in and started putting small bits of paper into the children's individual drawers.

Presumably for them to pass on to their parents who, when they were new, always eagerly checked the drawers at pick-up time; at least for the first week until they realized that small slips of paper tended to be ransom notes – demanding time and/or money in return for playground kudos and a little less parental guilt.

Having finished, and it was fair to say she did it at speed, Marion came over to Rosy. Completely ignoring the fact that Rosy was in the midst of a teaching activity, she started to bark at her.

'Thank you for letting me do that.' As if there had been a choice. 'But it really is desperately important to get some new blood. All my best ladies went in July, and honestly, the lot I'm left with, well, they couldn't organize a fire in a match factory. I've tried everything in the run-up to this term, incentives, days out, even an online star chart and PTA member-of-the-month award. But they're all so wet. No gumption or initiative. Beth had a meltdown this morning because she couldn't work out how much of my personalized PTA scent to spray on each note – a spritz is exactly as it sounds. I had to do three myself just to show her. Then she had the cheek to begin to question why. Pah! I shut that down fairly quickly, I can tell you. And to cap it all off I caught her popping these onto Sheila's desk for her to do after school, something about not wanting to disturb your teaching. Ridiculous. Sheila, for goodness' sake! I'm not sure how that woman manages to breathe and walk at the same time, and then Beth's palming off this job on her, which is really quite a responsibility. Ludicrous.'

'I am teaching, Marion,' Rosy responded, nodding her head towards the rapt faces of the small group of children sitting on the floor with her. Although she did concede that Marion might have a point about Sheila. The school secretary was an institution at Penmenna but was barely capable of turning the computer on. In fact, experience had taught Rosy that things ran a lot smoother when she didn't.

'Yes, but they're hardly going to master counting on the first day, are they, dear? And besides, as I said, I need new blood from the latest intake of parents so just wanted to remind everyone about the meeting next week, to welcome them into the fold, as it were.'

A small squeal emitted out of the mouth of Ashleigh, one of the youngest in the class, at the word 'blood', which when followed by the word 'parents' led to her starting to sway.

Rosy arched her crossest eyebrow at Marion before turning to soothe Ashleigh.

'That one's parents are bound to be useless.' Marion shot a dismissive look at Ashleigh, who was starting to cry. 'Oh no, no, no, no. No!'

Before Rosy could intervene, Marion was racing across the classroom to where Ellie and Sam were standing by the sand tray. A large brightly coloured jeep was held aloft in Ellie's hand, Alfie was bawling loudly and Sam was looking all deer-in-the-headlights.

'Absolutely not, young man. What do you think you're doing?'

Oh, dear God, Marion's new bond with Rosy obviously was making her far too comfortable in the classroom. Rosy signalled Pippa, the teaching assistant, over to help with the group she was with and went to intervene before Marion did something illegal.

'Of course she walloped you with it you, stupid boy! Good girl, Ellie. Angelina was quite right. You have to stand up for yourselves in school. Or they walk all over you. All girls together, eh? Do stop your bawling, young man, for goodness' sake – you're giving us all a headache. Come on, Ellie, your friend too – odd-looking boy but I'm sure you know what you're doing – I think you've just won the sand tray for yourselves. Go on, the rest of you, go and play somewhere else.'

'Mrs Marksharp! I'll take over here, thank you.' Rosy didn't think she had ever had to raise her voice in such a fashion, not in all her years of teaching.

'Oh no, don't worry, Rosy dear, I have it all in hand. In fact, now the leaflets have been done I can stay and help in the class if you like, we're so lucky to have young Ellie. Her father is quite a catch, you know. Oh, of course, you've met him. Quite a catch.'

'Alfie, come back here, love. Ellie, you stay right here too. Marion, out, out now! Although I will want to speak to *you* after school.'

Once Marion had gone, Rosy had de-escalated the sand tray situation and had made a mental note that Ellie, who hadn't been to the day induction the previous term, could need quite a firm hand.

The morning then reverted to the calm it should be. Time whizzed by and it wasn't long before story time was over and the parents came in to pick up their babies. Being the first day, Rosy and Lynne handed over the children individually, reassuring each parent on how the day had gone. Rosy had to explain to Alfie's mum why he had a large red blotch on his forehead on the very first day, but thankfully she was remarkably understanding about it whilst a parent behind her muttered something about karma.

She saw Lynne hand Sam over to Sylvie, who was hiding behind big sunglasses but whose grin was infectious as her son bowled into her legs, so excited by his morning. She saw Alex trying to start a conversation with her, but Sylvie seemed to smile politely, nod a bit and make her excuses. Rosy had wondered about the two of them this morning, but now her interest was definitely piqued. Marion was right, Alex did seem to be rather eligible, and it wasn't often that a handsome single father pitched up in the playground. She felt almost sorry for him; she gave him maybe another two days before the rest of the mothers worked out he wasn't married and moved in for the kill. Interesting that Sylvie seemed to be showing no interest whatsoever. The playground, the parent side of it anyway, was often a bit of a soap opera, and she was interested to see how this chapter would unfold.

And there he was standing in front of her as Ellie stood by her side. This bit she hated, but she needed to make it quite clear that Ellie had been aggressive today and that such behaviour had no place in school. Privately she thought Alex might want to keep an eye on Ellie's number one female role model as well.

–

Even though the first day for Class One was only half a day, it was always an exhausting one. With the new intake gone home there were only a few of the older children left in the class for the day so Rosy left them with Lynne for some focused literacy work and headed off to her office to start organizing some of the logistics for the new term.

Being a village school with a small roll meant that instead of the seven classes – one for each academic year – that a larger school might have, Penmenna School had four main classes, divided largely by Key Stage. Class One, overseen by Rosy and Lynne, had the Reception age children and some of the younger children that would be in Year One but were better suited to a little more Early Years teaching before moving up to Class Two. Class Two was taught by Sarah Fielding, who would be retiring next year, and was the sweetest teacher Rosy had ever encountered – perfect for teaching the five-, six- and seven-year-olds in her care. The remaining two classes were overseen by the most contrasting teachers one could imagine. Harmony Rivers had the younger ones, those that would be in Years Three and Four, and Amanda Adams was responsible for the eldest children in the school, and used distinctly Victorian methods to get them through their final-year SATs. Amanda was pretty fierce, but remarkably fair, and Rosy knew that she regularly went above and beyond for those children in her class but without making a fanfare about it. Unlike Harmony, who would like to dab every child with sage before they came through the door if Rosy would let her and make sure everyone knew why.

Rosy knew that every school had its share of different teaching methods, and it was fair to say that Penmenna was certainly diverse, but she did enjoy shepherding this raggle-taggle bunch. Most days.

Amanda rapped authoritatively at Rosy's door, which was open, and waited until Rosy called her through. The expression on her face so grim that even Rosy was startled and wondered what she had done wrong.

'Miss Winter.'

'Rosy.' She knew she would never win this battle over first names; Amanda wore formality as most women wore knickers, as a matter of course, and never removed in the workplace.

'I'm afraid we have to talk. I appreciate that this is our first day teaching, and it's only lunchtime, but I'm afraid I do believe speed is of the essence in situations such as these.'

Oh no. Please don't let Marion have gone to Amanda's class after Rosy had kicked her out. The last time she had done so Amanda threatened union involvement, although if she did let the two women battle it out, it would be a close call as to who would win. Amanda Adams in the blue corner dressed in pinstripe and sporting a fetching ballerina bun or Marion Marksharp in the red corner, in a new season Cath Kidston dress spotted with ladybirds and her trademark fuchsia lipstick. If they could just hold off a couple of months then she supposed it would liven up the Christmas Fayre.

Pulling herself out of her daydream she tried to focus on Amanda's very concerned face. She did hope Toby's mum hadn't sent him in with only a bar of Caramac and can of Red Bull for lunch again. Last time Amanda had felt compelled to ring her and dictate a recipe for vegetable soup down the phone. Rosy had sent her on a training course immediately afterwards about working with parents and to Amanda's credit, she had managed to rein her judgement in and made a real effort to build bridges with the parents. It was just a shame she always looked like she'd be more at home jangling keys in a prison camp as she did it.

'Which situations, Amanda? Here, do sit down.'

'I would have brought it to your attention on the training days but I didn't have the news for certain until yesterday afternoon and I wanted to confirm before I said anything.'

This didn't sound good.

'Go on, how can I help?'

'I need to come and tell you that I am due to have tarsometatarsal fusion surgery – the bones in my foot are arthritic as a result of sports injuries when I was younger. I was very sporty and things sometimes got rather competitive. I have been for both steroid and local anaesthetic injections into my foot to see if that helped, but unfortunately neither provided any lasting relief.'

'Oh, Amanda, I'm sorry. That doesn't sound very nice.'

'No, it's not. It is very painful at the moment and I appreciate I may be a little grouchier than usual.' Rosy was thankful her professionalism won through at this point, preventing her eyebrows from bouncing through her hairline. 'However, I shall ensure it doesn't affect my teaching, except for the time off required for the surgery, which I'm afraid could be anything from twelve weeks to six months. I anticipate being back after twelve weeks – I am not a woman that is happy to admit weakness of any kind…'

'I wouldn't define it as weakness. Your health is vitally important and it seems to me that one can't help being in pain. I know you take a very stoic view, Amanda, and I respect that. However, as well as making sure there is cover for your very necessary time away I think that if you are in pain, which you must be, I cannot in good conscience allow you to carry on teaching PE. I know you believe in doing so in a very active fashion…'

'I do. I expect my children to undertake PE properly, not merely throw some beanbags through a hoop.'

Rosy fought to keep the grin off her face; she knew exactly what point Amanda was trying to make. Harmony didn't believe in competitive sports of any kind and it had been a constant battle to get her to teach it a little more robustly. In fact, addressing the imbalance in PE delivery was one of the top things on Rosy's to-do list for this term.

'Absolutely, so I think we need to get cover for you. We can't have you in a worse state because of your teaching, and we want you back quickly so it makes sense that we get some proper cover for you, right up until, and possibly after, you're back.'

'I know when we drew up the action plan for this year I agreed to help you develop a more robust whole-school policy on PE, and I'm happy to do that. But I do appreciate you raising this. I have been concerned about delivering it personally to either my class or in a mentoring capacity to those who need it.' Amanda arched a brow to make sure her message had gone across. 'Alice could of course take over that side of the curriculum for me with my class, but I can't have her out of the classroom doing everybody else. Those children come to me very strong on their PSHE skills. They are, to be fair to her, emotionally intelligent when they leave Harmony's class, but their physical capabilities are barely developed beyond Class Two.'

'Yes, I know. The fact that we all have such different contributions to make is why Penmenna turns out such well-rounded children. It is a blow, Amanda, I will admit, that you can't wholly implement it – you are certainly the most skilled. But you could definitely oversee it still.

You're right, Harmony can't do it, and I don't want to ask Sarah – I'm trying to decrease her load up until retirement, not add to it – so it will have to be you and me or Lynne. And you know she does nothing but curse the day she trained as a teacher whenever she's put on the sports field. Lynne is excellent in the classroom but no natural athlete. Leave it with me. You and I can work on the Action Plan but I'll arrange coverage of your lessons and get someone in to do some extra provision. I don't want to take the teaching assistants away from their current roles. I'll see if County will help.'

'OK, thank you. And you'll have someone to cover me from tomorrow on?'

'Alice will have to cover you this week, but yes, I'm on it. And keep me posted about anything I can do to support you in the run-up to surgery.'

Amanda nodded curtly and left the office as Rosy gulped and stared at the phone. Ringing County for cover involved calling Edward Grant, a school improvement officer, who Rosy had tangled with earlier in the year. Rather like Gargamel from *The Smurfs*, the man oozed grease, prejudice and (since Rosy opposed him when he had tried to close Penmenna) cold vengeful fury. Wincing, she knew sooner was better than later and pulled up his number.

'Edward Grant.'

Rosy took a deep breath before speaking into the phone.

'Hello, Mr Grant. I'm glad I caught you, it's Rosy Winter here from Penmenna.'

'Ah, Rosy Winter from Penmenna, what can I help *you* with?' Rosy could hear the glee in his tone, almost see him rubbing his hands together, the grease on them making a squelching noise as he did so. Any hope that he might decide to be professional and supportive quickly vanished.

'I was calling to discuss the provision in place to support us in improving our PE teaching this year. It was on the School Improvement Plan when we submitted it. But our lead teacher is now unable to deliver it, so I was hoping that you could generously rejig the scheduling, perhaps send an Advanced Skilled Teacher earlier than planned?' Her brow furrowed as she pled her case; she really hated him, but if obsequiousness was needed then she could serve it up, if only for a minute or two.

'Well, as much as I'd love to help you, Miss Winter…' squelch, grin, squelch, '…I'm afraid all our PE AST's have been allotted for the year already and Penmenna is not on the list.' Argh! Edward Grant and his poxy lists. The man was obsessed.

'It's the first day of term, Mr Grant. And we were already on the plan for PE improvement. I'm not sure how we could have been overlooked.'

'Miss Winter, I appreciate that you are used to getting your own way, but in this instance, as I have already said, we cannot help you. Obviously if I could, I would…' Rosy wished she could screech, 'Liar!' down the phone but there was no way he was driving her to unprofessional behaviour, proving his belief that as a woman and especially one under fifty she shouldn't be allowed anywhere near the Senior Management Team of a school let alone be in charge of one. '…and perhaps if you had managed your School Improvement Plan properly then this wouldn't have fallen through the net. I'm afraid that even in the face of, and the expectation of, your ineptitude and lack of professionalism, there is nothing I can do. Nothing at all. You'll have to find another solution. And fund it out of your existing budget. I am so terribly sorry, Miss Winter…' he oozed out of the handset, unable to contain the joy in his voice, '…I just can't help you.'

## Chapter Six

Sam's first week had gone by so smoothly that Sylvie couldn't quite believe her luck. Not only had he been keen to get up and ready super-quick every morning, but he had still been beaming every afternoon when she picked him up. This evening, however, they were heading back to the school as there was a special PTA welcome for all new parents, and even though Sylvie wasn't particularly involved in the local community she wanted to show support tonight. Pass the message to Sam that she supported his school, and that school was important. Plus, her life had changed so dramatically in the last few months that it was probably time that she got herself a bit more involved with things, maybe make some friends.

She had been a bit of a loner when she was at school here, the odd one, the one the other girls played with when their friends were off school ill for the day. But the truth was, she wasn't really interested in the other girls' games. She was quite happy twirling around on the school field or the playground on her own; she would be a fairy queen or a sprite and dance her way through her adventures. Whenever she tried to explain her games to the other girls they would just look at her as if their worst fears were confirmed and wander off.

Then she had moved from infants to juniors and started taking her ballet seriously, eating, sleeping, breathing her dance moves, the stories, watching famous ballerinas from years gone by on a crackly VHS, completely enchanted and only vaguely aware of her mother nipping in and out. Her favourite times were those rare moments when her mother would stop, come and scrunch up next to her on the battered old sofa as she watched *Swan Lake* for the millionth time and they would ooh and aah together.

Then when she had won the scholarship and headed off to study ballet in London, she left any potential friends behind, catty girls quick to say she had always been weird and Alice, who she had a tentative friendship with, always away with her family when the holidays came around. In the city she had found her tribe and didn't mind the absence of that whenever she came back to Penmenna. She was there so rarely she was happy to spend every minute with her mum. Felt she should.

She thought it would be different for Sam though, and wondered what her life would have been like had she had an Ellie, who she could see he was keeping his eyes peeled for as she walked him to Class One. The children were being looked after by a couple of members of staff, whilst the parents were due to be indoctrinated by the terrifying woman in bold prints that Sylvie had seen flitting around the school.

'Hey!' Sam had spotted Ellie and flew from his mother's side, straight to the sand tray where she noticed Alfie and Harry already were. She watched as the two bigger boys stood back and let Sam through to the front before they continued their play. She felt a smile creep on her face; something had certainly shifted there and she was fairly sure it involved the determined little girl who was currently scrunching up her face with concentration as she built sand tower upon sand tower, the three boys around her as devotees.

Turning, she left the room and headed back out across the quad towards the main hall. If Ellie was here then there was a strong chance that her dad would be too. She managed to miss Alex every morning but in the afternoon he made sure to come and chat, and she had to admit it was kind of nice. Easy conversation – he managed to make her feel remarkably at ease, which considering their initial first day was quite impressive – with no hint of predatory behaviour. Nor any hint of a wife yet, and Sylvie had to admit her interest was piqued. Her money was on an immaculately groomed, terribly professional wife, who shot around all over the place being practically perfect in every way. Bar childcare, it would appear.

'Sylvie.' And as if her mind, and her uncharitable thought, had conjured him, Sylvie could hear the pad of his shoes as he chased to catch her up. Her head turned in welcome as she paused so he could reach her, and she could feel the grin take over her face. Along with the pale – she hoped it was pale, it was now a daily occurrence – flush that flared across her cheeks. With any luck, he'd just assume it was a medical condition.

She told herself that she wasn't *that* attracted to him, and that her response to him on the beach had been some freaky anomaly, completely unrelated to him as a person. She just had a habit of blushing at inappropriate times, at the postman, the vicar and occasionally at John, one of Tom's farmhands. Pretty much any male in the vicinity, and under seventy. Experience had taught her they didn't even have to have all their teeth, let alone their wits. It had been causing embarrassment ever since she was a teen, but she hoped she might grow out of it any day. Surely?

She watched as he smiled his greeting in return as he came alongside her; the way his eyes crinkled in the corner as he did so, and how the T-shirt he was wearing fitted his shoulders just so. Everything about him seemed so effortless, whereas she found it difficult enough to find matching socks of a morning.

'Those two are having a whale of a time together. I'm so glad we… Ellie was lucky enough to meet Sam on the beach that day. Having a built-in friend already has made coming into school so much easier for her.'

'She's definitely had an influence on Sam, he's growing in confidence every day. So if either of us owes a debt of gratitude, it's me. I think your Ellie would flourish anywhere. She has this shining charisma that pulls people in, bewitches them. If she keeps that up she will always live a charmed life.'

A flash of something flitted across Alex's face. A microsecond of bleak sadness that seemed completely out of context before he replaced it with his characteristic cheerfulness.

'She's certainly very confident. Though talking of confident, we'd better head in and see what Marion has in store for us.'

'Marion? The PTA woman? I didn't realize you knew her.'

'Oh yes, I met her when we were students, and she and her husband are good friends of a friend of mine. That's partly why I decided to send Ellie to Penmenna.

Chase invited Marion around and she bullied me into considering it.'

'Bullied you. You don't look like you're easily bullied.' Yep – there was the flush again; she hadn't meant in relation to his powerful physique but his air of utter self-assurance.

'You'd think. But honestly, she is something else. Trust me, if I hadn't acquiesced quickly she might well have brought pliers to pull my fingernails out next. In this sort of situation I'm a moral coward, I like to take the easy route.'

'In torture or sign-here situations, I can see why you might do that.'

'Don't mock me, you'll see. Any second now, I should imagine.'

He pushed open the door to the school hall and Sylvie couldn't help but gasp. Of course she had been here before, throughout her entire childhood for example, and more recently when the school had had its television debut a few months earlier – the children all involved in a gardening project that had proved to be peak-time television manna – and for the induction day. But this was something else. She spun around to look at Alex and saw his smug grin, belied by the twinkle in his eye.

'I expected a few dozen cheese straws, but this is ridiculous.'

'Told you, she's a force!'

'I will never doubt you again.' Sylvie stood, still rooted to the spot as she saw parents milling about in the hall, which was decorated to within an inch of its life. The big whiteboard attached to the wall showed sliding pictures of laughing children and beaming parents, and tables either side of the hall littered with foodie delights that would make any winner of *MasterChef* proud. There, as a centre-piece, was a cake of Penmenna School and next to it one of Penmenna Hall which had already had some, very neatly cut, slices taken out of it. One side of that was a chocolate fountain with mounds of glistening fruit around it, jewelled berries piled high and shiny grapes, chunks of pineapple and a jumble of popcorn. Its counterpart, the other side of the cakes, were three cheese fondue sets, equally spaced for access, and a pile of breads, soft squidgy white, a canary yellow cornbread and seeded wholemeal, all in delicious little squares desperate for plunging cheesy death.

By the interactive whiteboard Marion Marksharp held court, surrounded by women who looked very similar to her. In fact, two were spookily alike, their hairstyles almost identical to Marion's, coiffed, mid-length and blonde, and their outfits clearly picked with each other in mind. It was all just a little bit Stepford.

Sylvie discreetly directed Alex to them with a nod and then had to nonchalantly wander off to examine the cake as he burst into laughter.

His laugh meant that Marion's head spun around and Sylvie watched as she smiled a particularly welcoming smile at him. She resembled the Enormous Crocodile from the children's book and Sylvie watched, impressed that Alex didn't visibly gulp, look flustered in any way or indeed run. Marion carried on grinning, gave the room one last check, tapped her microphone – a microphone for goodness' sake – and cleared her throat.

'Hello, Penmenna parents and staff. I think we're all here now, so let's begin. Please do take a seat and feel free to help yourself to refreshments *afterwards*.' She said the last bit rather forcefully, and Sylvie couldn't help but giggle, but as the two Marion lookalikes glared at her she turned it into a little cough. It was rather like being back at ballet classes with an absolutely terrifying woman at the front barking commands and rapping a cane on the floor to back them up. It would appear that Parent Teacher Associations were a whole new world that the uninitiated had no clue about. Sylvie, up until this point, was very definitely uninitiated.

'Now, I'd like to welcome you to Penmenna School.' She gave a little nod as she said this and a rather sullen-looking acolyte with dark hair behind her pressed a key on the laptop to reveal a picture of the front of the school. She saw Rosy, who was sitting at the front alongside Marion, look around at the sulky brunette and try to give her a cheery smile.

'Penmenna is a school to be proud of, and I'm sure you're aware it has received more than its fair share of media attention recently, as we guide the school through the choppy waters of today's society, never failing to deliver a top-notch education and a raft...' Marion stopped as a GIF of a raft clicked onto the screen and the ladies behind her obediently tinkled. Alex's eyebrows shot up.

'Do you think they're robots?' he whispered.

'I'm happy to answer all questions at the end.' Marion beamed directly at Alex whilst Sylvie felt a strong need to cast her eyes down and fidget with her skirt. 'As I was saying, a raft of outstanding and exceptional extracurricular activities. The Penmenna Hall Restoration Project, which I'm sure every one of you...' again she paused as the PTA nodded vigorously and the new parents in the audience, who realized their obedience was expected, joined in, '…has watched on the television recently. None of this would be possible without our leading lady, Miss Winter…' Marion paused again as her minions led a round of applause and Rosy, managing to look both mortified and resigned, smiled back at the audience, '…and her amazing teaching team steering the school. However, this level of excellence is not unaided by our marvellous PTA…' the ladies all beamed on cue, with the exception of the brunette at the back who was somewhat aggressively hitting the keys on the laptop at appropriate points in the talk, '…who do a marvellous job of fundraising…' Marion continued to talk evangelically about how Penmenna PTA was not just outstanding in every way, but also a rare opportunity to hit a social pinnacle, a life-changing opportunity.

Sylvie was beginning to worry it was a bit cult-like. She was definitely going to approach the brunette and get the real low-down. She tuned back in to Marion's burble.

'And of course, the Penmenna Restoration means that our children get real-life media training, so important from a young age in today's society. I believe it's only a matter of time before my own dear boys are snapped up by a Hollywood agent. And you'll see it invigorates the school, attracts a new calibre of parent, as this year's intake surely demonstrates.' Sylvie watched as Rosy rolled her eyes heavenward, if only for a millisecond, and Marion's gaze seemed to have lit upon Alex again. Shit, should she know who he was? Or was that Marion woman delusional? Sylvie had a strong sense both might be correct.

The speech came to a close, with all parents being urged to sign up and make a difference before hitting the chocolate fountain and decimating the school-shaped sponge cake.

After rapturous applause Marion made a beeline for Alex, who looked at Sylvie in alarm.

'Oh no, an old friend you said. You're on your own.'

'Don't leave me,' he said as forcefully as one could speak out of the corner of their mouth.

Sylvie considered it but decided the entertainment factor of watching him squirm as Marion approached, rictus beam upon her face and dragging one of her cloned minions behind her, made it worth sticking around. Plus, she was intrigued; Marion's not-at-all-hidden mention of celebrity in the room had aroused her curiosity. Perhaps Alex's wife was dead famous. Although notably, still missing.

Marion clearly had no intention of including Sylvie in her intended conversation and with the determination and strategy that generals the world over would envy she managed to manoeuvre herself and her coterie into Alex's personal space whilst cutting Sylvie entirely out.

Clone number one muttered something about keeping one's clothes on as she closed the circle around Alex. Did someone in this hall have a penchant for stripping in public? This would make the PTA considerably more interesting. She wondered who it could be.

Sylvie grinned over Marion's shoulder, gave Alex a thumbs-up and headed for the cheese, eyes peeled for any potential nudity.

Five strawberries covered in chocolate, at least two handfuls of popcorn and half a loaf of bread dripping in melted cheese left Sylvie feeling like the Very Hungry Caterpillar; she had signed up to join the PTA and had let Rosy Winter know that she would love to come in and help with reading. She had also tried to pump the sulky brunette for the inside track on the PTA and whether it really was run as tightly as Stalin's Russia. But the woman, Beth she introduced herself as, stuck to the party line and merely said it was an honour to be part of such a committed group of parents, with *very* high standards of behaviour. Sylvie half expected her to murmur, 'Run,' discreetly and through clenched teeth, or semaphore for help using only her eyebrows, but alas neither of these things actually happened.

What was amusing though was watching Alex from across the room. Marion and her Marion Mark Two were only the first to pin him down; he was now surrounded by an awful lot of mothers, all jostling for attention, flicking their hair and laughing very loudly. Every now and then he would peep a look of desperation at her, puppy-dog eyes pleading for rescue, at which point she'd giggle and eat something else.

However, as much fun as it was laughing at his plight, she did need to go and get Sam, so she turned and left the building.

'Oi!'

She hadn't even got out of the door as Alex broke free, rather like a Labrador shaking off water droplets, scattering simpering women to the four winds.

'I thought we were friends.'

'I never said that,' she teased.

'Friends don't leave friends to be eaten alive by marauding hordes.'

'That's no way to describe the upright citizens of Penmenna, selflessly devoting themselves to community only to be slandered so heartlessly.'

Alex quirked a brow, and she couldn't help but giggle again.

'Hey, Ellie and I haven't eaten yet, we were going to make some pizzas. There's plenty if you and Sam would like to join us.'

Sylvie felt herself flush again before she responded. For goodness' sake, this was ridiculous!

'That sounds lovely.' And it did, but she was split. Firstly, she would love to have a look at where they lived, find some more clues out about him, and Ellie's missing mother. And although she understood the invitation was a platonic one, she was worried about crossing the line and getting too friendly. For all her talk (to herself) about how she wasn't even slightly attracted to him, she was self-aware enough to know she might be fibbing. Just a little. She didn't need to complicate her life even further. What she needed was a job, and some independence, not material to feed any romantic and wildly unhelpful crushes.

'But I've already promised Sam fish and chips on the beach as a special Friday night treat. Thank you for the invite, all the same.'

'No worries. We can do it another time.'

They reached the classroom and as they entered Sam and Ellie dropped the book they were browsing together in the library corner and hurtled at them at top speed.

'Hey there, big guy.' Sylvie dropped a kiss on Sam's head and for the first time ever he looked up at her with abject horror. Her boy was growing up. She'd have to remind herself to keep her displays of affection limited to the house from now on.

'Mum, can I go to Ellie's for tea? We're gonna make pizza and everything. And she got so much stuff to put on *and* we get to throw them.'

'Throw them. Sounds exciting. But what about the beach?'

'We could do that tomorrow, after you're home from work.' She couldn't fault his problem-solving skills.

'The invite still stands and you would both be very welcome,' Alex murmured into her ear, lending his voice to the appeal, whereas Ellie took a far more flamboyant approach by jumping up and down on the spot and shouting, 'Yes, yes, yes, yes. Pizza, pizza, pizza, pizza.'

'Plus, I know from experience that she won't stop that until you do as she wants, and in this particular instance I'm on her side so I'm going to let her. Go on, come. Unless the fish and chips thing was an excuse and there's another reason you can't?'

Um… how about because if I see you being all domesticated and perfect then my currently teeny crush will escalate to unimaginable proportions, said Sylvie. In her head.

'OK, that sounds good.' Were, thankfully, the words she actually spoke. 'You'd best lead the way.'

# Chapter Seven

Ellie grabbed Sam's hand and raced ahead, leading the way from the school, past the church, the corner shop and the butcher's to their house overlooking the beach. Alex knew she loved their new house, because she told him so, about twenty times a day. Apparently, the quirky curves and slightly bumpy walls made it a fairy-tale cottage. He wasn't so sure that damp featured quite so heavily in fairy-tale cottages but was assured by Lottie who worked in the village shop that, in Cornwall, it absolutely did.

He glanced quickly sideways at Sylvie walking alongside him, her wavy red hair falling across her face, covering the small smattering of freckles. There was something elfin about her, otherworldly. Words like *graceful* and *ethereal* sprang to mind when he wanted to describe her; everything she did was measured, contained and beautifully done – until he had seen the way she attacked the cheese fondue. That had made him want to roar with laughter. There he was surrounded by women chattering in high-pitched tones at him, like a chorus of very noisy and irritating starlings. And there was Sylvie, ripping into the bread rather like a bird of prey would a mouse. There was a lot more to her than the reserved image she showed to the world, and he was looking forward to finding out who the core of her was.

His daughter's friendship with Sam was delightful and he was grateful for it. But it was Sam's mother who intrigued him. This juxtaposition of ethereal combined with a laugh so hearty that it just didn't fit the body it emitted from, was fascinating. The captivating woman he had met on the beach versus the one that had run away from him on that first day of school, pretending she couldn't hear him calling after her and never alluding to it again. He had a feeling that there were many layers to Sylvie and he was charmed by each one. Or rather imagined he would be.

Her company was easy and she had a way of making him laugh, particularly cute because most of the time she wasn't trying to. Bringing up Ellie was so much fun, but it could be lonely at times. Chase was great, and Angelina too – although in her very own unique and not-quite-fit-for-children way. But neither had kids of their own and sometimes it took another parent to understand the highs and the lows. Sylvie was doing this all on her own too, or so he assumed from Sam's hilarious request on that very first day, and she seemed to just get it. Truth was, she seemed to just get everything. Pizza night was going to be fun.

Ellie stopped outside their front door, still bouncing on the spot, her favourite thing to do at the moment, and remarkably never leaving her as exhausted as he hoped it would.

He clicked the key in the lock and felt Ellie whoosh past his legs, dragging Sam behind her.

Grinning, he held the door open for Sylvie.

'It's still a bit of a muddle. I only got the keys last week and the stuff from my London flat isn't fully unpacked yet, so if you don't mind manoeuvring around the odd box or two then do come in.'

'Ha, I don't mind. We're at opposite ends of the box spectrum – you're unpacking and I'm filling.'

'Really, how come? Coffee? Tea?' He led the way through the tiny hall, into a dining room, floored with slate that in turn led to an archway into a kitchen, complete with exposed granite walls and a gleaming Aga.

'Yes, please, tea would be lovely. Since Sam started school, I've been sorting through my mum's things. I have been too scared to do it for months and then had some kind of epiphany on the kid's first day.'

'Oh, I'm sorry. I didn't realize.'

'Oh no, don't worry. Of course you didn't. She passed in February after a long illness. She had motor neurone disease so we all knew it was coming, prepared for it even and my goodness she put up a fight, but still, grief hits us all in unexpected ways. And I was just frozen. Have been frozen. But I'm putting things in boxes now and have even been able to cry, which hadn't been happening. Sorry. Burbling. Don't know why. Anyway, boxes, yes. You do seem to have a lot of them!'

'I do, they feel never-ending, but burble away, it's good for the soul. Here you are. Drink and burble.'

'I'll just drink if that's OK. So, tell me about your London place. Have you moved everything down now?' She looked around the kitchen, as if she were both sizing it up and looking for something specific.

'Pizzaaaaaaaaa!' Ellie came roaring in and started banging on the table. 'Pizza! Pizza! Pizza!' Sam stood behind her in the archway, looking utterly entranced by her naughtiness.

'Hey! Stop that, Ells, or we'll be doing it without you. If you want to make pizza then you need to get everything together. Without banging.' Alex used his firmest tone. He hoped it would work; experience taught him it could go either way but it was worth a try. He had to at least attempt to get her to behave, especially with witnesses.

Sam was a great friend for Ellie, and he was hoping he might calm her a little. He didn't want Sylvie thinking Ellie was a brat and stopping them playing together. Honestly, managing a five-year-old was way harder than negotiating war zones. The minute he thought it that same repeated scene, the one where he first set eyes on Ellie, flashed into his mind; he felt his body involuntarily shudder, his eyes close and his breath whoosh out. Compelling him to make a silent apology for thinking something so stupidly flippant.

'What do we need?'

'What do you think we should get?' he answered Ellie, thankful the memory had passed so quickly. It didn't usually, sometimes it liked to stick around. He felt Sylvie's eyes on him, gentle, sympathetic but mildly quizzical. She was far more intuitive than most, it would appear; however, glossing over this was a skill he had perfected and not even the cutest sprite in the forest was going to get that close.

'Sam, what do you think?' Ellie shifted responsibility to her friend.

'Um… tomatoes?'

'Yeah, tomatoes. What else, Sam?'

'Uh… um… cheese? Oh, and I like sweetcorn.'

'OK, have we got sweetcorn, Dad? We really *need* sweetcorn. Like *really* need.' He exchanged a smile with

Sylvie. How Ellie could sound quite so like she was thirteen was always a bit of a shock.

'I reckon I could rustle it up – even better, why don't you get those things from the fridge, ooh, and more tomatoes from the pantry, the corn should be there too. What else?'

Alex could feel Sylvie's eyes on him as he prompted the kids to get everything they needed and lay it out on the table.

'What can I do to help? I love a pantry, not many houses have them now.'

'Yeah, I do too.' He admitted, 'I was brought up in the country, well, Essex, but a country bit of Essex, and when I saw this place had a pantry I was sold. They remind me of childhood.'

'So, if you've only just taken this cottage, where were you staying before, when we met on the beach? Oh, sorry, I guess that's none of my business. Forget I asked, sometimes my curiosity means I overstep.'

'No, not at all, we were staying at my friend Chase's house. I think Ellie would have liked to stay there for ever, it's pretty swish. But I felt if we were committing to staying for a bit, we should commit properly. And Marion, yes, Marion from tonight, suggested this was coming onto the market as a rental and would make a perfect place until I was ready to buy, or move on.'

'Got them!' The children came out of the pantry, overloaded with jars and cans.

'Hmm… do we need all of that? Butter beans, really? Tinned fruit?'

'Yes. I think so.'

Alex decided to appeal to Sam, in his role as Ellie's voice of reason. 'You want tinned cherries on your pizza, Sam?'

'Um… uh… um…' The poor boy looked so torn Alex felt guilty for putting him on the spot.

'How about we start with the basics, make the dough, make the sauce, pop on tomatoes, maybe some onions, sweetcorn for Sam, and then… Ellie, do you like mushrooms? Great, mushrooms then, some cheese…' Sylvie stepped in, patiently listing more traditional toppings.

'Lots of cheese.'

'Lots of cheese, and then we can see how it looks and if we still want beans, and cherries and um… coconut milk, we can think about it then. What do you reckon?'

Alex watched, impressed, as Ellie considered Sylvie's words and nodded.

They lined up all the ingredients and Alex went and found a large mixing bowl. Sylvie showed the children where they needed to get the mark to on the old-fashioned scales and flour was weighed, olive oil and water poured, with Ellie shrieking in delight as it splashed into the pristine flour, making patterns on the top. Sam stood back a little, as if not that keen on mess. Alex figured he'd better get used to it if he was going to be Ellie's friend.

They all took it in turns to stir and then pulled the dough out to knead. Sam wasn't mad keen, despite all of Sylvie's gentle coaxing. He liked the fact that she didn't force it on her son. Lots of parents did – he'd noticed that with some of his peers in London, and swore he would never do it himself when the day came – more concerned for their own ego than the non-verbal messages their children were sending out.

With the three of them giving the dough a good working-over, Sam decided to give it a shot after all, and when he stepped back to let the little boy do so, Alex found himself watching Sylvie's face as she watched her son.

'Hey, this is fun!' Sam began to really pummel the dough and quickly beamed over his shoulder at his mum. Sylvie beamed in return and turned to face Alex, who found it impossible not to grin back at her, caught up in Sylvie's pride and Sam's enthusiasm. Time seemed to pause – just for a second or two – as Sylvie's eyes found his and the two of them stood there, smiling at each other, eyes locked and sharing the moment.

Alex was momentarily struck by all the different shades in her eyes, green, grey, hazel, but more than that, the recognition that this wasn't a mere sexual-pull gaze – he'd had enough experience of the power of those in his life – this was different. This struck something deeper, a soul-bind born of a moment, creating a sense of belonging, an in-this-together feeling which right here, right now was like nothing he had ever felt before. He wanted them all to eat pizza, the four of them to curl up by the fire and stay for ever.

His heart was bowled over regularly with intense joy when Ellie did all sorts of things, both when she was ridiculously clever and really very naughty. He had never fully understood the term 'pride and joy' until he had Ellie in his life, but these days it was something he experienced with frequency. Sharing those moments, however, as he was right now, with another adult, an adult who under-stood the occasional but utter bliss of being a parent, that was like nothing he had experienced before.

The bliss was clearly too much for Sylvie who suddenly broke her gaze, and hence the spell, and muttered something he couldn't quite make out before turning her full attention back to the children, who with the skill that all kids have, had picked up on their parents' brief concentration lapse and were both now beating seven bells out of the dough.

'Whoa! Hold on, I reckon that's ready now.' Sylvie waded in and gently batted both children off and rolled the dough back into a smooth ball, ready to pass to Alex. 'Here you go, what's the next step?'

'Leave it to prove.' He reached out to take the dough from her and accidentally grazed the side of her hand, feeling her flinch in response. He flicked a look at her but she merely turned to the children and suggested they start making the tomato sauce.

The easy camaraderie returned as soon as they started chopping, stirring, spreading and layering and it took no time until there were four individual little pizzas lined up on baking trays ready for the Aga.

Alex placed them in gently and turned to see the bottoms of the children's feet as they flew through the archway and clattered up the stairs.

'Wow! Look at the state of it. They're not stupid, are they?' The two adults stood and surveyed the kitchen, pristine when they entered, now covered in a sheen of fine flour with giant globules of tomato sauce on the table, the floor, the worktops, sliding down the door of the Aga and most of it adorned with the odd sprinkling of bits of chopped vegetables.

'On the upside, they've managed to miss the ceiling. It won't take us long to sort it out.' Sylvie smiled, the nervousness of earlier completely evaporated.

'You know we're going to clean it and then the pizzas will be ready and we'll have to start all over again.'

'Such a ray of sunshine.'

'You've never seen Ellie eat before. Swear she's like some kind of flesh-eating gorgon who manages to get her entire supper not just on her face but on her shoes, in her hair, in different rooms of the house. She's a walking, talking version of Mr Twit's beard.'

'Harsh!'

'Harsh but fair. You wait.'

'Well, I won't be able to even look at her as she eats now. I'll laugh and give her a complex.'

'I think it would take more than a giggle to give that girl a complex. She loves her food.'

'And that's a bad thing?'

'Oh no, no, no. That's totally a good thing. I don't think there's anything healthy about people who pick at their food and worry more than they enjoy.'

'Good, I was beginning to think you were some kind of food Nazi. I'm a big fan of food too. I had years of having to watch everything I ate – trust me, if we're talking of really unhealthy eating attitudes, the culture within my industry is insane. One of the better things about coming back to Cornwall is indulging as much as I like without the fear that people are watching, judging, reporting back. Or maybe it's that I just don't care what they think any more. Believe me, when a Cornish girl has been forcibly denied pasties, clotted cream, and Trevathien's ginger ice cream – oh, have you tried that yet? It's the best – then they're not holding back once they get home!'

'You're going to love me then, I've got that ice cream in my freezer and what's even better is that Ellie doesn't like it so there is some left and you and I have pudding sorted.' Alex watched her flush again; was it because he had used the word *love*? He knew she blushed a fair bit so should be more careful with what he said. Regardless of the look shared a minute ago, this had to be a child-based platonic friendship and he didn't want to blur boundaries. He had worked so hard to create stability for Ellie, he wasn't going to blow that all up now for a beautiful pair of eyes and an imagined sense of belonging. He supposed he was just so relaxed in her company that he wasn't monitoring every word used as he usually did. He quickly changed the subject. 'But tell me more, what industry stops you trying to eat? Jockey? Model?' Her build suggested either were possible.

'No, hardly a model, and I'd love to have been a jockey but I'm afraid not.' Sylvie's answer made Alex wonder, not for the first time, why so many women were so hard on themselves? However, before he could say anything she continued. 'I was a ballet dancer, absolutely loved it. But you know how life is, things don't always pan out as you expect. And do you know what? I'm pretty happy being back in the village with a son who has brightened my life beyond compare and surrounded by pizza mess. I'll take the swap.'

'Wow, it's not easy to become a professional ballet dancer, that's so impressive. But I know exactly what you mean, we spend our twenties pushing, pushing, pushing for professional excellence in fields that are not forgiving, or at least I did, live and die in the excitement, the buzz of the second-by-second lifestyles, only to find proper happiness in the mundane, in a sleepy village in Cornwall.'

'True. Apart from the sleepy bit – you were at that PTA thing with me earlier, weren't you. That's not sleepy, that's downright terrifying.'

'Terrifying? You weren't the one that Marion forced into a corner and tried to get you married to some sort of freaky clone.'

'Hahaha! Was that what she was doing? Someone definitely mentioned the taking off of clothes, was that about you? Ha!'

'I don't know for sure if that was the plan, and I know that makes me sound like an ego-riddled arsehole if I say yes, but honestly, yes. At one point, she told me that Jenny, that was clone number one's name, was not only a great homemaker but very skilled with her hands. Honestly, I didn't know where to look and you were no help.'

He smiled as Sylvie let out the loudest laugh, then clapped her hands over her mouth.

'No, that's fine, you keep amusing yourself at my discomfort. And when I looked to you for support you were too busy scoffing some delicious-bloody-looking cornbread to come and save me from the clutches of those rampant mothers. I tell you, it's frightening.'

'You knew in advance she was frightening, in fact you warned me of it! You can't complain now.'

'I didn't know I was going to be her number one target.'

'Yeah, right. It must be tough being the prettiest boy in the village.'

'Prettiest boy, huh?' Alex could feel the smile take over his face, radiating out of his eyes.

'Well, there's the vicar, he might have the edge on you. And truth is, I have appalling judgement, so I'll just take that back, and um… we'll pretend I didn't say it. Otherwise you'll label me predatory like Marion and I promise I'm not, I'm really not into you like that… ah, I'm making this worse, aren't I?'

'Well, you started quite nicely, but now you've managed to rip my ego into shreds in two short seconds.'

'How about we stick to pizza instead?'

'OK, although this is quite good fun.'

'Teasing me?'

'I was under the impression you were teasing me, actually.'

Beep. Beep. Beep.

'Bloody hell, that's the timer.'

'No way! We haven't even started on the kitchen yet. Here, you grab the pizza and I'll wipe down the table, that'll do for a minute, won't it?'

'Yeah, although you know what, it's a really nice evening still – why don't you grab the pizza, I'll fetch a blanket and we'll have a picnic in the garden instead.'

'You're on!'

'Picnic!' Alex hollered up the stairs so loudly and with such enthusiasm that it was a miracle the pictures on the walls didn't shake.

# Chapter Eight

Sylvie followed Alex out to the garden where he lay a large check blanket underneath a low-hanging tree she recognized as a grey willow. The garden itself was beautiful, larger than she had imagined those belonging to these cottages would be. So close to the sea you could smell the salt and the seaweed in the air but it didn't seem to have too much effect on the things growing.

Being September it was coming to the end of the season, but Sylvie could see the raspberry canes from the summer, next to a host of other fruit bushes. There were remnants of sweet peas that had clambered up trellises throughout the early summer months and now were ready to be cut down and composted.

A huge Cornish palm tree dominated the far corner of the garden where there was a large shed, painted a pale seaside blue, and a woodshed, with all the logs chopped and arranged in higgledy-piggledy rows ready for the coming winter.

She watched as Ellie and Sam came out through the wooden kitchen door, balancing pots of salad bits that Alex had instructed them to bring from the fridge, a green salad, beetroot and goat's cheese, coleslaw.

Everything was placed in the centre of the blanket and then they all slowly munched their supper, content with the last of the day's sunshine warming their skin.

Sylvie fell into her usual evening meal routine with Sam, without even thinking. It was a time the two liked to catch up on all that had been done in the day, and today had been so hectic that they hadn't done so yet.

'So, Sam, Ellie, have you had a good day? What did you do at school?'

Sometimes Sam would just murmur *nothing* and sometimes he would tell her in great detail, every possible second covered of what he had been up to. She never knew which it would be, but from his face this evening, it looked like it would be the latter.

'Oh, we did a wishing tree, didn't we, Ellie?'

Sam put his pizza down, unlike Ellie who nodded and made an uh-huh-yummmm noise as she gave him a thumbs-up and carried on eating her pizza at an alarming speed.

'A wishing tree. Sounds cool. How does it work?' Alex joined in.

'We all think what we'd wish for most in the world and then we write it on a leaf, a leaf made of paper...' Sam liked to be accurate, '...and hang it on our wishing tree. Miss Winter says mummies and daddies can come and see, so I can show you next school day. That's not tomorrow, is it?'

'No! Tomorrow is Sat-ur-day,' Ellie was interested in that enough to pause eating, 'and Daddy's taking me to see Angileeena!'

'That wasn't a promise, that was a maybe,' Alex clarified.

'What if I make it a wish, then it has to come true.'

'That's not exactly how it works,' Alex qualified and the children looked at him, horrified. As if he had kidnapped the tooth fairy and hidden her in a cupboard somewhere.

'So, what did you both wish for?' Sylvie tried to divert them.

'I wished for an elephant.'

'OK,' grinned Sylvie. 'To have for ever? To see one? What do you want your elephant for?'

'I want an elephant 'cause we have the same name nearly so we'd have to be friends…'

'That's not tru…' Sam interrupted only to stop, horrified by his own daring.

'Go on, Sam, what were you going to say?' Alex prodded gently. Sylvie tried to avoid scrunching her face up, her go-to reaction when she was worried about what might happen next. Sam did not like being put on the spot; he could retreat back into his shell so very easily.

But instead he looked at Alex, swiped a quick glance at Ellie and spoke.

'Just that I know another Sam from gym club and I didn't like him…'

Ellie scowled.

'…but I 'spect your elephant will be different, Ellie.'

'Of course it will. And we're going to be friends, and it can sleep in the shed, and it will give me rides to school and then everyone will be like… Ellie, I want to be friends with you 'cause you've got an elephant and I'll say I'm sorry, I might let you stroke him but he's my elephant and he only likes me and Sam, so there.' Finally, she stopped to take a breath, Alex looked like he wasn't sure what he was supposed to do or say in this situation and Sylvie had to fight back the laughter, both at Ellie's conviction that this was going to happen, and any day now; and at Alex's fear that that might be the case!

'That sounds great, I can see why you'd want an elephant, Ellie. Although it would be a long way from home if it came to Cornwall. He might get a bit chilly.'

Ellie narrowed her eyes at Sylvie. The child did not like to be challenged.

'I'd give him a blanket.'

'Good idea, we might have to put lots together, so it was big enough. What about Sam…' Sylvie made her tone gentle, '…did you have a wish?'

'Yes.'

'Did you want to tell us?'

'Um… um… do you have a wish, Mummy? Alex?'

'Alex?' Sylvie echoed her son.

'Oh, I don't know. I'm pretty happy with things, I don't know what I'd wish for. I suppose I should go big, I don't know, world peace? Yep, I'm going to use my wish on world peace.'

'That's cheating, we all want world peace, don't we?' Sylvie laughed loudly and the children nodded vigorously, although they didn't really know what she meant.

'It's not cheating.'

'OK, it's not, and it's a very admirable wish. But what about something more… more personal.'

'Oh, ah, I don't know. Do you know what, actually I do. I've had an idea bubbling and I don't know if I'm ready to verbalize it yet. I don't want to jinx it before I've seen if I can get it off the ground.'

'Maybe we can help you get it off the ground.'

'Maybe you can.' Alex found himself giving her a glance that was far too flirtatious. OK, he was going to have to explain now, give it some context, so he didn't look like a complete creep. 'I've been toying with doing some fundraising, serious fundraising to help kids caught up in civil war. I'm just not sure how yet, it's the beginnings of a plan, a kernel, that's all.'

'That sounds like an ace plan. I'd love to help if I could. Let me know when it takes shape and I'll help in any way I can.'

'Only if you promise not to be bossy.'

'I can't promise that.' Sylvie scrunched her face up mischievously.

'Yes. Don't be bossy to my daddy.'

'No, Ellie, I was teasing, of course she wouldn't. She was being helpful and I was just joking. I shouldn't have said that and thank you for standing up for me but you mustn't be rude to our guests.'

Ellie didn't look convinced.

'I promise not to boss your daddy about.' Sylvie smiled.

'OK. What about you, Sam's mum, do you have any wishes?'

'Do you, Mum?'

'Yes, I suppose I do. Although now I feel bad because they're pretty selfish compared to Alex's. I'd really like to get the chance to learn more about Berber, North African, dance – it's always fascinated me. I was going to be part of an educational exchange thing when I was working but then became pregnant and someone else had to go instead...' She was aware that Sam was watching and listening to every word. '...and I had my baby, which was the best thing in the world, far better than any dance stuff, and now I'm the happiest mummy ever.'

'That's good, it's nice to be a happy mummy.' Alex smiled down at Sam before continuing, 'But you'd still like to explore it? What sort?'

'Yes, that's hard to answer, there are so many different types and I guess that's part of what fascinates me. There are three main types of Berber folk music, and the dances are often tied to rituals and have meaning. They can be to celebrate masculinity or femininity, obviously some are for ceremonies such as weddings, some have been repurposed and in modern use have become quite political. They even have a dance for exorcism and their musicians are seen as doctors for the body and soul. It's fascinating, I love it, I love the way dance is an embedded and valued part of culture, I could ramble on about it for ever. I used to dream about it. I guess it's just an itch that hasn't been scratched.'

'I like dance too. Is that your best wish?' Ellie asked. They were obviously no longer mortal enemies.

'Hmm, I guess whilst I'm wishing, a house in the village for me and Sam would be great, oh, and a new job to help pay for it. That's three wishes. Am I allowed that many or does it make me greedy?'

'Oh no, that's OK, three wishes is what it is in stories,' Sam reassured her.

'That's true.'

'I wished...' Sam spoke quietly but was obviously now happy to share, 'I wished Ellie would be my friend for ever.'

'Course I am! For ever and ever and ever and ever and ever.' Ellie's mouth dropped open and her eyes widened as if she couldn't believe what she was hearing, and then pulling herself together rubbed his shoulder quite hard as she answered. Hard enough to almost unbalance him. 'Wanna go play teddies? We could take them some of your pizza if you don't want it.'

'I'm full, they can have it.'

'Come on then, race you.' And she bounded up, grabbed the pizza crusts from his plate and hurled herself into the house in typical Ellie fashion.

'Glass of wine?'

'Oh, thanks but no, my car's at school, I should get Sam home. Let me help you clear up, and then we'll make a move.'

'But Ellie's teddies are *starving*! How could you be so selfish? How about we have a coffee – I've got decaff as well – and then they can have an extra half-hour, we can enjoy the last of the sun and I'll clear up on my own later.'

'That doesn't sound very fair.'

'What if I make it a wish?'

'Really.'

Alex raised his hands. 'Yeah, I know. But Ells is having such a nice time, I reckon half an hour and she'll be ready for bed, so you spare me the horror of her jumping on me demanding stuff by letting her play with Sam instead.'

'So, you're saying me staying for a drink would be a kindness, charity even?'

'Ha, yes. That's it. I'm in need of all the help I can get. I love her, but oh my! Will you help?'

'You make the coffee, I'll wipe down some surfaces and you're on.'

'OK. And then we're going to work out how to get you a new job! I've already got an idea.'

Coffee made, they headed back to the blanket. The sun was beginning to set and the sky was alive with the boldest pinks and oranges there could be. This really was heavenly, she couldn't remember feeling this relaxed in the evening since, well, since for ever.

'So, earlier you said you needed work and ideally a home in the village.'

'Yup,' said Sylvie, not really willing to give any more away and wondering where he was going with this.

'So, if you were a professional ballerina in London before you moved back down, what do you do now? Or are you concentrating on Sam and not working at all at the moment?'

'I'm definitely prioritizing Sam but with him in school that gives me a bit more flexibility, and obviously up until recently I was helping care for my mum. But I do teach a couple of classes as well – I have two evening classes in adult self-defence and I run a couple of ballet classes for little ones on a Saturday as well, both at Roscarrock leisure centre. In fact, that's how I know Rosy Winter a little bit – she took one of my defence classes a few years ago.'

'Self-defence from ballet seems a bit of a stretch.'

'I can see why you'd think that, but the truth is I did ballet, taekwondo and jiu-jitsu from a really young age, and they do both have quite a lot in common in terms of discipline and flexibility. I went into ballet professionally but I still do the martial arts, still do gradings and stuff.'

'What grade are you?'

'Um… I'm a black belt third dan in taekwondo and fourth dan in jiu-jitsu.'

'So you could completely kick my arse if you needed to?'

'I could *completely* kick your arse any time, big man.'

'Do you know what?' Alex held her eyes and she couldn't bring herself to look away. Those eyes really were something. Glancing at them was enough to make her tingle, but staring into them – a girl could get utterly lost. Alex continued speaking and it took all her self-control to concentrate. 'I believe you utterly. I'm no fool, there's no way I'm putting it to the test. OK, so what would you like to do if you had your own way?'

'I love teaching, I love little ones…'

'You're a natural with them, it's impossible not to notice.'

'Oh, I don't know about that, but I do enjoy their company so. Your Ellie is a joy, she's a real firecracker. She's done Sam such a world of good in one short week, I'm very glad she's in his life.'

'She's certainly something. And I'm very grateful Sam is in her life too. So, you want to teach young children?'

'Not as a teacher teacher. I don't want to go and do my training but I would love to teach ballet properly, here in Cornwall.'

'Well, why don't you do that then?'

'I'm hoping to. When I started teaching my ballet classes I rang the village hall and it's booked absolutely solid, no appropriate slots at all, so I needed to find another location and Roscarrock was the easiest. But I'd really like to start something locally, rather than always driving miles away. Plus, staying local would mean I could increase my hours and ultimately I'd like to build up from running classes to having my very own ballet school – but that's my ten-year plan, not for right now.'

'Oh, you are speaking to the right man, I do love a plan. But first steps, what about seeing if you could rent the school hall, use that as a community space? The village hall doesn't have to be the only option. You should talk to Rosy about it.'

'That's not a bad idea.'

'You know who you really need, who could round up a veritable army of customers desperate for their little ones to study with a proper ballerina?'

'Don't say it. Rosy has already said it.'

'You need…'

'No! Don't! Black belt, remember. I swear to God I'll suffocate you with this cushion.'

'You. Need.' Alex brought up two cushions in front of his face to defend himself. 'Marion.'

Sylvie attacked him with the remaining cushion, laughing so much that her tummy began to hurt, Alex laughing alongside her as the tears ran down her face.

# Chapter Nine

'Hi, Rosy.'

'Hi, Lynne. Come in. Is everything OK?'

'Oh yeah, the kids are fine, they're just out for break at the moment.'

Lynne and Rosy shared the responsibilities for teaching Class One and Mondays and Fridays were Lynne's turn in class enabling Rosy to do head-teacher-y office-based things.

'I thought I'd whizz over and talk to you now. I had planned to do it at lunch or after school but honestly I'm just so excited I can't wait.'

'Go on.' Rosy turned in her swirly chair as Lynne pulled one of the visitor's chairs alongside her and did the cat-scrabbling-on-a-knee-thing to Rosy, as she always did when she was excited about something. They had been firm friends ever since Rosy's first day in Penmenna when Lynne had found Rosy hiding in the stationery cupboard, alternately deep-breathing and ramming huge wedges of chocolate orange in her mouth, before she introduced herself to the staff for the very first time.

'I couldn't tell you last night when I found out because I was waiting for Dave. When he got in and I told him, well, then… anyway, I didn't get the chance to call. And then this morning I was going to be so professional but

I just can't keep it in any longer. I'm going to absolutely burst if I can't tell you now!' The scrabbling was getting quite fast, and she was grinning so wide and gritting her teeth with such sheer excitement that Rosy's heart was quite filled with love for her friend.

'That sounds like it could get super-messy. You'd best tell me right now!'

'Right now?' Lynne stopped scrabbling and smiled.

'Oh, my goodness. Go on! You can't build up like that and then tease me and withhold. You ratbag.'

'I'm pregnant!'

'What? Oh, my goodness. Pregnant? Oh, wow!' Rosy jumped from her chair and flung her arms around Lynne's neck.

'Hey, if I want to be a mother you have to let me breathe,' Lynne giggled with excitement as she tried to bat Rosy off.

'I'm so sorry, I just can't believe it. I'm so excited. Woohoo! Wow.'

'Did you really woohoo me? I've never heard you woohoo.'

'Is everything OK?' Sheila the school secretary popped her head around the door.

'Oh yes, yes.' Rosy regained her composure quickly and sat back in her chair with her most authoritative face on. She knew Lynne well enough to know this wasn't news to be shared just yet. 'All's fine. Thank you, Sheila.'

Sheila did not look convinced as she headed back to her office, shutting the door behind her.

'Thank you, Rosy. I swear that woman can smell baby-related news. Had I not taken a test I could have just stood at the front desk and let her sniff me. If she finds out for sure I'll have three pairs of knitted lemon booties in my pigeonhole by home-time and everyone in a ten-mile radius would have been informed of my predicted due date.'

'Truth. Sweet as she is, it does seem the only thing she can do efficiently.'

'Ouch! That's not like you.'

'Oh, trust me, I've had a morning of it. Do you know she emailed the parents' newsletter to the school nurse, and printed out a hundred copies of Jade James's medical notes for the PTA to put in the trays. Then made me a cup of coffee as a peace offering once she heard Sarah from the PTA asking what she should do, but put salt in it by mistake, so we now have a hundred copies of Jade's confidential notes covered in coffee needing to be shredded, and a dry-cleaning bill for Sarah Sutton's white dress.'

'Hahahahaha, brilliant. I mean, oh dear. That's some morning. Ooh, that reminds me, you'll never guess what Pippa and I overheard this morning, the juiciest titbit! I know you do the whole disapprove-of-gossip thing *but* in your role as head you *do* need to know what's going on.'

Rosy raised an eyebrow and smirked. 'In my role as head I *should* know what's happening across the school – go on.'

'Well, we heard Marion talking to Sarah. Marion was telling her all about her plans.'

'No, please, not another one! She has been awfully quiet of late. Go on.'

'She is determined to keep Ellie's dad in Penmenna, something about cachet, good looks and a media profile. Anyway, apparently she has decided the way to do it is to get him married within the village. The poor man doesn't stand a chance.' Lynne's face was alight with delight.

'No, she hasn't! And you're right, he doesn't. I feel we should warn him?'

'You have no duty of care, he's not a pupil. I say he's an adult who can sort himself out and you have always refused to get caught up in parent politics.'

'True.'

'Apparently, she's already tried to push Jenny on him but, and I quote – "I did try and guide him Jenny's way, but he's a man of such good taste he clearly saw her as a pale imitation." However, she's not giving up. She reckons she'll have him married by next summer!'

'She probably will. Poor man. You're right that I shouldn't get involved, it's got nothing to do with Penmenna School as such, but thanks for telling me. At least whilst she's playing Cupid she's not trying to mess with school policy. Now, let's talk about you, and mini-you. Tell me all you know!'

'OK, it's very early days and I guess most women wouldn't be telling anyone yet, and you know the history here, Rosy, that is the only reason I'm telling you. I think I'm only about eight weeks, but I did a test last night and have an appointment booked in with the GP this afternoon after class. I'm going to ask for an early pregnancy scan, just to rule out… well, you know, just to make sure everything is OK this time.'

'Of course. Let me take class this afternoon so you can get off.'

'Bless you, no. It's not until five and I want to keep busy so I don't overthink and start to worry. Let's just keep everything normal for now. And between us. But obviously if everything is OK then I'm going do my utmost…'

'Lynne, you don't need to explain. I will do everything I can to help you. Starting with stopping you doing all of Amanda's PE work.'

'I'm sure it will probably be fine, it's not the nineteenth century. I can probably carry my own shopping as well.'

'Ha! As if Dave is going to let you do that.'

'He insisted on carrying my morning tea to the table for me this morning. I mean, I know I should be grateful, and it's cute and all, but really. And then he stood over me and made me eat porridge. And I found he'd put my Nutella in the bin.'

'Oh, I think that's going to get worse. I can't control what goes on at home but you and I both know working with young kids is hard physical work. The whole point of this new PE curriculum is that it's very, very physical both for the kids and the staff. I can't force anything on you but I would feel better knowing you were as protected as you can be. Anyone else who was expecting, then of course PE is fine but Lynne, with your history, if I were to have my way you'd be on bed rest for the next seven months. I'm on Dave's side, I'm afraid.'

'I think that's the first time you and he have agreed on anything,' Lynne giggled.

'It's not my fault he has abominable music taste, but exactly, and Marion Marksharp has rubbed off on me. Don't think I'll have any qualms about becoming the next school Machiavelli and finding all sorts of methods of getting my own way on this. It would be so much easier if you just played along.'

'OK. Although I'd like to point out that in Dave's defence his medieval music helped bring you and Matt together.' Her friend sighed and smiled, but Rosy knew her well enough to know that Lynne was relieved to be let off the hook. The loss of her other pregnancies had absolutely devastated Lynne, who had been plunged into a deep depression after the last failed pregnancy a year and a half ago. Dave had proved an enormous support throughout it all and the two had loudly declared that they had made their peace with not being parents and talked hyper-loudly about cruises and sports cars. But it had taken Lynne a long time to recover, to return to her usual zestful self, and Rosy couldn't blame her for wanting to be cautious this time around.

'So he may claim. There's an argument we would have been dating quicker if Matt hadn't butchered "Greensleeves" in my garden.' Rosy knew this was utterly untrue but it was fun to tease. There were lots of reasons her and Matt hadn't got together as quickly as he had wanted and Dave certainly wasn't one of them. That, Rosy had to take full responsibility for. 'Anyway, no more PE, I'll find someone to cover. I understand you don't want it being public knowledge and I understand why, but how about we let Pippa know? What do you think? Then she can jump in in any class situations that look like they're going to get tricksy.'

Pippa was the TA for Class One and both Rosy and Lynne trusted her utterly. Teaching young children was not as simple as standing at the front and barking at them, especially the young ones. Most of the time you'd be getting down on the floor with them, and interacting, not just teaching them a love of learning to help shape their whole future school career – for many it was also about teaching behaviour in school, setting firm boundaries and seeing them through. Of course, schools should be a haven of peace and calm, where a tranquil absorption of facts and the ability to critically think took place. But the truth was that every year group would have children who would struggle with this, especially as they were first settling in and usually through no fault of their own. In Rosy's teaching career she had been kicked, hit, punched, bit, and even walloped with a chair. This was what she was determined Lynne could not engage in. Admittedly, there were fewer of these incidences in Penmenna than some of the schools she had worked in before, and she and Lynne were highly skilled at heading off this sort of behaviour before it escalated but still, she needed to be prepared and protect Lynne at all costs. Pippa needed to be in on that team.

'I think that may be a good idea. Little Harry has a habit of running into people at full tilt and whilst I think we've managed to stop that, it's early days and he is still very unpredictable. And Ellie, as cute as she is, can be quite tempestuous. I think we may have more to see from her yet.'

'Right, consider it done. Pippa can ensure you're good in the classroom, I'll get cover for the new PE curriculum. Lynne, your news is so amazing. I couldn't be happier for you. Let me know what the doctor says every step of the way. You've got this!' And standing again she enveloped her friend in another great big hug and pretended to ignore the single tear of relief that trickled down Lynne's cheek.

# Chapter Ten

Sylvie walked back into her mother's room for one last time. It smelt fresh again and she had managed to condense the things she held most dear into one large box that she could take with her when she actually managed to move out, although that felt like a fast-fading dream at present.

It was nearly the end of September and she had been hanging on for winter lets to come available next month, far from ideal but at least something, a stopgap. Only to be told by the letting agency yesterday that they had nothing at all, not in that village. She could hear his voice now, a young man barely out of college with a smug look and lilac tie – perhaps she should try further afield, Penmenna might not be the best choice for her budget. She had wanted to take the sheaf of paper sitting on his poxy glass desk and scrunch it into the air, letting each sheet fall as she maintained eye contact – but of course she didn't.

Penmenna had been her home since birth until she had fled to London. She hadn't expected to be priced out upon her return. But she couldn't really stay at the farm much longer, and neither did she want to. Not only did it feel like living in the Dark Ages – neither her mother nor uncle seemed to have understood the term 'decorating' or 'natural light' – it wasn't fair on Tom either. She glanced around the room one more time before shutting the door and heading back downstairs. She had dropped most of her mother's clothes to the charity shop before braving the agent's and the furniture in the room would remain in situ, each bit a part of the farm's history, here long before the word *flat-pack* had been dreamt up, and bound to remain in place for many more years yet.

Tom was ten years younger than her mother and had been dating Julie, who lived at Brokenshire Farm, three farms down the lane. They had been dating for years now and it appeared to be a relationship strongly rooted in a bygone age, that revolved around country walks, holding hands and home-baked pies. It was not, she imagined, a relationship that felt the need for new furniture. It was however one that was perhaps waiting upon Tom's niece and great-nephew to sod off so he could make an honest woman of his sweetheart.

She left the room and went downstairs to the writing desk situated in the dining room; again, like the farm itself and Tom and Julie, it harked back to a former time. She knew her mother had done all her correspondence from there, preferring to write letters by hand and using cheques to pay for feed, vets and all the other things the farm required. Her father had bought them a computer, a big old heavy-backed monitor and tower that would still burr and whirr as it fired itself up, but as far as she was aware her mother certainly never used it and Tom only did so for a basic spreadsheet facility. Alongside it sat a printer which looked as if the ink might have dried up some twenty years ago. It was only as Sylvie moved back home that they had even countenanced the need for Wi-Fi, and even then she had known it was to humour her.

She sat at the desk and saw how at odds the outdated beast that took up so much space was amongst the floral notelets that her mother favoured, watercolours of violets, roses and carnations sacked up in a neat pile next to a pad of blue Basildon Bond and matching envelopes that Margaret had also used. Her mother had been forty when she had had Sylvie, but her rural upbringing had such an influence she appeared older than the other women her age that Sylvie had met and known in London. They wouldn't have been seen dead with a floral notelet. They would have been Biba and Mary Quant whereas her mother would have been ecstatic about a new mid-calf polyester skirt.

Sylvie let her breath out slowly and counted to ten before returning to the task in hand. She knew she didn't really need to go through this bit of the house, but after clearing her mother's room and having a wildly unproductive kitchen sort-out, this was all that was left. Then everything would be done, bringing an air of finality, of closure, that Sylvie needed.

Maybe with all this done her mind would be free to magic up a new home for her and Sam regardless of budgetary restriction and snotty letting agents. Unlikely as it was maybe it was this, a formal goodbye to the farm and her mother's life within it, that was holding her back.

She pulled open the first drawer and saw nothing of note – receipts and account books, all to do with the farm. Some had the neat cursive script of her mother's hand and some had Tom's scrawlier scribble, but there was nothing that needed to go. She pulled each walnut side drawer, some stickier than others, and all but one contained farm things. The bottom one had her mother's driving licence, a passport that had expired years ago and other bits and bobs that could be brought out to go into the memory box.

She leant back in the high-armed chair, letting her upper body be encircled by the wood, and looked at the passport photo. She could remember their one trip away as clear as yesterday. It was meant to have been the start of many family holidays, a plan that could never come to being once Tom's ashen-faced arrival in the farm kitchen had occurred.

She didn't want to dwell on that day, the day that shaped her mother's determination that Sylvie must escape the farm and make the most of any opportunity, whatever the cost. The day that cemented in her mother's mind that sending Sylvie to board at the Royal Ballet School at eleven was the best way to guarantee her a bright future. As an adult Sylvie had wondered if this was in homage to her father, as much about the past as the future. Ensuring her father's dreams for her came true as much as Margaret's. Today though she turned her mind to their holiday, the one the passports had been issued for.

There had been so much excitement; they were a family that never left the farm, so when her father decided enough was enough and booked tickets for a week in France, neither Margaret nor Sylvie could believe their luck.

After arranging cover for a week with John, who was a casual farmhand at that stage before the necessity had turned him into Tom's right-hand man, they had boldly caught the ferry to Roscoff.

Just the sway of the water had felt so glamorous to Sylvie, and then to discover it had not one or two but three restaurants and a cinema on deck. And signs that were both in English and French. She felt like Cinderella, and it was not outside the bounds of possibility that there could have been a French prince just waiting on board for a Cornish maiden to appear and make his dreams come true. It was all so bewitching she would have been happy to spend their week away just exploring the boat.

Instead they'd stayed at a campsite just outside of Morlaix and there had been a water slide and swimming pool and boules. The list of new treats had been endless and the chatter of the families around them was exciting, not just their own Cornish accent, but English accents from up and down the country, intermingling with the French, Germans, Dutch and Spanish. Sylvie had felt she was in a multicultural mecca and resolved that as soon as she was old enough she would be leaving Penmenna and exploring the delights of the world. She was sure there were probably even more campsites in France to see.

Having made friends in the pool and the children's club – the girls being entranced as she flew across the grass lawns almost pulling off a grand jeté and the boys equally so as she threw the biggest one to the ground when he had laughed at her – meant that she was sure she could shake off the shackles of Penmenna and mix internationally from here on in. Not a bad lesson for a nine-year-old.

She chuckled at the memory, her mother's passport still in her hand, and forced her mind back to the trip, revelling in the memories of her father. How they had crammed themselves with French bread and cheese, although Sylvie wasn't quite sure of it, all squidgy with a different smell from that which she was used to but her mother and father had loved it, talking about new adventures and new things to try which had led to a heady night where the two of them had tried snails, green and oozing with garlicky butter. A step too far for Sylvie.

Her parents had been so happy and playful that week, different people from when they were at home and the burden of the farm was upon them. The three of them had sat on the grass outside their tent on that last day and Sylvie had made them do a pinkie promise, a promise that they would come away again. And spent her return journey feeling replete, secure in the fact they would have so many more adventures, and that maybe there was more to her parents than she had thought.

Life had different plans for the three of them.

# Chapter Eleven

It was Friday afternoon and Rosy was wandering through the school. This was traditionally when the children had Golden Time, an activity that was extra fun or of their choosing. This week she had asked Sylvie if she'd come in and show Class Four some basic self-defence moves. Whilst she knew Amanda ruled them with a rod of iron there were some fairly feisty characters in the class so she thought she should maybe just have a meander through and make sure all was going well. With Alice out for the afternoon and Amanda at a medical appointment, she needed to check that Sylvie hadn't been bound and gagged and held to ransom by Rafe Marksharp, Marion's oldest son. He had form for such behaviour. He was the quietest of the three of her boys but still entirely capable of planning and enacting a classroom revolution. He had never been as rowdy as his brothers but he was certainly the one who had inherited the most of his mother's skills.

She walked through the library, gleaming as always thanks to the strong work of the PTA, whom she had successfully dissuaded from installing CCTV to monitor who was doing what where, and which child had dared, dared, to leave a crisp packet under the brightly coloured beanbags. She spotted a small group from Class Three accompanied by their teaching assistant sitting in the corner taking it in turns to read from *The Lion, the Witch and the Wardrobe*, and couldn't help as the corner of her mouth turned up. This was what it was about, those kids right there, engaged, happy, captivated even.

As she pulled the hefty wooden weight of the old door, ever so quietly so as not to distract, she saw the whole of Class Four in the hall. One half sat on the benches watching the other, paired up and performing a very basic martial art move onto the colourful foam mats on the floor. Sylvie moved quietly from couple to couple, instructing in a very gentle manner – her low voice pulling the children in to listen hard. As she righted each pair, she would then explain to those on the benches the positive things each one was doing, or why she had made a correction. She used simple language but without babying them and invited them to verbally participate. Rosy leant against the door jamb; not a single child had turned to see who had come into the room, so enrapt were they with the lesson unfolding in front of them. It was as if they were caught in the siren spell that Sylvie's calm tones had woven.

Even Jade James and Rafe, who somehow Sylvie had paired together, were following her lead and doing as they were told. She was using them as an example and their promotion to a position of authority was working. Amanda did not usually give them the chance to even wiggle out of place, let alone lead the others, and it looked like Sylvie's method was by far the most effective. They were choosing to stay and learn rather than being metaphorically pinned down and forced.

A few minutes passed and Rosy watched as Sylvie smoothly managed a transition as those on the benches took their turn to practise. Jade and Rafe were quelled with a smile when they began to giggle between themselves on the bench and Rosy stood in awe. Sylvie was displaying the soft skills that every teacher needed and often took years to learn. She had noticed when this mum was supporting reading in Class One that she had a natural style with the children, able to encourage and increase the confidence of the children she was listening to with no great fanfare or ego. The children that often struggled seemed to migrate naturally to her and Rosy could feel the flourishing of an idea that had begun to germinate the minute she walked into the hall.

Sylvie looked up, as if knowing she was being considered, and grinned at Rosy.

'Good afternoon, Miss Winter. We're having a real nice afternoon, aren't we, everyone? Do you want to join us?'

'Do you know what, I just might, but only for a minute. Now I should warn you, Miss Williams has taught me self-defence before, so I'm not a complete newbie. Who wants to take me on as a partner?'

'I will, Miss Winter.' Rafe jumped off the bench, ready to have another go.

'Does that mean you can beat Matt up, miss?' Jade couldn't help herself. All the children in the school knew Rosy's partner from their work at Penmenna Hall over the last couple of terms and it hadn't taken long before the news that their head teacher was dating the television gardener had spread around the village. It had taken Rosy a little longer to accept the fact that everyone knew and that was fine.

'I don't need to do that, Jade, he's not daft!'

'Are you the boss then, miss?'

'I wouldn't say that. We work together.'

'She's the boss then,' Rafe said knowingly as Rosy arched her eyebrows and considered flipping him to the ground. Her professionalism was stronger than her desire to beat up small children but she couldn't resist teasing him as she pretended she was about to do so.

'Whoa, miss!' Rafe bellowed as he thought he was going to fly through the air, only to giggle as she pulled him back to straight up again on the mat. 'Whoa, you scared me for a minute there.' He grinned at her. 'Got it, you work together.'

'Yep, that's the one, Rafe.' She joined in with the class for a bit, glad to see that Sylvie didn't seem particularly fazed by her presence. As the hall clock started to edge towards three o'clock Sylvie got the children to tidy away the mats and benches and change from the PE kits they were wearing. It was accompanied with a lot of groaning and, 'Oh, miss. Do we have to?' and, 'Can we do this again next week?'

Rosy lugged the last mat back against the wall, helping Ollie who had been hauling it across by himself.

'Miss Williams, that was so much fun. If you've got a minute – and I know you've got to get Sam – could we have a word in my office after?'

# Chapter Twelve

Sylvie ran from the hall towards Class One, her feet tripping across the quad at super-speed. She had never been late for Sam before, she hoped he wasn't one of the first out. Rounding the corner, she saw him standing next to his teacher, Mrs Rowe, but paying her very little attention as Ellie stood by his side chattering away about something at such a speed that Sylvie couldn't begin to make head nor tail of it.

Alex stood listening, seemingly intently, to Mrs Rowe until he saw Sylvie approach, at which point his face lit up. She couldn't help it as the corners of her mouth turned up and formed themselves into a huge grin. She had been trying to exercise a bit more self-control of late; she found she couldn't help grinning like something possessed whenever she saw him, and even more so since the night they had cooked pizza and had a picnic. Her initial appreciation of him was fast becoming an enormous crush that would hurtle out of control if she didn't get a hold of herself and soon. However, her mind didn't seem to be communicating this fact effectively to her body.

Him beaming at her like that was not helping.

She tried to force her features into a slightly stricter look, and attempted to issue her thanks in a gruff and serious I'm-not-smiling-like-a-lunatic-because-I-have-a huge-crush-on-you-I'm-just-naturally-grinny voice.

'Hey, thanks for keeping an eye on Sam. I got caught up with Mrs Adams's class.' She wasn't convinced that had sounded as gruff as intended.

'No worries, what are you doing now? Wanna come play?'

'Isn't that what the kids are meant to say?'

'Are you suggesting I'm past it, not down with the youth?'

'Well, I was suggesting that perhaps you weren't eight, but if I'm wrong I apologize.'

'I think I should keep a log of the apologies you need to offer me.'

'A log, a log of apologies owed? Are you joking me? I have been nothing but a perfect friend to you since your child swore on the beach.' Sylvie caught Mrs Rowe's smirk. 'Oh goodness, Mrs Rowe, she didn't swear, not really. I was just teasing Alex.'

'Mmm, yes, I can see. And don't worry, I wasn't listening. Have a lovely weekend the both of you.' Lynne smiled at them, ruffled Sam's hair and turned to go back in the classroom now all the children, bar Ellie and Sam, were gone. Sylvie felt that the smile Mrs Rowe gave them suggested she had very much been listening, and drawing all sorts of incorrect conclusions indeed.

'And now you've got us in trouble with the teacher, really. That also needs to be logged.' Alex nodded seriously, as if this was a crime beyond words.

'Twit.'

'Oh my goodness, I'm going to need a whole forest's worth of books at this rate. Anyway, if you could hold fire on the insults for a bit the invite still stands. Wanna come over for a cuppa and let the kids play for a bit? I could do with a pal, truth be told.'

'Um, I would, but I've got to go and see Miss Winter, she asked me to come to her office after I got Sam.'

'Did she? See, you are in trouble with the teachers, that's why you were trying to drag my poor darling Ellie…'

'Yep.' Ellie looked around at her name.

'Nothing, just chatting. Are you and Sam coming? School's finished for the week, you know.'

'Come on then.' Ellie skipped down from the granite school step upon which she had been standing and motioned Sam to follow. Which obviously, he did.

Sylvie was so pleased that Sam had grown in confidence since his friendship with Ellie, but she really hoped he developed a way of not just slavishly following the little girl everywhere. She just needed to find a way to word it that was appropriate for a four-year-old.

'…as I was saying, you were obviously using my daughter to divert attention from your own misdeeds.' Alex finished his sentence, pulling Sylvie's attention back to him.

'Caught, officer. That was it exactly. I'm a bad girl.' Without thinking she put her wrists up in front of her, as she would have had she been messing about with one of her old friends in London. 'Oh no, I'm not, oh, um… I don't know why I said that, oh, for goodness' sake!' Sylvie flustered that she had said something so flirtatious. Thank God she had stopped before suggesting he discipline her! Although that would be quite nice.

'Do you want me to bring Sam back with us whilst you talk to Rosy? If you're only a minute you can run and catch us up, and if you're longer you don't have to fret about him waiting.'

Sylvie shot him a grateful smile for glossing over her faux pas so gracefully.

'Do you know what, that would be really helpful.'

'OK, Sam, you're coming back with us, is that OK?'

Sam gave him a massive thumbs-up.

'And…' Alex continued to speak but leant in close to Sylvie as he did so. She tried to concentrate on his words, and standing up straight, but both were very hard as his breath flitted across her ear, '…when you come and get him you can help me formulate a last-minute exit plan to escape Marion's clutches. I've been really stupid, Sylvie, and I don't know how to get out of it.'

'Marion's clutches? Something stupid? Oh, I am so intrigued. You'd better get that kettle on and I'll be at yours as soon as I can. Although I can't promise to help. Laugh though, I can promise to laugh.'

'Cheers for that.' He smiled again, still quite close, and she had to use all her self-control not to grab for a wall to lean on. There was something quite special about that man's smile. Something quite sinful.

Alex was seemingly unaware of his sinfulness, or in any need of a handy wall to support him, as he spoke. 'No rush, Sam will be fine.'

She stopped. The four of them had reached the head teacher's door, situated as it was by the entrance to the school.

'Right, I'd best go in. Thanks for this, Alex, see you in a bit, and you…' she grabbed Sam before he wandered off and planted a big kiss on his head, 'I'll see you…'

'Aw, Mum! Mum! Urrghhh! You said you wouldn't do that any more. C'mon, Ellie, let's go see if that lollipop lady has any lollies today.'

Sylvie grinned at Alex and the two children sped out of the school door with determination writ large across their faces. Alex gave her an uh-oh-there-could-be-blood smile and followed after them.

Sam was so literal that he got very cross when things weren't as he assumed they should be. She'd have to try and explain this again. Parenting manuals never warned you about the constant, and it was constant, explaining that you had to do. Made worse by television representations of families, usually dressed in beige and white (as if), with smiling parents explaining concepts to clean and grateful-looking children who nod, happy in their new-found understanding. It wasn't like that for Sylvie. Last time she had tried to explain that the lollipop lady was there to help people cross the road safely rather than dish out sweets Sam had looked at her as if she had tried to serve him some of the farm kittens for dinner.

Miss Winter's door was slightly ajar so Sylvie knocked and flicked a smile to the school secretary, glasses atop her head and a frantic expression on her face, who seemed to be chaotically moving piles of paper back and forth on her desk.

'Come in,' called Rosy and Sylvie felt the same trepidation she used to feel whenever she had been summoned to see the artistic director. However, Rosy was lovely and approachable and had been nothing but nice to her. The artistic director was an evil old crone who very probably did eat farm kittens for dinner. Or at the very least hit them with the metal-tipped cane she was always tapping in anger on the floor.

'Hi, you asked me to pop by once I had got Sam.'

'Yes, brilliant, thank you. Where is he? He can come in, or have you left him outside with Sheila?'

'Oh no, he's um… Alex McKenzie has taken him for me. Is Sheila OK? She looks as if she may have lost something.'

'Ah, quite probably. Excuse me for a second.' Rosy smiled at Sylvie before bellowing, 'They're on your head, Sheila, your head.' Her tone reverted to normal. 'Sorry about that. I wanted to have a chat with you. You have such a natural skill with the children and I wondered if you'd be able to help me out. Last time we spoke you said you were hoping to find some work more locally, maybe do some dance classes in Penmenna.'

'Yes.' Sylvie's answer was tentative as she looked at Rosy a little suspiciously. She wanted to help the school out and really enjoyed coming in to do reading with the little ones, and this afternoon had been lots of fun, but she couldn't keep giving her time for free. Now she had sorted her mum's things out she needed to crack on and find more paid work. Plus she wasn't very good at saying no, so she was worried about the direction this was heading in. 'I still am looking for work, and when I asked I found out that the village hall is fully timetabled out – it only has some late-night slots which wouldn't work for ballet for the children. So I'm still looking.'

'Excellent. Well, obviously not excellent about the village hall, I imagine that's very disappointing, but I meant excellent for us. Hopefully. I have a suggestion then. I need someone to help with PE provision in the school. Mrs Adams has drawn up a new, very active PE curriculum but unfortunately can't implement it herself at the moment. It would only be a few hours a week, but all our TA's are full-time and there just isn't any wiggle room in freeing them up from their current responsibilities, plus I'd rather have consistency in delivery. As it's only a temporary position rather than a full-time permanent one I have flexibility about who I offer it to, and after watching the way you worked with the children this afternoon, I'd like to offer it to you. Would you be interested? I don't need an answer right now, but it would be great if you could let me know sooner rather than later. What do you think?'

Sylvie thought she couldn't believe her ears. This was amazing – jobs didn't fall into laps like this, not even temporary ones. Especially ones that occurred during the school day with no need for childcare. Wow. And any money at all would be useful at this point. She still needed to save a deposit for a house to rent but this was going to make her life an awful lot easier. She could feel the grin spread across her face but realized as Rosy continued to look at her that the head teacher might require an actual verbal answer.

'Oh yes. Yes, please. I don't need time to think, that would be fab. I'd love to.'

'In that case, congratulations and welcome to the staff team at Penmenna. If you're sure you don't need longer to think about it we can sort out all the formalities now and get things moving. I can give you a copy of Amanda's PE plans that cover all the classes and you can familiarize yourself with it all before you start. Also, just thinking aloud, but if the village hall is unavailable why don't I ask the governors about renting you the school hall for a few hours on a Saturday? They'll have to clear it, but it is supposed to be used as a community space, and I can't see why anyone would have any objections. There would be lots of benefits for you, being able to do ballet from here. Should I go ahead and ask?'

Sylvie couldn't believe it. How had one five-minute meeting after school suddenly handed her all this opportunity on a plate?

'Really?' She felt like a fool as she heard the words slip from her lips, but this was all so much. She could get the ballet school up and running, and Rosy was right —the school hall would be perfect, easy to find and somewhere local children were very familiar with. Plus it would have the unspoken implication that the school supported the classes.

'Ha, really. Don't look so surprised. I was impressed when I studied with you in evening classes a couple of years ago and as I say you have a really natural way with the pupils. You've already had your DRB check so we know you're cleared to work with the children. I'm not the only one to notice you either. Trust me — staff gossip about the parents as much as parents gossip about the staff, and others have commented on how good you are in the classroom. This is a no-brainer for me, and you're actually doing me a favour stepping into the breach. So I'm guessing that "really" is a yes. And as luck would have it we have a governor's meeting scheduled for next week. So I'll wait until then to raise the hire of the school hall but I can't foresee any problems. If that's OK?'

'Miss Winter, I don't know what to say. This is amazing.'

'If I were you I'd start with yes and swiftly follow it with your national insurance number. Oh, and Rosy, please. Miss Winter makes me sound like a character from Dickens, and whilst it's fine in front of the children, using Rosy the rest of the time makes me feel less like some kind of stern workhouse matron!'

Sylvie giggled at this; the woman in front of her couldn't have looked less like an evil character from Dickens had she tried.

'OK, Rosy, thank you. I'm going to be the best PE person you've ever seen.'

'I don't doubt it, and trust me, you'll be the only staff member I've ever had that I know can do the splits when sober. We're going to love having you here.'

## Chapter Thirteen

'Hey, you look like you've run all the way here,' Alex said, opening the door to her with that crinkly-eyed smile he had.

'Oh my goodness, I have. You're not going to believe what Miss Winter wanted with me.'

'Ooh, true, but my mind is conjuring up all sorts of pictures.'

'Oi.' Sylvie punched him on the arm. 'Don't be filthy!'

'I wasn't.' Alex looked surprised but then followed it with a smirk. 'But now you've said it… No, don't hit me again, obviously I'm joking, and you started it. Come through. The kids are in the garden. They've built some kind of athletics course for Ellie's teddies, who are silently pleading with me to do a risk assessment, close the whole thing down for health and safety and send them back inside so they can just lie there having cake rubbed on their faces rather than being hurled through the air.'

'I think you're spending too much time with the children. You need some adult company.'

'Alas, you're not the only one to think that. But I'll tell you my tales of woe after you tell me what's made you sprint down Beach Road like an escaped prisoner.'

'Can I have a cup of coffee first?'

'Of course, coffee is always available. What did she want?'

'Oh, just to offer me a…' Sylvie started nonchalantly as she pottered over to the coffee machine. And then to increase the drama, she spun on her heel and grabbed Alex by the arm as she started to jump up and down next to him. '…a job! She offered me a job!'

'Wow! That's amazing!' He grabbed her other arm too and they jumped up and down in tandem. 'You must be over the moon, obviously you're over the moon. I'm so happy for you. Can we stop jumping now, I'm beginning to feel a bit sick.'

'Haha, yes, of course. Thank you.'

'What for?'

'For being someone I can share my news with. I'd be lucky to get a grunt from Tom, and Sam can't possibly really understand.'

'Well, I do. And I think we should celebrate this, it's fantastic news. What do you want to do? Let's go to dinner. Although I can't tonight, I'm afraid.'

'OK, Sam would love that. Thank you, that's a great idea.'

'Oh, oh yeah, OK. I'm sure Ellie will as well. You'll have to choose where and we can do it next week.'

'OK, now your turn. What are you doing tonight that you're so scared about? How has Marion got her claws into you, and what have you been stupid about? Come on, spill all. Oh, let me just go and check Sam's OK and then we can sit and you can tell me what you've got yourself into!'

Sylvie ventured into the garden and was narrowly missed by a purple bear whizzing past her ear as her son was jumping up and down on the spot further down the garden, fists clenched in sheer excitement and looking very similar to how she had in the kitchen just seconds ago. Ellie was standing on a plastic chair with another bear in her hand.

'Just this one and then it's your turn. I think Purply is the winner so far!' They were so caught up in their 'Olympics' that they didn't even notice Sylvie come into the garden.

'Hi, that was one speedy bear!'

'He's got long legs, it helps,' Ellie said from her chair, nodding knowledgeably.

'I don't wanna go!' Sam bawled as soon as he spotted his mum.

'Whoa, you're OK for a minute, boy. But hello would have been nice.'

'We're not going?'

'Nah, I'm having a coffee first.' Sam ran at her and gave her legs a big cuddle before turning and running back to where he had been standing.

Sylvie headed into the kitchen to find Alex had put some cake out next to her coffee.

'Black, one sugar? And some carrot cake.'

'Wow! Today really is turning out to be the perfect day. I like that you now know how to do my coffee. And cake as well. Jobs, cake, occupied children. The day doesn't get much better!'

'For you maybe. The cake is a bribe so you stay here longer and help me come up with a plan.'

'With the greatest respect, you have never struck me as the sort of man who needs help with anything much, but definitely not to plan.'

'And I'm not, or I wasn't. Until I moved to this place and had to deal with the likes of Marion bloody Marksharp. Honestly, give me a tribal warlord any day of the week.'

'I mean, she's bad, I give you that, but warlord bad?'

'Oh, I know of what I speak.' Alex nodded, and looked almost hurt that she had accused him of exaggeration.

'I'm sure you do.'

'No, really, that is how I earnt my living after all. Until I chose village life, and trust me, she's up there. She may not have an automatic weapon strapped to her chest, but she has skills that could be classed as "enhanced interrogation". Honestly. I've got myself out of some spots but for some reason I'm faced with Marion and speech dries up and pure survival instinct kicks in which means I just nod and say yes and pray for escape.'

'OK, there's too much here for me to take on at once. What do you mean how you earned your living? You've never told me. You're really open in so many ways,' she nodded to the coffee and cake, 'and pretty private in others, so I don't know what you do for work. I've just been taking the he'll-tell-me-when-he-wants-to path. So now I'm a bit worried – tribal warlords, automatic weapons. Tell me I'm not drinking coffee with a fully paid-up assassin, and then we can discuss Marion.'

She felt the smile play at her lips, but half of her was serious; she knew very little about Alex, and had built a friendship with him based on instinct rather than any real knowledge. She hoped she hadn't made a mistake. Obviously she was joking about the assassin bit but she wasn't entirely sure what he did do, plus he had rocked up in Penmenna with a child of a markedly different ethnicity and no mother in sight. Maybe she should have asked a few more questions?

'Put your mind at rest right now, I promise I'm not an assassin or mercenary. I'm a – or maybe that should be was a – journalist. To be honest I'm not sure where I stand when it comes to definitions at the moment. No, I am a journalist, have been for ever, and right now I'm working on a project to substantially fundraise for and raise awareness about the victims of the South Sudanese civil war. That idea I mentioned on our first ever pizza night, well, it has grown legs and has become an actual thing. Prior to this, for the last five years I was the Central Africa correspondent, so yeah, I know a bit about warlords and hotspots or at the very least have witnessed some truly horrific scenes. I was being flippant, of course, Marion isn't an equivalent. Of course she isn't. But does she scare the bejesus out of me when I should know better? Then yes, damn right she does. Which is why I need your help.'

'OK, but can I ask you more about the journalism thing after we've sorted out Marion?' She wondered if that was why she had felt that jolt of recognition when she first saw him on the beach. She must have recognized him from the television, reporting from a war-torn world as she cooked dinner with the TV on in the background.

'I don't think we have the power, even combined, to ever sort out Marion! She was frightening enough at twenty when I met her, and she's had nearly two decades to hone her powers. She's virtually indestructible.'

'No, you're probably right, but we can give it a go. I mean it, though. You've sat here the last few weeks, getting me to tell you all about my life in London and on the farm and you haven't said a word about yours and now it turns out you've known Marion for ever. How come you know all about my ballet career and me but I have only just learnt what you do or did? Let alone that what you did involved travelling the world and probable tales of derring-do. You owe me an interrogation.'

'OK, you can have it. No derring-do though, I think that died out with Robin Hood. But can we talk about today now, please. I've only got a couple of hours and it will make it you giggle.'

'That I don't doubt. You may continue.' She sat back in her chair and looked at him through this different lens. A journalist – that made sense, and now that she knew, it kind of fitted. Central Africa can't have been an easy posting, and had obviously had a massive impact if now he was working with the victims of something she wasn't sure she had even heard of. There was a lot more to the man in front of her than she had perhaps realized. But then, wasn't there always?

She had seen him as an all-action-hero type but even more questions were raised in her head. Presumably he wasn't working overseas any longer because of Ellie, but she wanted to know more. Pushing was hardly going to be helpful and she recognized that it wasn't really any of her business, but she dared any human being not to have their curiosity piqued even further by his revelation.

'Hey, earth to Sylvie. I haven't even started yet and you look like you've zoned out. Not cool, Miss Sylvie Williams, not cool at all.'

'Sorry. I'm here, I'm listening. Now, tell me, what *are* you doing with Marion this evening?'

'Stop smirking, and stop being naughty. You know full well I'm not doing anything with Marion as such this evening. I'm just doing what I'm told.'

'Dear God, you tell me you're going to tell me and then do exactly the opposite. Are you going to give me specifics or what?'

'Give me a chance. Just eat your cake and listen for a minute. I can't tell you if you keep talking. No, no hitting!' Alex mock defended himself from an anticipated fictional blow.

'You're so bad. No one can see you, you know, and no one would believe I was as violent as you make out anyway!'

'Shhh. Now you know Marion has got it into her head to matchmake on my behalf?'

'Oh my! I thought she had dropped that idea.'

'I wish. Unfortunately not. Anyway, she came over at the weekend with those three hell-spawn she calls "her boys" and told me she had the most perfect date lined up for me. A colleague of Richard's, apparently.'

'Hahahaha. No!'

'Oh, yes! She knew if she came in person it would be harder for me to wriggle out of. Before I knew what had happened she had not just found a woman but booked a bloody table at a restaurant of her – her as in Marion, not the date's – choosing. For tonight. I can't even begin to imagine who she's found. And whether or not the poor woman has been coerced as I have. Although I suppose that wouldn't be too bad. We could just bolt dinner if that was the case and escape. Will you stop laughing? It's not funny, this is my life!'

'I'm sorry, but this is joyful. Alex McKenzie, foreign correspondent brought to his knees by the head of a village PTA.'

'I think we all know there's more to her than the one role.'

'Hahaha, still hilarious.'

'Well, when you've finished amusing yourself perhaps you could help me. I don't want to be rude to my upcoming date, but how the hell do I get out of this?'

'You can't.'

'What do you mean I can't? You're supposed to be helping.'

'I am. How is being dishonest or lying to you helping? You have to go and hope this woman has a modicum of common sense.' Sylvie paused to laugh again as Alex gave her a piercing look indicating exactly how likely he found this. 'She might have! Anyway, with any luck she has some basic human understanding and you could try to tell her that you find her charming but this was very much Marion's idea and you're not interested right now.'

'That seems a bit lame.'

'Look, Marion's already picked and booked the restaurant. Just face it, she's utterly emasculated you already. This is the most sensible way. And besides, seeing as you are normally very optimistic, have you considered that you may actually be attracted to Marion's pick? It is a possibility.'

'No, no, it's not.'

'Yes, yes, it is. From what I understand, she's pretty thorough. She's not going to find you someone that's not suitable, so this could be the start of something beautiful.

You're looking at this all wrong. You should be embracing this opportunity.'

'Are you taking the piss?'

'No, maybe a little, but not really. Consider it. This should be exciting, not terrifying. Your perfect woman waiting for you, right there, tonight. This time next year I could be buying a hat and you might ask Marion to be your best man.'

'This isn't funny.'

'Why are you not looking on the positive? Why are you sabotaging this? I wish I had someone to set dates up for me. I've forgotten what going on a date is like.'

'Really?'

'No, not really, I haven't got time for that sort of thing at the moment. Imminent homelessness tends to rejig one's priorities.'

'You're not really imminently homeless, plus today you got a job and the opportunity to set up your ballet school. If we're talking about this time next year, you could be a millionaire.'

'Hahaha.'

'It's as likely as me marrying Claudia.'

'Oh, the gift that keeps giving. Is she called Claudia?'

'It's a nice name.'

'It is. And we shouldn't judge on names. But it's not really very approachable, is it? It's not Sarah or something. I'm already a bit intimidated and I haven't got to meet her.'

'Idiot. Judgemental idiot at that.'

'Yep, but seriously, give me three good reasons for not marrying Claudia.'

'I've never met her. I reckon that's a good reason.'

'Nah, arranged marriages actually have quite high rates of success. Two more, please.'

'I think not having met her is pretty strong. How about, I don't want a relationship of any type right now.'

'Why on earth not? You're an attractive man.' Sylvie was very glad her blushing was more under control, but he was a very attractive man. She fell asleep most nights thinking about how attractive he was. Probably best not to mention this here. She kind of agreed with Marion, it did seem a shocking waste. Not only was he ludicrously sexy but he made great coffee, was fab with kids, and as yet she hadn't been able to find a single flaw. Although perhaps this was it. Perhaps he had commitment issues. Perfect. That was definitely a flaw. She had that one as well.

'Well, thank you, I think. But that doesn't mean anything.'

'It does.'

'Yeah, in a last-century attractive-people-are-duty-bound-to-procreate kind of way. And we're not in the last century, we're living in a time where as long as all choices are consensual then anything goes. And my choice is not to date.'

'Well, you're not doing very well at that, are you? Oh, this cake is delicious. If you marry Claudia is she going to stop me coming around every day?'

'If you don't shut up about Claudia *I'm* going to stop you coming around every day.'

'Um… Alex, the children are very quiet. Should we be worried?'

'That's a good point. See, I can't have a relationship – the one female I have in my life takes every minute of every day. How on earth is there room for any more?'

'Yeah, for all my teasing, that's exactly how I feel. I kind of need to get to grips with the parenting thing and make sure Sam gets the best of me – that seems a lot more important than dating right now.'

'Right. Exactly, so you do understand. That's what I'm saying.' Alex got up from the table and wandered over to the kitchen window. 'Oh, look, they're fine. No trouble at all. Still playing teddy Olympics.'

Sylvie pushed her chair back and came and stood by his side, having to squidge up quite close to be at the correct angle to see Sam and Ellie. Alex didn't move, but seemed happy with her squidging.

'Is Ellie in the tree? Should she be?'

'Oh, yeah, that's fine. She does it all the time. I know it looks like laissez-faire parenting but I'm actually teaching her to manage risk and assess situations.'

'Is that what it is?' She smiled up at him, aware of her closeness and really wishing in that moment that she was Claudia and that Alex *was* looking for something. In this moment, she'd probably take anything. Just standing next to him, he seemed so big, so masculine, and she had always been so attracted to big and masculine. And then on top of that he was him, and she *really* rather liked him.

'That's exactly what it is. Look how happy they are.' And without seemingly even thinking he popped his arm around her shoulder and pulled her in. 'See, it's perfect.' And he wasn't far wrong. Sylvie found herself thinking she could stay like this for ever and used every ounce of self-control not to breathe him in. That way danger lay. Plus, what if he thought she was trying to sniff him? That would just be weird. Why was breathing normally suddenly so difficult?

She thought she heard a funny scraping noise behind her, but nothing was going to get her to break this squeeze up now. You had to take the tiny pleasures in life where you could find them.

'Coo-ee, only me. Thought I'd let myself in. Oh. Oh, dearie me, no, no, no, no!'

# Chapter Fourteen

Alex's head spun around as he heard Marion walking through his dining room. Seriously?

'I thought I'd let myself in, it was on the latch. Hello, Susie, how are you doing?'

'Hello, Marion, it's Sylvie. Very well, thank you. How nice to see you.'

'Um, Marion. Hello?' Alex stared at Marion with disbelief. He knew things were different in the country to living in London, but still, letting oneself in?

'Hello, darling. It occurred to me that with the boys' schedule for this evening – Rufus has karate and Rupert and Rafe will be going to diving club – it made much more sense for me to come and get Ellie now. Do you have a bag ready for her?'

'I can see. But I don't have to be in Truro for another two hours. I thought I was dropping Ellie to you.'

'Well, that was the plan, but as I say the boys' schedules meant this was far the better option. Now, pyjamas, tooth-brush, any special bear or book and we'll be off. Then you've got plenty of time to get ready at your leisure. See, much better. I'll just take Ellie now.' Marion beamed at Alex, pleased that she was so helpful before smoothing down her skirt and beaming at him again. Alex wondered if the full-force beam had some kind of magical power because he felt compelled to go upstairs and pack a bag immediately. But something deep within him fought back and made his feet resist.

'Marion, I haven't fed her yet.' Yes, he still had some self-determination left in him, fading but fighting.

'Not to worry. I had planned to give her supper along with my boys. Friday is sushi night. It's so important they are exposed to all cultures, isn't it?'

'Well, that's very kind of you.' There was no way in the world Ellie was going to happily eat raw fish. He quickly looked to Sylvie.

'Marion, it sounds like you've got an awful lot on, why don't I take Ellie? I had actually nipped in to suggest a sleepover, Alex. Sam has been relentless in asking and I think they hatched up a plan at school. So if I step in, Marion, then you can see to your boys, and not worry about another. Four is an awful lot of children to be dealing with. What do you say?'

'No, I don't think so. I'll have Ellie, it's all arranged. Thank you. I understand you applied for a spot as one of my new ladies, didn't you? Well, I fear it's only fair to warn you, we do have *very* exacting standards.' Alex watched as Marion looked Sylvie up and down as if she was lucky she was speaking to her, and then finished the look with a dismissive nod that managed to convey an awful lot in a very short space of time. What was that all about? Marion had many faults but he hadn't seen her do that before. Sylvie clearly didn't give a shit and looked at her straight back.

She might be slight in build but that girl had some balls. She had managed to stand firmer against Marion than he had. Feeling emboldened, he decided he had had enough of dancing to Marion's tune. He wouldn't refuse to go on this date – he would follow through as anything else at this late juncture would be rude – but here, with Sylvie at his side, and the thought of Ellie spending the night with the Marksharp boys, that was a hill he was prepared to die on.

'Fabulous, Sylvie, I'd really appreciate that. Although I'll pick her up when I'm finished so you won't have her all night. Thank you.'

'But…'

'Marion, I'm so grateful to you but I just can't keep taking, it doesn't sit right. You've done so much, please allow me to let Sylvie share some of the burden.' Jesus, he didn't dare look at his friend or his faux sincerity would disappear and he'd be in giggles instead. Manly giggles, but giggles nonetheless.

'I'll just go and let them know.' Sylvie grinned at the both of them and hotfooted out to the garden to give the children the news and seal the deal. Alex thought Sam would be pleased and he was fairly certain Ellie would prefer it to playing with Marion's sons. He hadn't spent much time with them but the village grapevine said they were more than a bit of a handful. He was fairly sure he had heard a tale recently about the middle one, Rupert, having set fire to the vicar's shed.

'Are you sure Sylvie is the influence you want around Ellie, dear?' Marion took advantage of Sylvie's absence to dig the knife in, pulling at her own shirt as she did so and doing weird stuff with her eyebrows. What *was* her problem?

'Yes, pretty sure, thank you, Marion.' Alex's attention was distracted by a whole lot of whooping, and he even thought he heard Sam join in – he hadn't had him down as a natural whooper – when Ellie came steamrollering into the house and launched at him with such force he nearly toppled over.

'Is it true, am I really going on a sleepover to Sam's? Really?'

Alex laughed at her enthusiasm. It was impossible not to, she was utterly contagious. However, he still needed to peel her off him; slate floors did not make a soft landing for either of them, and she was rocking back and forth making them both teeter.

'Yes, yes, yes. Not all night, I'll come and get you, but you'll probably fall asleep there. If that's OK with Marion?' He felt a bit guilty now, it felt like out-and-out manipulation and it was. But his daughter trumped all and she would not only be happier, but potentially a lot safer, at Sylvie's farm. She could attempt to ride a combine harvester and even still it would be a safer something than spending time with Rufus, Rupert and Rafe.

'Well, she clearly wants to, although my boys will be disappointed.'

Yeah, damn right they will. Her boys would have probably tied her to a train track and twirled their pre-pubescent imaginary moustaches. He had never been that comfortable with it as an idea but as with the date he had been steamrollered into it. This was a much better solution and one he wished he had thought of himself.

Sylvie and Sam reappeared from the garden just in time to hear him muttering apologies to Marion and hoping that the boys would be so busy with their clubs they would forgive him this once.

'So, go and pack a bag and get yourself ready then.' He addressed his daughter, having safely got her to the floor. She nodded quickly, as she did everything, and turned to her friend.

'OK, Sam, you'd better come and help me. I need to know what toys you have. Should we bring some of mine? Do you have a TV in your room? I've got my own Netflix account you know… although Dad has a silly rule about watching it in bed. Does your mum?' Her voice, seemingly never stopping, continued as she led her friend up the stairs and off to get her pyjamas.

'Well, I suppose I had better go then.' Marion addressed the both of them, still looking a little shell-shocked. Alex wondered if she had ever been team-tagged quite so effectively before. Hats off to Sylvie; he doubted anyone else would have been so brave.

'Once again, Marion, I'm so sorry, but thank you anyway.'

She pasted the big Marion beam back onto her face, and grinned at him, managing to exclude Sylvie utterly as she spoke.

'Absolutely no worries, Alex, so lovely to have you in the village. Now, all you have to do is enjoy yourself tonight, and in Claudia's company, you certainly will. Charming girl and absolutely perfect for you.' At this point she did manage to shoot a triumphant look at the redhead still standing beside him, before turning on her heel and letting herself back out again.

As soon as she had gone he turned to Sylvie and the two dissolved into giggles; it was like being back at school. He couldn't remember the last time he had laughed like that, although it was partly out of relief as much as anything else.

'Thank you. I was more worried about Ellie than I was the actual date.'

'Well, now you don't need to worry about Ellie and you can concentrate on panicking yourself stupid about Claudia.' She pronounced his date's name with that sing-song voice you used in primary school but before he could comment about her being a cat she carried on speaking.

'Although I don't understand why I can't have Ellie all night. If this date goes well you don't want to be rushing back to pick her up in the middle of the night. Once she's asleep she may as well stay asleep and you can come and get her in the morning. That way you can have a drink, relax, enjoy yourself. Driving to the farm at silly o'clock makes no sense.'

'I know, and that would be really nice, but I just can't.'

'There's no such thing as just can't.'

'Ooh, you sound like a teacher already.'

'Haha. Doesn't stop me being right though.'

'As much as I suspect you're always right, in this situation you don't have all the facts.'

'Never stopped me before,' Sylvie retorted in full imp mode. She really was adorable.

'I don't doubt it. But Ells, well, not so often now, but she has night terrors, not nightmares, night terrors. She used to wake up screaming and screaming. Admittedly she is loads better, but it's still a huge risk. It used to be all through the night, every forty-five minutes or so when I first brought her home, but now it's a couple of times a week max and we have a system in place. Her counsellor says it's normal in kids who have had a traumatic start, and trust me, Ellie had a traumatic start and…' He paused. Everyone always wanted to know all the details but Sylvie didn't interrupt him in a quest to find out more, she just waited for him to continue. '…and I will tell you more but not today, but she could well wake the whole farm and that's too big an ask. It's possible that without the security of our routine it could easily trigger her. She may want to be in her own bed.'

'OK, well, you know your daughter best, but at some point she is going to want to sleep away from you and I *am* a safe place. Sam will be fine. If he can sleep through the cows mooing as they go to be milked – and they're noisy buggers, let me tell you – and the cock crowing, he can sleep through almost anything. And I'll be there to reassure her and get her back to sleep. Again, it's up to you, maybe let this be a test run. I'm saying I don't mind being woken. You know Ellie feels safe with Sam and me, and if it gets too bad I'll call you from your slumber with Claudia.'

'Easy, there'll be none of that!'

'Then you're a disappointment! But I *can* call you. You will still have to stay sober just in case, but how great would it be if you gave it a shot and everything was OK? You're teaching her to manage risk, well, maybe this is one you could take tonight. It's up to you, but I think it's worth a try.'

'Um… I don't know.' And he didn't, he just wasn't sure. He had wanted to try before, and had toyed with leaving her with Chase and Angelina to see how it went, but the fear of making any changes, especially with everything going so smoothly up to now, stopped him at the last minute.

Since he had adopted her they hadn't spent a night apart. The truth was that for all the years, almost three, that she had been in the orphanage, he had spent most days and nights there. Trying to push the adoption through, bonding with her, ensuring she was well-cared for and safe, making her smile; these had been his raison d'être. When his extraordinary leave, mandatory after the event he had witnessed, had run out he had known he wasn't ready to return to work. To witness and report events as they unfolded, an observer not a participant, that was a role he could never undertake again. Finding Ellie had meant any objectivity he had once possessed was no longer part of him.

But they were not in Africa any more, they were in Cornwall, building a secure and stable life for the both of them. He was aware that there was a danger in over-compensating, that he had resolved to treat her in as normal a way as possible, not to mess with her head by treating her like a victim. Had he got them to a point where they could progress on to the next step? If the last few years of his life had been about making sure Ellie felt secure was it now time to take teeny-weeny steps towards helping her be more independent?

'At some point you may have to go away for work, an emergency may arise.' Sylvie's response brought him back to the present and he focused in on her words. 'Wouldn't it be good to know there was somewhere you could leave her if you had to and not worry about the night terror thing not being dealt with properly? Look, we've got rid of Marion and the perfect chance for a dress rehearsal has arisen. Plus, it frees you up, if you want to, to spend the night with someone and not worry about Ellie's screams waking her up. I really don't mind. Just talk through what you do, how you manage it and would want me to, and then if you're happy, we can ask her. Not that I'm in favour of the child ruling the parent but she should have a say – there's no point trialling this if she's not secure enough to want to. Train me now, then ask her when she comes down. What do you think?'

Alex thought. And knew she was right. It was possible that this insistence they sleep under the same roof every night was him mollycoddling Ellie and making himself feel indispensable. Which in itself wasn't healthy. Maybe this was a golden opportunity. And there *was* a chance he could get called to London, especially now his foundation was beginning to take shape, and then what would he do? Drag Ellie out of school because they couldn't spend the night apart? That wasn't conducive to a secure start.

He looked at Sylvie, and suddenly like a switch his decision was made. He'd run it past Ellie, and he might have only known Sylvie a month or so but there was no one he'd trust his daughter with more.

# Chapter Fifteen

With Ellie practically vaulting onto Sylvie's back, so keen was she for a real sleepover as she raced out of the cottage, Alex managed to get to Truro early for his date. He felt his tummy jumble a little with nerves, which was a reasonable expectation. Largely, he thought, because of leaving Ellie overnight for the first time but also because he hadn't ever been on a blind date before and couldn't believe that he was now going on one. Thirty-six years old, a father and feeling butterflies about meeting a woman he had zero interest in.

He had offered to pick her up but Marion had informed him that Claudia was coming straight from the train station, having travelled down from London to spend the weekend in her second home, which wasn't in Penmenna but in Treporth Bay, a small town along the coast, where she had recently bought a rather chichi flat (Marion's words) overlooking the new marina. Chichi and predictably spotless flats were all about Alex's history; his future seemed to be uneven cottages and an awful lot of mess. He knew which he preferred, although it would come as a surprise to all who had known him in his London life.

Heading into the bar, he ordered himself a drink and sat down to wait. He was quite early but hadn't been there long before he was approached by a startlingly attractive woman, dark hair bouncing as she walked, professionally dressed in a navy trouser suit that clung to every beautifully proportioned curve, and a silk shirt opened just a smidge, revealing honey-coloured skin and more than a hint of promise. Every other man in the bar turned his head as she entered.

She made a beeline for him.

'Alex, an absolute pleasure.'

OK, so she recognized him, which meant this must be Claudia. She was certainly exactly to his taste, and reminiscent of a girlfriend he had had in university. Slim with thick wavy brown hair and clothes that screamed a natural, and expensive, good taste. She knew how to dress and he accepted that Marion knew what she was doing. Matchmaker extraordinaire. He probably owed her an apology.

'Claudia, lovely to meet you. Can I get you a drink?'

'Fabulous, yes, please. But could we perhaps grab our table. I'd forgotten how hideous the train journey is and the buffet car only had a soggy-looking panini. I'm absolutely famished.'

'Of course, that sounds like a great idea. I've got so used to eating early recently that my tummy is considering eating the plate as well.'

She gave him an odd look and he reminded himself not to talk to her as if she were five. Spending all his time with Ellie meant his vocabulary had become a little childlike and considerably less man-about-town. Men about town very definitely had stomachs.

'Well, we'd best get something to eat then.' OK, he seemed to have got away with that, and he wouldn't be repeating that mistake again. He was an adult, on an adult date, with possibly very adult consequences. He flourished his hand and she took the cue and walked through to the restaurant, whereupon the maître d' guided them to their table before asking for her coat which she shrugged off her shoulders with the ease of Grace Kelly.

Alex couldn't help but smile as he pulled out her chair and she sat down, again oh-so-gracefully before smiling up at him, a smile that would have most men falling to the floor. Luckily, he wasn't most men, but he acknowledged its power. He also hadn't failed to note that the smile was reserved only for him – she hadn't so much as bestowed a glance on the maître d' or the waiter who was now hovering with a menu and an air of teenage devotion.

Taking the menu with a nod, she focused her full attention on Alex as he sat opposite her.

'I must say I was very happy when Marion called and suggested we have dinner. I'm sure you hear this a lot, but I'm a huge fan.'

He didn't. Most people other than those in the industry didn't really know who he was. The juxtaposition between him always being seen on camera in a flak jacket and helmet meant that people struggled to place him when he was in the jeans and T-shirt he normally sported. Which made him very happy. He couldn't imagine anything worse than being constantly recognized and consequently treated differently.

'Oh, thank you. But you have the inside track here. Marion has told me very little about you.'

'Oh, that's easy enough. I live largely in London where I work as a hedge-fund manager. And I have a home here for down time. So important, as I'm sure you know.' She leant across the table and touched his arm, but instead of a sexual charge shooting through him, as he would have expected sitting opposite such a beautiful woman (especially due to the lack of sexual activity since he had arrived in the country), he merely felt a shiver, almost of warning but so faint he queried himself.

Experience taught him to listen to his intuition. He sat back in his chair and looked at her afresh. The waiter, hovering nearby, wasn't unsure at all and was looking at him with outright envy.

'I try and get down here as often as I can. I like to get out on the water. Do you sail?'

Before Alex could answer the waiter approached to see if they were ready to order.

'We haven't had a chance yet. Could you give us a minute?' Claudia smiled sweetly at Alex after she had addressed the waiter who, mortified, slunk off to the other side of the restaurant. 'I'm sorry…' she really didn't look it, '…but I can't abide being pestered. Although I suppose we should have a look.'

Alex smiled back and opened his menu, reminding himself that maybe she was nervous.

'Ooh, it all looks lovely, doesn't it?'

'It certainly does.' He scanned the menu and then snapped it shut.

'Oh, have you chosen already?'

'Yes, I'm ravenous so I know exactly what I want.'

'That's a good sign, I always like a man who knows what he wants.' She shot him an X-rated look as she reached for her wine glass. 'In that case, I had better make my mind up quickly, best not to keep you waiting. I wouldn't want to make you impatient.' She continued holding his eye as she spoke and was delivering each line with a slightly breathless air which instead of reeling him in, left him itching to ask if she needed an inhaler. If Sylvie were here, she definitely would do.

Claudia finally tore her eyes away and looked down the menu, occasionally tutting, before she closed it and looked around the restaurant. The young waiter was serving a table nearby but before he could finish Claudia had clicked her fingers and rolled her eyes in Alex's direction.

'Looks like I was right about the staff.'

The poor waiter scurried over and the two of them ordered but not without Claudia breathlessly explaining that she wouldn't have a starter because she was looking forward to getting to the pudding, shooting Alex another very pointed look whilst rubbing her feet against his leg. The waiter nearly passed out.

'Really, they should hire staff who are a little less pubescent. Did you see that poor boy?'

Alex grimaced and nodded. What had looked like it could be a dream date in the initial seconds was turning into a bit of a nightmare. He was increasingly as keen to leave as she was, just for very different reasons.

'So, I haven't seen you on screen for quite some time. Rumour has it you're on an extended sabbatical.'

How the hell did she know that?

'Yes, you could say that.'

'So, what prompted that then?'

'I've been in the job for a long time and thought it was time to have a look at what I wanted to do next.' He delivered the standard answer, designed to give no real information at all.

'Mental health then? Don't you worry, I'm very good with this sort of thing. My sister-in-law is an absolute loon, howling, licking windows, the lot.'

'And how does she feel about you labelling her like that, then?' Alex couldn't help himself, she was just getting increasingly unpleasant. Who on earth thought such things, let alone vocalized them?

'Hohoho, she knows I say that. She and my brother get a bit tetchy but you often find that, don't you – some people simply don't get a joke. I can tell you and I share the same sense of humour.'

'Hmm.' His dad had drummed it into him that a gentleman was polite at all times but it was becoming a bit of a struggle.

'So anyway, your sabbatical. I had heard a whisper that you had rescued some orphan Annie out in Africa and that's why you have buried yourself down here, but I've been watching you for years so I told the person who told me, that it was abject nonsense. Of course you wouldn't, you're much savvier than that. I said, look, orphans are ten a penny. Alex McKenzie, he knows he can make much more of a difference using his celebrity status to raise awareness rather than just plucking one child out of obscurity. And I mean, we both live in the city, neither of us are stupid people, what on earth would anyone want a child for? Poor Richard seems to have dozens, emotional vampires the lot of them. I'm like you, I'm a good judge of character. After all, I could hardly make a living in the financial markets if I couldn't read people, could I? Hedge-fund management is all about good judgement, sorting the weak from the strong and acting accordingly. Do you not like your steak?'

'I seem to have lost my appetite.'

'Well, we can't have that, can we? We need you all strong for later.' She winked across the table at him and this time her foot moved up from his leg and into his groin. That was enough.

He was all for people being sexually confident but as far as he was aware dinner did not mean consent. What she was saying was offensive and if he had put his foot in *her* groin during dinner then she would rightfully be able to claim assault. Sorry, Dad, being gentlemanly was one thing, but sometimes one has to draw the line. He pictured Marion's face as he told her that Claudia was not just a loathsome individual but had also come on far too strong and crossed the line into harassment.

Maybe that was harsh, maybe she had made a mistake – that might be all it was. The least he could do was finish his dinner, be polite, not make anyone uncomfortable but get his message across very clearly.

He started by pointedly putting his knife and fork down, lifting her foot off him and dropping it back on to the floor.

'Let's just eat, shall we?' Surely that wasn't rude, merely clear without being impolite?

'Oh, of course. I do apologize.' She had the grace to look abashed as she returned to picking at her salad. OK, that was easier than he had thought. Hopefully the rest of the evening would proceed in a dignified fashion and then he could hotfoot it back to Penmenna. Alone.

'I should have realized, Alex McKenzie is a man who likes to take the lead. I'll tell you what, I'll make it up to you later.' Oh, for Christ's sake!

His mind immediately took him back to Ellie with her hands on her hips on the beach. Oh no, maybe it was him who had taught her to swear and not Angelina after all! It did seem to be something he was thinking quite a lot recently; maybe he had been saying it as well. Did this mean he owed Angelina an apology?

Then he conjured up Sylvie's face. That day on the beach had been their first meeting, hadn't it? Yet now it seemed like she had been his best friend for ever. He wondered what they were all doing now and glanced at his watch. Eight. They should be tucked up in bed, although he knew there was no guarantee – they could be doing farm-like things, frolicking on hay bales, riding on tractors or whatever it was people did on farms in Cornwall. He was fairly sure it was different from the farms he had seen in South Sudan. Then Sylvie would bathe them and curl up on their beds as she read them a bedtime story.

He looked across at Claudia, still twirling a bit of rocket on her fork whilst babbling on about something terribly important in the City. He should probably concentrate, after all she had had the grace to leave his groin alone for the last ten minutes.

'…and so whilst I'm not one to office gossip, and I'd appreciate it if this went no further, but I think Marion may need to back off on the amount of time she spends niggling at Richard. It's no wonder he's spending more and more time in his city flat, if you know what I mean? I know he talks about how they have a wonderful relationship but if you ask me that is because he's hiding something. I mean, who really is *that* happily married? What is it now, umpteen years and like I said, all of those children, I mean it's no wonder he's looking elsewhere.

And I'm not one to judge, but the man deserves a medal. I don't know how he does it, always so cheerful and she really is a dreadful old harridan. Are you OK? You look funny.'

'Um… yes, I'm fine. I thought you were Marion's friend? That was the impression I got. She did arrange this date.'

'Hohohoho, well, of course I am, but you know my connection is more to Richard and when you think about it, what is friendship these days? Everything is so fluid, isn't it?'

'Um, well, I see things differently.'

'You know what they say, opposites attract. Now, what was I saying?'

'You were saying, I believe, that you didn't have high hopes for the Marksharps' marriage. But I think I would rather change the subject. *Both* Richard and Marion…' he shuddered inside a little at the lie, but from today on he would make it true, '…are my friends and I feel distinctly uncomfortable with what you are saying. I've known them for ever, at least since university, and I should imagine they are as strong now as they ever were. Now, tell me what else you like to do in your downtime apart from come to Cornwall and sail.' He was proud of himself for managing not to add 'and bitch' – he was fairly sure that was high up on her agenda.

Claudia outlined the sorts of things she enjoyed, all of which seemed to involve vast sums of money, although he was relieved that making purses out of puppies didn't appear to make the list. But then he supposed she was on her best behaviour.

As the evening came to a close he began to worry a little about how best to end it. He needed to make it absolutely clear that he wouldn't be coming home with her or inviting her to his for a nightcap, but if she lived in Treporth Bay and had come by train then he felt somewhat responsible for getting her home safely.

As the bill came and he paid, Claudia gave him yet another knowing smile over the brim of her wine glass and he wondered how on earth he was going to phrase this, deciding the best way was just to come out and say it. The maître d' helped her back into her coat and again she was as graceful in her movements as she was graceless in her interaction. No thank-you, no smile for staff. Not once, the whole evening.

They exited the restaurant, their cheeks hit by the brisk early October air. The days had been unseasonably warm so it was a shock when the evenings developed and reminded you that autumn was well on its way.

'So, Alex…' Claudia turned to him under a lamppost and looked up at him with her big brown eyes, '…thank you for a lovely dinner. Shall we go for a drink somewhere else or shall we…'

He was surprised she was being so reticent, but was grateful as it meant he didn't have to start an awkward conversation, he just had to finish it.

'Yes, thank you for your company. I've had a lovely evening.' He paused for a second, waiting for lightning to strike him down, but it appeared, this evening at least, that God was on his side. 'I've really enjoyed meeting you, Claudia, but I'm afraid I must get back to Penmenna for the babysitter.' Another enormous lie. If anything, it would be odd going home to an empty house after so long and he knew Ellie would never forgive him if he rocked up at Sylvie's house to claim her back before the morning.

'The babysitter? Really?'

'I'm afraid so, yes. But do let me drop you home.'

'Fabulous idea, and you could come in for a coffee.'

'No, I'll just be dropping you at home, Claudia. I won't be coming in.'

'Another night then?'

The polite thing would be to nod in the affirmative and imply that yes there would be a second date, but as polite as Alex was (and quite frankly he felt he deserved a medal for tonight), there was a time when honesty trumped politeness and that time was right now.

'Probably not, Claudia, You're an amazing woman…' that bit was certainly true, she was quite breathtaking; stunningly beautiful on the outside and mind-numbingly hideous underneath it, '…but I'm just not sure we're compatible.'

'Not compatible? Are you mad? Look at me!' Her outrage was beyond palpable, it was virtually sonic booming from her as she used her hands to indicate her body. 'What is wrong with you? No, don't answer that. I was warned about you when my friend heard Richard's stupid bloody wife had set us up. She said, that Alex, he may look like some kind of God – and trust me, you're not all that, I could do so much better. Anyway, she said it was common knowledge that you had had some sort of breakdown after that Sudan thing, lost all professionalism and adopted that stupid bloody African child, I mean, who does that? I can't believe I agreed to this! That'll teach me to always look on the bright side! You have wasted my entire evening – do you know how much my time is worth? Absolutely fucking shambolic. Don't think I'll be keeping quiet about this. Oh no, the whole City will hear about this!' She was spitting, her rage-strewn words tumbling over themselves in her fury.

'I think that about sums it up, Claudia. However, you still need to get home. Can I assume you won't be wanting a lift?'

'No, I fucking shan't. I've got friends in Truro, I'm going to do my best to rescue this waste of an evening.' And pulling her phone out of her bag she gave him one long look of disgust and stalked off up Lemon Street, spitting venom about what an absolute waste of space Alex McKenzie was into her phone.

# Chapter Sixteen

Alex had waited until nine o'clock. It was a Saturday morning after all and he didn't want to be so early it was rude, but neither did he want to wait any longer so he pitched up at the farm eager to get Ellie and share the story of his hell date with Sylvie.

As he arrived he saw that everyone was already up and about, sitting around the wooden circular table in the garden and eating cake.

'Cake for breakfast? That sounds like a grand idea. Can I join in?' If he expected Ellie to race to him shouting, 'Daddy, Daddy,' with glee, over the moon to see her parent after her first night away since the adoption, then he was sadly mistaken.

'Hey, Dad,' came the lukewarm reply as she looked up from the big piece of paper she and Sam were drawing on as they ate. 'This is crib – that's Cornish for elevenses but you don't have to have it at eleven, so it's much better. We had breakfast hours ago.'

'Ah, OK, hours ago?'

'Yeah, hours ago,' Sylvie confirmed, smiling a greeting and gesturing that he should sit and join them. 'There's tea in the pot if you fancy. You've just missed Tom but it would seem your daughter could make a cracking farmer. She's even enthused Sam, they got up at five…' she smiled the thin smile that in parent code that said, oh yes, they really did, '…and insisted that Tom let them milk the cows.'

'Five,' said Alex loudly for impact whilst mouthing at Sylvie, 'I'm so sorry, you are a saint.'

Sylvie smiled a very saint-like smile.

'You got up at five to milk the cows? Was it fun?' Alex continued, addressing the children again.

'It was *so* fun,' his daughter replied in her not-quite-teen-speak. 'You know that old story book where they sit on a stool and milk the cows, well, that's not how you do it in real life at all. It's loads different, and there are twirly bits and hose bits and I know how to do it.'

'OK, well, that is impressive stuff. I'm thirty-six and I don't know how to do it that way. You'll have to tell me all about it when we get home.'

'Oh, I'm not coming home, am I, Sam?'

'Um.' Sam looked like he wanted to crawl under the table but found his voice, 'Um… I think you are, but not today.'

'No, Ells, you do have to come home today.' Alex was firm.

'Well, I'm going to town to do lessons with Sylvie and then the beach for a late-afternoon swim. You said, didn't you, Sylvie?'

'No, I said it would depend on what your dad wanted to do. You promised you understood that it wasn't for sure, just possible that you might be allowed to come with us.'

Ellie narrowed her eyes as she looked at Sylvie and then decided the best way to play this was with her somewhat belated best-daughter act, and she slid her legs around from under the table and clambered onto Alex's lap, pushing his cake plate out of the way and wrapping her arms around his neck.

'Ah, Daddy, I've missed you. It's nice to see you. I love you.' She pecked him on the cheek and put on her most winning Ellie smile. 'Can I go to the dancing and then the beach with Sam and Sylvie, please? You can come if you want. He can come, can't he?'

'He can, but he may have other plans. I tell you what, why don't you and Sam finish your cake and go and get your things and I'll talk to him and we'll see.'

For some reason Ellie didn't seem to argue with Sylvie, like she would with every other adult she had ever encountered, and Alex was most impressed as she slid off his lap, rammed the last bit of cake into her mouth, and turned around to face him, putting her big grin on again, cake crumbs falling from her mouth as she plaintively said, 'Please, Daddy, please,' before heading back into the house with Sam.

'Wow, that was easy. How was she?'

'She was a joy, she really was. And she slept through the whole night, I promise she did. Tom has taken a huge shine to her, and I've never seen that before. She is so high-spirited it's infectious, and he was more than happy to show her the milking. He's been trying to encourage Sam for ever but one word from Ellie and Sam is up with the lark and putting on his wellies. Your daughter has some serious skills. She could be running the country by twelve years old at this rate. It really has been an absolute pleasure. She's brought sunshine to the farm and I'm tempted to ask if I can keep her. But don't let her bully you into coming into Roscarrock and then having a swim if you've got things to do. I know how powerfully persuasive she can be.'

'No, although I thought your classes were fully booked? Is there room for the kids? The beach will be nice, but it's October, isn't it a bit late in the year?'

'Ah, what's the matter with you? You can tell you're not local-local. Best time of the year, all the tourists have gone home and the sea has had all of summer to heat it up. And the weather this weekend is stunning. Don't tell me you're not enjoying the heat on your arms – you're in a T-shirt so you can't argue that it's not gloriously hot for this time of year. It's about to turn so Sam and I wanted to make the most of it and get in the last swim of the season. And as to work, then I usually leave Sam with Tom but I was going to let the two come and be extras just this once. I really don't mind. Especially as you've had a date and it's kinda early in the morning for you to be joining us, don't you think?'

She gave him an eyebrow wiggle that definitely hinted that he should be at home doing rude things.

'Haha, you're so bad! And no, it isn't! I cannot tell you how horrendous last night was.'

He could be mistaken but he thought he saw the glimmer of a smile, different to her usual one, play at the corners of her mouth.

'Oh, that's a shame. I had high hopes of Claudia. Did she have three heads?'

'Ha! Stop it! No, she didn't, she was just my type actually. All tall and dark-haired with these deep brown eyes and well, she was physically very attractive.'

Another indecipherable flicker.

'So, what went wrong? Your perfect woman turns up and you say it was horrendous.'

'I don't think I used the word *perfect*, and how shallow do you think I am? Yes, she was very attractive but my God, her soul – pure evil. Not even Angelina – oh, you haven't met her yet, have you? I'll introduce you, so you know what I mean – but not even Angelina evil which is bad but quite amusing and with redeemable features. No, Claudia was pure evil. She referred to my decision to adopt Ellie as a nervous breakdown and she was rude to the waiters. That's a definite no-no.'

'A nervous breakdown? Ellie? Wow. I know you're not supposed to hit people on dates but did you hit her?'

'No, of course not, but my goodness, I couldn't get out of there fast enough. And when I let her know there would be no nightcap she really exploded. Didn't I know how valuable her time is and how lucky I was to even be in with a chance? I am apparently absolutely shambolic – she was going to tell all of London what a loser I was.'

'Oh no, don't.' Sylvie was laughing so much, her eyes crinkled at the sides and her shoulders heaved.

'Well, I'm glad you're having a giggle at my trauma! What is worse is that I got a text from Marion this morning saying she had heard it hadn't gone well but not to worry, she had another one lined up for me next week!'

'Bwahaha, this is too good.' A little bit of cake was spat across the table.

'Stop or I shan't come to the beach with you this afternoon or even entertain this madness of swimming in October!'

'Barely October, and as you're not proper Cornish, I'll let you wear a wetsuit – but as far as I'm aware it was only your daughter that *I* invited!'

'Ouch!'

'OK, you're welcome. But only as long as you don't display your more shambolic tendencies.'

'Funny.'

'On a serious note though, you had never said that Ellie was adopted…'

'I tend not to talk about it. She's my daughter, I don't see what it has to do with anybody else. Sorry if that sounds a bit brusque.'

'It's fine. I understand what you're saying and you're right. It isn't anyone else's business.'

'Thank you. You have no idea how refreshing that is to hear. Most people just want to push, push, push for detail.'

'Well, just don't tell them.'

'I don't.'

'I can imagine. However, I'm going to contradict myself now, but not to do with you and Ellie. I've been trying to pin Tom down all week to talk to him about moving out, and all that entails. Now I've got a job, the next step is to get Sam and me a place of our own.'

'Excellent idea. Get one near to Ells and me.'

'That's very cute, and actually exactly what we'd like, but I do need to talk to Tom about it. We've been here for nearly five years now. It was never meant to be long-term but it doesn't feel right making plans and not discussing it with him first.'

'And he doesn't want to?'

'Well, he's not madly talkative anyway and he hates to discuss money. You know what farmers are like, land rich and cash poor, and I think he's got some weird ideas in his head because you'd think he'd be dead keen to get rid of us. But when I tried to broach it one evening last week he just did his Maid-I'm-shattered-and-my-head-is-banging-I'm-off-to-bed routine and escaped. Then the next thing I know he's hired an extra hand for a few days and hotfooted it to Dartmouth with his girlfriend for a midweek mini break. He's never done that before He is not a man who spends money frivolously – the mere thought brings him out in a rash. I don't want to be paranoid and think he's taking crazy steps to avoid me but...'

'But he's taking crazy steps to avoid you.'

'Yeah. Right. I think so. And then of course he got back yesterday but I had the kids last night and this morning he had them milking cows so I couldn't even jump him for information at dawn. He knows I have Sam all day so he's safe until tonight, and I'll be interested to see how he dodges me this evening when Sam's in bed.'

'Why don't I take the kids after dance class, if you're sure we can still tag along, and then you can catch him afterwards and meet us at the beach? What will he be doing later this afternoon?'

'Far field, I think, there for most of the day, something about fences.'

'Right, it sounds like we've got a plan. What time were you heading to the beach?'

'I thought two-ish but if I'm coming back to speak to Tom, maybe half-three, four-ish?'

'OK, I'll meet you in Roscarrock and then we'll head to the beach for that sort of time and you can come and join us at your leisure. That'll give you the element of surprise, plus if you need to, you can take as long as you like before meeting us, plus...'

'That's a lot of pluses.'

'I'm a man full of them, so... plus, if your talk doesn't go to plan you can rant at me afterwards.'

'Alex, you are amazing, that would be so helpful.'

'Amazing rather than shambolic, I think I prefer that. Thank you. And you're very welcome. But in return you have to help me stop Marion's matchmaking.'

'Argh! I'll do whatever I can to help, but I don't have super-powers!'

# Chapter Seventeen

After class and with the children bundled off with Alex, Sylvie headed back to the farm thinking about how she was going to approach Tom. This shouldn't be so difficult, she was simply trying to have a conversation. It was just that every time she had tried to have a serious chat with him since her mum's death he would scuttle off like a beetle as a log was lifted. On the upside, if he realized her plans this afternoon it was likely to make Julie's day; after hiding out in the hay barn for a bit he'd probably be booking a month in Blackpool.

Her best approach was softly-softly; she needed to catch him unawares. What if she were to make him a drink and take it down to the far field? No, that would definitely warn him something was up. She was better waiting at the house and catching him when he came in for his afternoon crib. As a creature of habit, he was due back soon. She parked the car and quickly checked her mother's watch, now proudly on her own wrist. She had about half an hour and then he'd be back in the farmhouse, settling down for fifteen minutes with a cup of tea and a saffron bun. She could whizz around and have a quick tidy-up, make the kitchen as sparkly as it could be without an entire battalion of cleaning staff and a lorryload of bleach.

Tom liked the house clean yet it never seemed to occur to him that he could possibly pick up a duster himself. She was fairly sure Julie's ability with the Flash and Shake'n'Vac was one of the things that had attracted Tom initially, although now Sylvie was fairly sure he loved her for considerably more. She baked daily, for a start, and Tom was a sucker for the smell of fresh cakes and a neatly pressed apron.

True to form Tom turned up in the kitchen half an hour later and Sylvie cunningly slid a tray of fresh scones out of the range as he walked in.

'That smells fair good, maid.'

'Yeah, I made a batch for Sam, you know how much he likes them. He's going to be sad when Ellie goes home. And I figured you wouldn't mind one or two.'

'She's a cracker that one, isn't she? Natural with the cows as well. Did you know she told me her name wasn't just Ellie but Elechi or something like that and where she comes from cows are money and people steal them. She says I should keep an eye out for thieves because our cows have very pretty faces. She does make me chuckle. Now I don't know much about Africa or if she just has a grand imagination but she was certainly keen.'

'Hmm, she is quite a character, that's for sure. And very good for Sam, she's bringing him right out of himself.'

'Aye.

'Seeing as they're ready, do you want a scone with your tea, Tom?'

'Aye. That would be nice, maid. Thank you. Kitchen's looking grand. You had a tidy-up?'

'Yes, Sam has gone off with Ellie for a couple of hours so I thought I'd make the most of a little bit of free time at the weekend. Here you go, let me just grab the cream and jam. I wanted to talk to you anyway, I've got some good news and of course I want to hear all about Dartmouth.'

'Dartmouth was fine. What news?' Tom looked a little suspicious, but then suspicious was his resting face.

'Well, I've been offered a job at the school and I've said yes. It's only short-term at the moment but you know what these places are like, once you've got your foot in the door then more and more opportunities come your way.'

'That is good news, bit more money coming in.'

'Right. Plus the headmistress has offered me use of the school hall so I can get my ballet classes up and running in Penmenna. So with any luck I'll be able to save like mad and try and find somewhere in the village for me and Sam.'

'Aye.'

'And then you and Julie could maybe, you know...'

Tom looked up from his scone and fixed her with a look.

'Aye.'

'So you're fine with me looking for a place and us going fairly soon?'

'That depends.'

For goodness' sake! It would be easier to pull her teeth out with the rusty pliers she had found on the kitchen table during her quick clean-up than it would to get a simple answer from her uncle.

'Depends on what, Tom?' She gave him her most patient smile.

'Well, maid, I ain't got any money. So regardless of what anyone says I can't be helping you move and I ain't got anywhere to move to meself – this has always been my home.'

'Tom, I don't know what you're thinking but I'm not asking you for any money. I know the farm limps from one quarter to the next. This isn't that. This is me asking if you'd be all right without me and Sam here.'

'Yep.'

'That's fine then, that's all I needed to know.'

'And you don't want money?'

'No, why on earth would I?'

'Well, the will like.'

And suddenly it all fell into place. Tom was avoiding talking to her because he thought she wanted to discuss the farm's future. Her mother had left her half of the farm to Sylvie and Sylvie had every intention of passing it on to Sam, she just hadn't told Tom. It hadn't occurred to her that she'd need to.

'Oh, Tom, did you think I wanted you to buy me out?'

'I can't do that. I can't raise any more finance on the farm, maid.'

'Of course you can't. Tom, listen to me now, this is Lovage Farm. It's yours way more than mine, whatever the legal facts of the matter. I am not asking you to buy me out. I am not asking if I can buy you out. I want the farm as it is, as it's always been. This is Mum's and yours and one day, I hope, Sam's. And who knows, you could have children and then it will be theirs and Sam's.'

Tom laughed then, a great big laugh straight up from the belly, his mouth open, showing two gaps where teeth should be. It took him a while before he could speak.

'I ain't having no children. Dear me, don't be saying such things. Julie will out-and-out leave if she thinks I expect children.'

'Would be a punch in the eye for medical science, that's for sure. Although I'm sure I read an article about some women giving birth in their fifties these days.' The colour drained from Tom's face. 'You could give it a shot, get yourselves both in the newspapers. The *Cornish Guardian* would probably want a full feature.'

Sylvie stopped and glanced across at her uncle.

'Breathe, Tom, breathe. I was only teasing. Don't make me have to do CPR in the kitchen. I was teasing. I don't think Julie has any intention of getting pregnant.'

'I don't think that that is a subject to joke about, maid. I know attitudes are more relaxed these days, but oh my goodness, I think we're well past that!'

'I'm sorry. Will you move Julie in?'

'What is it with you today? Not everyone wants to live in sin. I shall have to see.'

'I don't want you to be lonely, Tom, if Sam and I go, and we will be going at some point.'

'Lonely? You mean I won't have to be tripping over them damn blocks or needing nine different shampoos in the bathroom? I think I'll manage.'

'Huh, you're a bad-tempered old bugger. I'll miss you.'

'Humpf. Then you need your head examining, maid. You're not going anywhere today, are you?'

Tom stood out of the old low-slung chair and patted her shoulder as he walked past towards the open kitchen door. He turned as he got there and Sylvie looked up from the flagstones on the floor where she had fixed her gaze as she felt his eyes upon her.

'Scones were good, maid.'

# Chapter Eighteen

Sylvie was jolted by the sound of a text coming through. She saw as she looked at her phone that it was just past four which meant she had been sitting there for nearly an hour – she must've fallen asleep after Tom had left. He was a funny old thing – fancy thinking she had any intention of hurling him out of Lovage Farm!

Sitting here was not helping get on with the afternoon; she couldn't remember the last time she had dozed during the day. She hit play on the voice note she had received and heard the voices of Sam, Alex and Ellie singing, 'We're all going to the beach right now, beach right now,' pretty tunelessly. Sam managed to fit in a properly hideous crescendo at the end that made her grin. He was her future, there was no way she would be selling the farm off when it was the security she had for Sam, the one thing she knew she could give him, even when he was but a twinkle.

Shaking her head, hoping it would get rid of the sleepiness, she got to her feet and headed to grab the beach bag by the back door. She boiled the kettle and made herself a coffee to take in the car with her – maybe that would also help clear the fug. A quick check in the hallway mirror, and she decided to slosh some cold water on her face just to make sure.

It took a mere ten minutes before she was parked in Penmenna village and walking to the beach, the sun beating on her face and the pink Fowey Pride still in bloom and poking out of the walls. As she turned the corner by the ice-cream shop she could hear the squeaks of Ellie and Sam before she saw them tiptoeing by the water's edge, playing the racing-the-tideline game and deliberately losing. Alex was down there with them, their giggles occasionally interspersed with his deep rumbly laugh. An orchestra of sound when combined with the crash of the waves and the noisy caw of circling gulls. It brought a smile to her face for the second time and she felt her pace pick up as she headed towards them.

For some reason, the very shape of Alex struck her today. She had experienced that flutter yesterday when he had put his arm around her, but today she was deeply aware of his sheer physicality. The way the T-shirt shaped his abs, and the way the top of his arms filled the sleeves to bursting was possibly her favourite bit. She was used to beautifully toned young men – after all she had been dancing with them her whole career – but there was something even stronger about Alex, something that made her tummy flip when she studied him, butterflies not merely fluttering their wings flirtatiously but practically colliding and bouncing off the wall of her stomach.

Why was this hitting her today? Did she not have enough to deal with in her life right now? Could her brain not just give her a break for a bit? She had managed to accept that they had a great friendship and she had no intention of rocking the boat with lustful imaginings about a man who could only ever see her as a friend. A man like Alex dated Glamazons, women like Claudia or those who dashed from continent to continent with a camera slung around their neck looking effortlessly glamorous whilst still engaging in danger day to day. Not a single mum who lived in jeans and Converse and barely brushed her hair. And definitely not the single mum whose child Ellie was best friends with.

Neither of them were stupid enough to rock this particular boat, not with both their children so dependent upon each other. That way madness lay. Fabulous madness, but dangerous delusional destructive madness all the same.

She walked across the beach reminding herself of this fact. Alex is off limits. It will explode your life and ultimately break Sam's heart.

Alex looked up as she approached and she watched the grin spread across his face.

'Hey, all good?'

Three simple words. She felt herself suddenly strong, cocooned in the warmth of his support. Knowing she had someone who cared how things went, who was in her corner, made her feel that the world wasn't entirely gloomy and impossible and complicated. She had been a bit hurt that Tom thought so poorly of her, so the simple act of someone caring how talking to him had gone made her feel protected and a bit less vulnerable, a little less misjudged. Yes, this afternoon with Tom was a surprise but now she felt infused with spirit. She could handle other people's misperceptions, she could handle anything life threw at her; she had done so before and would not be beaten down by this. She took a deep breath and gave Alex the biggest smile she could muster.

'All good,' she said as she beamed like a lunatic.

Alex arched his brow and nodded slowly.

'Great,' he responded. 'We've had a busy old morning. I had thought they might be tired after their five o'clock start but apparently not. We went to do a food shop when we left you and before we hit the beach and I suggested I could put them in the trolley seats if they were sleepy. It was like unleashing the dogs of hell. They informed me they weren't babies and had no intention of riding in baby seats and instead took it in turns to push the trolley to prove it. And my own darling daughter decided she was in charge of what went in. You have no idea how many chocolate bars and crisps I had to put back on the shelves. I had to allow the popcorn just to prevent a full-on floor-bashing tantrum whilst your son very impressively put in things like hummus and satsumas. I'd quite like to keep him. You wanted Ellie this morning so we can swap if you want. Ellie pretended to cry when I point-blank refused to buy these things she had seen on the TV. Sam was almost as mortified as me and told her to stop. What was really impressive was that she listened, which was a miracle I was more than grateful for. You have no idea the sort of looks that women in supermarkets can give you when your child misbehaves.'

'Oh, I do. Trust me. Some women just dish them out.' She was so grateful for this torrent of babble; it further grounded her, cushioning her from earlier.

'Of course you do. You got one from Marion yesterday, didn't you?'

'I certainly did. I didn't know you had noticed!'

'Not notice? It was virtually a scarlet-red laser of disapproval beaming from each eye. Hilarious. However, this morning I was on the receiving end of quite a lot of them.

Most times I go shopping women give me these misty-eyed smiles and coo at Ellie, but not today.'

'Oh, it's a hard life being a dishy single dad.'

'That's the second time you've said that you think I'm gorgeous.'

'Dishy isn't gorgeous, and neither is ego. You want to watch that.' There was no way in the world she was going to let him know what she actually thought.

'How kind you are.'

'Known for it. They're having an amazing time.' She nodded at the children and used them to change the conversational subject.

'They are. Sam guided us to your spot. I didn't realize we had stolen it last time, however he has given us permission to use it whenever we want.'

'Oh, that's sweet.'

'Right. And you were so on the money about this being a great time of year to go in the water. I've only dipped a toe in but it's really not bad.'

'Do you know what? A swim is exactly what I need. If it's not that bad does that mean you're going to join me?'

'Do you know what, I might. But I'm definitely going in my wetsuit.'

'I'd tease, but truth is I've got my shorty on under this. I'll keep an eye on the kids if you wanna go and get changed.'

'Aha, I too have it on under my clothes.'

'Hmm, that sounds like deliberate planning.'

'A gentleman is always prepared.' Alex smirked as he quickly undressed in front of her, dropping his clothes to the sand.

'Really? I think I've just gone off you.' Sylvie matched him, item for item, trying really hard not to look too closely. But dear God, the man was stripping off in front of her!

She quickly summoned a picture of Marion in an attempt to slow her rapidly pounding heart, hoping it was as effective as a cold shower and might prevent her from panting out loud.

'Oh, hush your fuss. Last one in has a face like a turnip. Go!'

'Aaah… Sam… Ellie… come on in and join us… aaah…' and Sylvie and Alex pelted into the sea at high speed.

# Chapter Nineteen

By the time they had finished splashing in the sea, even Sam had dared come in to his knees, and Sylvie had taught them to build the biggest fairy castle imaginable by dripping wet sand on top of wet sand, enthralling Ellie, who wanted her to make it higher, higher, higher whilst Sam carefully etched doors and windows so the fairies could get in and out and see the sea. Alex was exhausted. He didn't know how the other three were still standing, but it was true about sea air being both invigorating and ensuring you got a good night's sleep – he was ready to curl up for a nap.

They were now packing up and he realized he hadn't had a chance to discuss Sylvie's inquisition and he needed to find out more about how Ellie's night had gone. Had she really been all OK?

'Thanks for a great day.' He smiled over at Sylvie as she helped Sam put his things back in his beach bag.

'Thank you. This afternoon was just what I needed. I swear the sea here has magical properties.'

'And here I was thinking it was our company. I'm sure you'll be as knackered as me, but do you want to come back for fish and chips?'

'Would love to, but I should head back, I've got a busy week next week.'

'You've got an exciting week next week. So we should celebrate and save you from having to cook for you and the boy tonight.'

'Nicely argued. OK, you're on, let's enjoy the rest of today and then tomorrow I can get ready for school.'

As soon as the kids had finished their fish and chips the four of them curled up in front of the television in Alex's living room, with Ellie dragging two beanbags right to the front of the TV, and Alex dragging them right back again, pointing out that he didn't mind relaxing his rules occasionally but there was no need to push it.

With a movie on, full tummies and a day full of milking, shopping and swimming, it was only minutes before both children were snoring outright.

Sylvie sat in the corner of the sofa and Alex got up to grab some blankets, two to drape over the kids and a great big fluffy one to give to his grown-up guest.

'Thank you.' She smiled up at him, her wispy red hair perfectly contrasting with the grey fuzz of the blanket as she pulled it up and tucked it under her chin. He couldn't help but melt a little; she looked so cute and he felt himself fill with a protective kind of love. He really hoped the morning had gone well for her.

'Listen, we couldn't talk openly earlier with the children there but...' she flicked a look at the two little ones as a snore came from Ellie, '...I think we're safe now. Ellie seems soundo. And we know nothing wakes Sam.'

'Go on.' Alex worked hard to mask the nerves in his voice as he spoke. Had she not been quite straight this morning? Had he made a dreadful mistake letting Ellie sleep over?

'I just wanted you to know that when I signalled that all was OK with Ellie last night, I meant it – it really was.' Alex's shoulders loosened at her words. 'She tuckled in and topped and tailed with Sam and the both of them giggled a lot, and I mean a lot, and then once she was asleep, she was asleep. I promise that she didn't wake screaming in the night. And I was ready, I stayed awake myself for ages.'

'You didn't need to do that.' He could see the earnestness all across her face, still peeping out over the blanket, as she spoke to him.

'I wanted to be there in a flash, I didn't want her waking scared and then being in a strange place and that making things worse, so I was awake for a fair while, and I had dug out Sam's old baby monitor and hidden it under the bed where they wouldn't see it but it would pick up any noise and I placed the other one right by my bed. I'm sure, a hundred per cent sure, that had she woken I would have known about it. I really think I would.'

'Oh, you would have done. When she has a difficult night she screams so loud, Sylvie, it cuts to your core. She screams in her sleep and then that's what wakes her. They're getting less frequent, I guess – and I hope that as she becomes more secure and has more and more memories made that they are pushing the old ones out, but I don't have much experience with kids. I look at her in the day and she functions like a child who hasn't had any trauma, but at night, when she sleeps, it becomes a whole different thing. Her counsellor says that the body can remember trauma even if the mind doesn't so I guess this is that working itself out. It's hard, though – the effects of this sort of thing are impossible to predict but as the terrors lessen I can only hope that she will be OK in the long term.'

'I don't begin to know how you cope with that, I really don't. And you know she couldn't have a better chance for recovery than you are giving her. But believe me when I tell you that last night she was fine, really fine.'

'Thank you, that means a lot.'

'It doesn't have an awful lot to do with me, Alex. It's you who's provided this secure beautiful world for her, the world that's allowing her to heal.'

'Hmm, thank you. I know I haven't told you the story yet, but I will.'

'You don't need to tell me anything. Really you don't.'

Alex looked at her with a little half-smile of appreciation. 'Tell me about yesterday. Did Tom respond well to you planning on moving out?'

'Do you know what? He did. But it was all a bit of a shocker. I discovered why he's been running from me.'

'Wow! Really? Do tell. Is it because he half expects you to be a cattle rustler? Um, could it be he thinks you're going to overrun the farm with even more small children? Oh, come on, tell me, what did he think you were going to do?'

'Funny you should mention it, but your daughter has already warned him about cattle rustlers. And I've enough on my hands with the one I've already got – children that is. So no, neither of these things.'

'I can't think of what else it would be. You're going to have to just tell me or we'll be here all night.' Which he would quite like.

'He thought – and I can't quite believe it – he thought I was trying to talk to him about probate and my mother's will.'

'Has that not been resolved yet?'

'It has. And as far as I was concerned that was exactly what it was, but Tom didn't think so.'

'I want to be supportive, but you're not making much sense.'

'Mum left me her half of the farm when she died. Tom owns the other half – their father split it between them when he died. And he assumed, just assumed, and yet he has known me my entire life, that I was going to throw him out, kick him to the kerb and sell the farm. Or at the very least insist he gave me half the farm's value in cash and that that was how I was going to set up a new home for me and Sam. I would never do that, Alex. I never would. I can't believe anyone who knew me would think I would do that and I guess I'm a little hurt. I know it's a silly thing, and all cleared up now, but did he really think that was who I am?'

Sylvie looked at him with her big green eyes and in them he saw confusion and hurt, making him want to padlock her into the blanket and keep her safe and stress-free for ever, wrap her up and look after her and fight anyone who thought ill of her, to cuddle her up at night and wake with her every morning. He knew that he couldn't. First of all, padlocking someone in your house was bound to be illegal, but he knew as he looked at her that she had too much on her plate right now to be worrying about anything other than finding a home that she and Sam could be comfortable in and earning some money. He would love to prove to her that no one could possibly see her as some money-grabbing monster, not even her uncle, that in his opinion she was as close to perfect as could be. But being a captive, despite his good intent, was not going to help her. Sylvie was nothing if not a strong independent woman and would want to sort her stuff out herself.

# Chapter Twenty

Alex had managed to put Ellie to bed and for once she had gone straight to sleep, although it could be less from exhaustion and more a wish to escape the sheer stress that was a Sunday evening. Making sure her reading had been done, her uniform was washed and ready and that no note had slipped out of her reading folder into a crevice in her school bag informing him that he needed to have helped create a Roman Colosseum out of loo rolls by Monday morning, was not as easy as it sounded. He was fast learning the truism that it's only ever on Sunday night that the children remind you that they need freshly baked cake/a fully completed sponsorship form/a piece of obscure uniform you have never even heard of, and that no matter how organized you tried to be every Friday, it was a universal law that things kicked off at six-thirty on Sunday evening and there wasn't much you could do about it.

However, tonight had gone relatively well, and she was now tucked up in bed and snoring which was a huge relief as he had invited the boys around for a catch-up.

Just as he settled on the sofa there came a knock on the door. He had been in the house for nearly two months now but this was the first time he had invited Chase over who, in turn, had suggested Angelina's brother come as well.

He opened the door and there was Matt standing grinning at him, beers in hand.

'Hey, mate, come in. Good to see you.'

'Thanks for inviting me. Shall I sling these in the fridge?'

'Great, thanks. Chase should be joining us shortly.'

'Yeah, I got a text from him earlier, he says he's bringing you a surprise but doesn't say what it is.'

'Oh God, that's always terrifying. Unless it's Richard – he was going to join us but has had to spend the weekend in London, work's been crazy for him recently. He's barely able to get back at weekends let alone weekdays at the moment. I'm not sure what they're doing to him up there but I remember when he took the job, the deal was he could work from home the majority of the time. It's getting so bad he's having to consider getting Marion a puppy for company, and he's been fighting that battle for years. He really isn't a dog person.'

'Puppy or divorce seems like a no-brainer to me.'

'Right? I said the exact same thing.'

Sitting and chatting they were startled by a deafening banging on the door, one that threatened to have it coming off its hinges.

'What the…?' Alex jumped out of his seat, both in alarm and anger. Who on earth would be that inconsiderate? As he swung the door open his jaw dropped. Of all the people – and of course it was!

'Hector! How? Aww.' Alex man-hugged his old school friend who he hadn't seen in years. The two shared a prolonged embrace and then with the age-old that's-enough-now pat on the back, separated and just stood looking at each other.

'You look exactly the same.'

'I am exactly the same, old man. You, however, have a definite sprinkling of grey,' boomed Hector, in a deep and *very* loud voice that screeched public-school privilege.

'Childbirth does that to you.' Alex winked.

'I heard about that bloody tomfool idea, but you've always known your own mind so I guess you had your reasons. Just don't bore me with them. Now, are you going to bloody let me in or do I have to stand in the fucking doorway all night? Always were a shitty host.'

'Get yourself in and stop making a fuss.' Alex grinned widely as he stepped to one side to let his old friend into the living room.

'Ah, so you must be the gardener.' He heard Hector address Matt. 'Anything to drink in this bastard house? Beer? No, thank you. Chase, where's that bloody wine?'

Chase had been standing in the doorway behind Hector and gave a what-can-you-do shrug to Alex. And he was right, Hector had been Hector since they had met him at twelve years old and was never going to change a whit. He was a constant in their ever-evolving world, even if it was a constant dressed in salmon-pink trousers that matched his complexion, a hideous braying voice that carried, and viewpoints that most people felt were outdated when Victoria was on the throne.

'The wine you left in the car and expected me to carry for you, Hector? That wine?'

'Yes, stop being such a girl. Have you got it or not?'

Alex caught Matt's eye and laughed. 'Matt, you'll get used to him. Just don't even try to bring him into the twenty-first century, it'll be a battle you'll never win.'

'Why would anyone want to live in the twenty-first century? As far as I can see it's all about bloody narcissism and over-sharing – social media has to be the biggest waste of time ever invented. A whole generation of men who like to rub oil on themselves and take photos. That sort of nonsense died out with Classical Greece and they at least did it without constant bloody sobbing and wanting "likes". I tell you, this world is going backwards, not forwards.'

'See,' Alex smiled, 'he just doesn't stop.'

'Just have a drink and sit down, Hector. Poor Matt isn't used to you yet, so maybe tone it down so he can adjust first.'

'Tone what down? Everybody loves me, you know it.'

'I'd argue you were an acquired taste,' Chase chipped in.

'Just open the bloody wine. Now, do I have to find myself a glass in this godforsaken house?'

As the evening progressed Alex was able to tell them about his plans and the work he was doing whilst on his sabbatical.

'The thing is, they're in peace talks again at the moment but every single time they break down. Meanwhile there are well over one and a half million displaced people, and tens of thousands of those are children who have lost their families. I was able to save Elechi because I *saw* her entire family killed and village razed, but there are so many families that need to be reunited...'

'You can't save every child, Alex. That's not how the world works.'

'No, Hector, but any positive impact I can have, surely that's worth something. And we sit here in this cute Cornish cottage with resources at our fingertips that can help these children, can help reunite them and give them the best start they can have. So shouldn't we? A good education and excellent pastoral care doesn't cost that much, not comparatively, not when you look at what wealthy families may pay for one child to attend private school here. I'm not trying to save the world, I'm not super-bloody-human, but if I can make a bit of a difference, help these kids a bit, maybe try and do something that stops the constant repeated circle of vengeance that you get in the aftermath of civil war, if it ever bloody ends, then yes, I'm going to do that. I have a voice, I have skills, I have contacts and I'm going to use them all. And you, Hector, are one of those people that I'm going to use shamelessly to try and make some headway in…'

'Oh, use me, boy, use me.' Hector aimed for a super-sultry tone.

'Ha, I will. We can talk about how later.' Alex winked at his friend. 'Actually, things are going really well so far. I've already got quite a lot in place in a short amount of time. I've set up the Elechi Foundation, sorted out the tax stuff and charity status. Just having Ells in school has freed up so much time, so I've started to organize a big fundraising gala thing. Yeah, I know, don't roll your eyes, you can do it for me and for Ellie, it's only one evening, All of you. Apart from you, Matt, you're off the hook seeing as I've only known you a couple of months.'

'Whoa, I'm more than happy to help – sign me up for anything within reason. Rosy will too, maybe we can build some links between the school and the orphanages. Do some local fundraising – even if it's just small-scale, it's better than none. I'll chat to her when I get home.'

'Thank you. The foundation is in place to raise awareness and educate as much as fundraise, although obviously the two go hand in hand, and I've been wondering about trying to involve schools in the UK, maybe get them to mentor new-build schools over there, fundraise or donate as part of some kind of global citizenship programme. Rosy would be a great place to start.'

'No worries, it sounds like exactly the sort of thing she'd be interested in. I'll get on it.'

'Now, Chase, your turn. With those Hollywood clients of yours, you could really help. They've already demonstrated they like to give their money away.' Alex winked at his friend.

'Hey, they get real value from… oh, hang on a minute…' Chase's phone started to bing. 'Hey, babe, yes, of course.' He spoke into it and then held it up and moved it around the living room. 'See, no strippers, just me and Alex, Hector and your brother drinking wine and working out how to save the world. And then I'm going to cook kebabs… Of course I'm missing you, but I expect I'll live with the trauma… Ha, yes, I may develop separation anxiety but I doubt it. Hang on, let me ask Matt. Hey, Matt, do you suffer any form of separation anxiety when you're not with your sister?'

'Dear God, no. Just an overwhelming sense of relief. Tell her to stop being so needy and leave you alone to have a drink with your mates or I'll ring the tabloids and tell them she's developed acne and a beard.'

'I think she can hear you, no need for me to relay that message.' The whole room could hear Angelina's furious squawking.

Matt laughed. 'Pass me the phone. Ange, leave him alone, for goodness' sake, the man's hardly likely to be anywhere else, and if he was I'd hardly be vouching for him. Now get off the phone and leave us in peace. No, you're not going to ring him one more time just to check. I mean it. Now sod off.' And Matt very decisively hit the end button.

Muffling his laughter, Alex jumped up and headed towards the kitchen. 'Chase, let's get on with the cooking or I'll be talking about my stuff all night. And I need you all awake and able to reach for your chequebooks!'

A couple of bottles, and despite Chase and Alex's kebabs, they were all more than a little sideways. Alex hopped up the stairs to check Ellie was still asleep – miraculously she was – and returned, reminding them to keep the noise down. It was worth a try and there was nothing wrong with optimism. Truth was ten years ago and his words would have fallen on deaf ears but the combination of his guests' maturity (bar Hector) and their respect for his new role meant they did try their best. It involved lots of shushing.

As he poured them all some more wine, having got everyone on board with his project, Alex found himself telling them about Sylvie and her quest to find a house in Penmenna.

'And the thing is she just deserves it, you know. She's been bringing up Sam entirely by herself – the father doesn't want to be involved at all from what she says and I've never heard her bitch about it, not once. Then she gave up her career and came home and nursed her mother for years, and now she feels the need to move out because it's very much her uncle's farm. She wants a fresh start for her and Sam, the life she had planned for them, and yet there's nowhere in Penmenna available in her budget.'

'Well, perhaps she should get a bloody job then? Can't her parents help?'

'I've just told you, they're dead, for God's sake. The mother did leave her half the farm, but she refuses to capitalize on it. She's adamant that she would never disrupt her uncle's life like that and besides which it's security for Sam. She has just got a job, thanks to Rosy...' Alex nodded in recognition to Matt, '...and hopefully will get her ballet school up and running, but that doesn't help out with the whole deposit and rent-in-advance thing. Do you know how hard it is to rent privately these days, Hector? No, of course you don't!'

'I do know how hard it is to get bloody staff – you should see the problems I'm having with my house in Morocco.'

'Yeah, it must be really tough. Don't be a twat. This is serious.'

'Sylvie needs a place to rent in Penmenna?' Matt leant forward as he addressed Alex.

'Yeah, she really wants out of the farmhouse and to be in the village. And it would be great to have her and Sam even closer. Ellie would love it.'

'*Ellie* would love it,' Chase said, with a completely straight face. Alex flicked a look at him, but he appeared to be genuine.

'From what I've heard, Ellie really likes the way her curly red hair peeps out from the blanket,' Hector added.

'I didn't say that. At no point did I say that, did I?' Alex looked at Matt and Chase for support.

'Not those exact words, no,' Chase helped. 'But she has been your main subject of conversation all night. I think we could probably tell you her shoe size and star sign if pushed.'

'And she's just had it so hard and she just needs looking after. A real good looking-after.' Hector guffawed as he made some pretty infantile hand signals.

'Shut up, Hector, that's not OK. Do you never learn?'

'Seriously, I may have a solution,' Matt interjected.

'Haha, so does Alex.'

'One more time, I dare you.'

'Hey, hey, hey...' Chase, used to being peacemaker between these two, held up both his hands for quiet. 'What are you trying to say, Matt?'

'I should probably talk to Rosy first, but I was going to suggest to her that we live together. I know it's quick but we both spend every night together as it is – I haven't seen the inside of my own house for more than fifteen minutes for as long as I can remember. I have planned a thing for her and was going to ask then. But if she says yes, and she might not – I still can't tell which way she's going to jump – and as you know, Chase,' he nodded at his friend, 'she has this thing about firm boundaries and compartmentalizing, but if she says yes, then we might have a spare cottage between us. If we were to rent to Sylvie I can't see us needing the deposit and I'm not sure about the month's rent in advance. But you can't say anything, because obviously I need to make sure Rosy is on the same page as I am with this relationship. But it could work.'

'That's a great idea. It really could. When were you going to ask her? Were you thinking soon?'

'Whoa, Alex. You can't push Matt into something for your convenience, especially not because you've got a crush on your daughter's friend's mum.'

'I haven't got a crush, Chase! What is it with you lot? I'm a grown man. I haven't said anything about a crush. I don't look at her in that way, I'm just looking out for her. Why do you assume I'm only being kind because I want to sleep with her? I've never said that. She's the mum of Ellie's best friend, for God's sake, why would I mess that about? And besides, she's in no place in her life to be looking for a relationship. She has got way too much on her plate. I'm not messing with her life when she's still trying to get the most basic security for her family sorted. And besides, why would I rock the boat with someone I respect as a friend, regardless of Ells, for a quick shag? No way. That's not it at all. None of you have any idea what you're talking about.'

'I don't know about the rest of you, but methinks the lady doth protest too much.' Hector chortled as he held his hands up to protect himself from the inevitable flying cushion.

# Chapter Twenty One

Rosy sat back in her chair. It was Friday afternoon and the week had flown by, and been a raging success. Human dynamics were fascinating; she had often noted how introducing one new member to a team could change the whole set-up, as had happened this term.

Sylvie had started three weeks ago and today was the last day before half-term. She had clearly spent a lot of time making sure she knew Amanda's newly designed PE curriculum off by heart. Her quiet gentle persona had rippled throughout the school, with all the teaching staff somehow miraculously softening their edges and adopting a slightly more Sylvie approach. Rosy didn't expect it to last but it was jolly nice whilst it did. Even Amanda, who she knew had observed Sylvie's first lesson with Class Four and made notes whilst she did so, hadn't found anything to tut about and had reluctantly admitted in the staffroom that the new girl knew her stuff. Although she did make the most of the opportunity to shoot an evil look at Harmony as she said it. Luckily, Harmony was too busy cutting out little rainbow flags for the woodlouse mansion her class were making to notice, and World War Umpteen was averted.

There had been no major incidences at all for a while. Marion seemed more muted than usual and with

Sylvie bringing in a little bead glasses-chain as a gift for Sheila, even the school secretary was appearing slightly less chaotic.

She was interrupted from this blissful, stress-free reverie by the ping of her email. Odd. No one in their right mind emailed a school past five o'clock on a Friday, especially with a holiday coming up, unless it was an utter emergency.

She smiled as it popped up.

> Dear Miss Winter,
>
> As both head teacher and close friend you are cordially invited by the curly-haired and slightly scruffy gardener and his dog to Penmenna Hall Gardens for a special event this evening. It should be added that this is a strictly not-for-television occasion and the dress code is informal, ideally very little. You are welcome to attend any time from five-thirty on and I would like to take the opportunity to remind you this is a personal invite. Pupils, colleagues and Marion are not required. RSVP.
>
> Yours,
>
> Green-fingered and Gorgeous, so I'm told.

What on earth was this daft man planning now? Five-thirty – that gave her just enough time to give the school a quick once-over and drive to the Hall.

He was too cute. They had started seeing each other in March this year, the same evening as the premiere of *Green-Fingered and Gorgeous*, the gardening show set in Penmenna Hall that the school had become involved with. He still winced every time the name was mentioned, which was rather a lot as he had quickly become a darling of the nation and couldn't even do a supermarket shop now without being attacked by dribbling women desperate for his autograph.

When they had first met he had been king of the romantic gesture, mocking up a Tudor cap from gardening kit and serenading her with 'Greensleeves', potting her up an orchid that he claimed flushed as beautifully as she did, preparing a romantic picnic with all her favourite things whilst they watched (or didn't – truth be told) *Gone with the Wind* in the Penmenna Hall orangery lit by fairy lights.

And she hadn't made it easy for him either. She was as embarrassed by that as he was by the name of his show. But since they had been together, their relationship had been nothing but easy. They were such a natural fit and everything glided by effortlessly, so naturally, that she could barely remember her life without him in it and certainly didn't want to contemplate a future in which he wasn't a key part.

–

She had butterflies in her tummy as she parked the car outside the orangery and went to find Matt.

'Hello.' She heard her call echo around the greenhouse. Matt's dog Scramble barked a welcome and she felt the huge beam spread across her face as Matt popped his head up from behind one of the big old wooden benches down the end.

'Hello, you didn't RSVP!'

'Oh, I'm so sorry! I thought I had. I must have been giddy with the excitement of the invite. But I'm here – have I spoilt the surprise?'

'Actually, yes. If you could get back in the car...' Matt came around from the table and came and gave her a kiss. 'Don't be daft, of course you haven't. You know Scramble and I are always happy to see you. Thank you for driving over.'

'Mmm, pleasure.' She spoke through a second kiss. It didn't matter how long they were together, she would always love the feel of his lips upon hers. He pulled back ever so slightly and looked her straight in the eyes.

'I've been tidying up the flower beds, pulling out some of the annuals and having a rearrange with spring in mind.'

'OK.'

'And I have done something very naughty and particularly selfish and I felt I should tell you.'

Rosy felt her heart dip but only for a second. The flash of fear had clearly flooded her face as Matt grabbed her hands.

'No, don't be daft, nothing to hurt you. I meant I had transplanted some roses whilst they were still in bloom, and all for my own selfish gain, which is pretty heinous but you can do it if you're careful which I was, obviously, just not with my words. How could you think I'd do anything properly bad and bring you here to talk about it? You must know me better by now.'

Rosy looked at his big grin that couldn't hide the love shining in his eyes, at his curly brown hair and his slightly wonky nose. Of course this man wouldn't deliberately hurt her – foolishly or not she had complete faith in him. Total and utter.

'Of course I do. It was just your choice of words shocked me, but only for a second. I know you. You know me. We are good. So, go on, tell me more about these roses and your heinous actions.'

'Come with me then.' He held his hand out and with Scramble obediently trotting behind, Matt led her to the rose garden, through its assortment of beds to the very middle where there were some beautiful bright, light crimson cupped roses – bold and red in the middle of October. As she got closer and stood so she could see over them she realized that Matt had replanted them, all close together and forming a clear heart shape. And there atop the soil in the centre, Matt had lightly sprinkled some more petals and placed a large old key on top of them.

She stood trying to work out what this was meant to mean as she felt him slip his arms around her from behind, resting his chin on her shoulder and standing there wordlessly as she looked.

Roses and a heart, that was obvious. The key, what did the key mean? She almost didn't mind what it meant, it was such a beautiful gesture and she knew that Matt wouldn't have messed about with the roses if it hadn't meant an awful lot to him.

'If you reach through you can pick it up.'

She did as he suggested, crouching down on the path and threading her arm through the wall of roses, feeling for the metal of the key. As she grabbed it and pulled it back, she stood and turned to face him. Looking down at the key in her hands she felt the length of it, the weight, turning it and looking for what clue it was meant to give. Then she spotted that it had something engraved into it. Bringing it closer to her face she could make out that someone, and she had to assume it was Matt, had etched the word 'together' into it.

Roses, heart, door key, together.

She looked up at him quizzically, her look changing as he laughed and grabbed the hand that wasn't holding the key.

'Rosy, it's not that cryptic. I'm trying to ask you to move in with me. I know we haven't been dating long, but I also know how I feel and I'm fairly sure I can't see that changing. Every morning I wake up thinking I can't love you any more and then every night I realize that I was wrong and I love you even more than I had that morning. We're right. I don't know how to say it in a way that's more flowery, so I thought I'd say it with flowers instead. You and I are right. We are right today, we were right yesterday and I know, with no shadow of doubt, that we'll be right tomorrow. We spend every night together and I don't ever want to think of myself spending a night without you, so let's cut to the chase, let's be bold and take the next step. Rosy Winter, I'm asking you to move in with me. The roses are to tell you I love you. I love you more than my biggest passion – oh shush, Scramble, apart from you.' He broke his focus for a millisecond to look crossly at the dog who had yapped as if he understood Matt's words, almost breaking the romance of the moment. Matt turned his full focus back to Rosy who was standing there, her heart racing and stunned in silence. 'And the key is to tell you I want to live with you. I want to wake up with you every morning and know that in every way I am home. What do you say, Rosy? Say something. Will you move in with me?'

'Um… um…' Rosy looked at this man who she loved, who she trusted, and who she wanted to spend the rest of her days with and gulped. 'Um… can we live in my house?'

'Of course we can live in your house!' Matt laughed. 'Is that all you have to say, can we live in your house?'

'Oh no, now that's clear. I've got an awful lot to say, lots and lots of words, and every single one of them is yes! Yes, Matt, I would love to live with you, properly and formally and for ever.'

'Right, now that's cleared up, come here.' And the two of them, not for the first time, spent an awful lot of time kissing in the gardens of Penmenna Hall.

## Chapter Twenty Two

Alex had never really thought about Halloween before, other than that it was a bizarre thing to make a fuss about, but this evening he thought he might change his mind. Half-term had swooshed by and it had been lovely having Ellie at home. The week was made up of lie-ins and late nights, littering all the nearby villages with flyers for Sylvie's new classes and then going on autumn walks with Sylvie and Sam in the woods, crunching on leaves and searching for conkers, before returning home and having experiments, seeping them in vinegar and cooking them for hours in the Aga.

In the evenings Sylvie and he had been cooking for the kids, having epic conker battles (which Alex was astounded to learn they weren't allowed to do in the playground these days), taking turns to read to them and curling up and having movie nights. He knew that she had still been desperately looking for an affordable place for her and Sam. It was not proving fruitful. However, he had just had a phone call that he hoped might make all the difference.

She and Sam were due any minute and he was fascinated to know what surprises she had up her sleeve. They had been discussing going to Roscarrock to buy Halloween costumes earlier in the week and she had said that she would take care of it all, but it was nearly the eleventh hour and Ellie was getting antsy.

'Are they here yet?' Ellie came running into the kitchen, just in case she had missed them in the three whole minutes it had taken her to nip to the loo. She was twirling one of her plaits around her finger and looking at him with a scrunched-up face.

'You know Sylvie will be here soon, she'd never dream of letting you down. What sort of costume do you think she'll bring?' Not only was his best friend perfect in all that she did, she had taught him to master the art of distraction.

'Ooh, oh, um… I want to be a cat… no, no, I think I'm going to be a ghost, oh, or a vampire like Mona, ooh, oh no, I know, I want to be a witch like Meg and Mog, oh, and like Sabrina, and *Room on the Broom*.'

'OK, well, I don't know what she's got in mind for you, but let's hope it's either witch, cat or vampire then.'

'Hey, hey, hey.' The latch clicked and Sylvie and Sam came through the door. Alex looked at her, her arms full of green and black and purple fabric and a great big wicker basket on her arm, and felt his heart swell. 'Happy Halloween.'

'Happy Halloween.' Ellie ran to their guest. 'What am I? What am I?'

'Weeelll, you're always a pickle but tonight, Elechi Ada McKenzie, you are going to be the witchiest witch of them all!' She pulled the fabric off her arm and it opened out to be the most detailed witch costume Alex had ever seen.

'Oh, oh, oh, oh. I looove it!' Ellie looked like she was going to hyperventilate as she pulled the dress from Sylvie's arms and held it against her. 'Look, Dad, I'm going to be the witchiest witch. And it's got pockets!' And it did – she had different-coloured pockets with outsized stitches all over the skirt.

'You certainly are.' Alex grinned down at her and then mouthed, 'Thank you,' over Ellie's head.

'Thank you, thank you, thank you, Sylvie.' Ellie was still quite breathless, her brown eyes shining with joy.

'They're for putting your charms and spell stuff in. We've got snails and frogs and all sorts, just pretend ones though, and there's more,' Sam said, a proud grin on his face. 'Mum's made you a hat, and a wand and even, you're not going to guess…'

'What? What? What?'

'She made you real witch's warts, look!' Sam leant into his mum's basket, rummaging so hard that she nearly lost her footing.

'Easy there, big guy. Here they are.' Sylvie triumphantly pulled out some prosthetic warts from the crevice of the basket. 'You learn a lot in the theatre – it's not all pink and white tutus, you know. Now you go and slip that dress on, although it should fit, and when you come back downstairs, and only after you've eaten some vegetable soup, then we can do your make-up and then we can go…'

'Trick 'n' treating,' the children screeched in unison.

'Uh-huh.'

'What's Sam going to be?

'I'm going to be an evil vampire, mmwhahahaha,' said Sam in a very evil vampire voice. 'Mine is in here. I've got a proper swishy cloak and fangs and Mum's going to draw blood running down my face and everything.'

'Ha, you're going look so scary.' Ellie giggled.

'He is. Now you two little ghouls go and get changed while we heat this soup up. Is that also in your magic Halloween basket?' Alex couldn't believe what Sylvie had achieved in a few short days; if nothing else that basket was like Mary Poppins's bag and Sylvie herself very definitely had magical properties.

'It is indeed. Veg before candy, them's the rules.'

If Alex thought he had been finished off by pockets then he was mistaken; his heart continued to melt many times as the evening progressed. The first time was after the children had noisily slurped their soup and Sylvie painted their little upturned faces, adding warts and blood as desired, Alex wordlessly changing the water time and time again as it became a green-brown murk. Watching them all in his kitchen he was overwhelmed with a sudden feeling of warmth, of satisfaction with life. And then, he realized, this was what family felt like.

# Chapter Twenty Three

As they wandered around the village Alex could see that trick-or-treating was fully embraced in Penmenna, with lots of the older couples, their own children having long flown the nest, making specially iced cakes, biscuits or candies for the kids when they knocked. Huge efforts had gone into the decorations with houses of horror popping up all over the village; badly sawn-off legs littered driveways and you could barely move for spiders, skeletons and elaborately carved pumpkins.

Sam's evil vampire bravado had a bit of a wobble once they left the house although Ellie was happily shrieking, 'Boo!' at everyone they walked past until Alex reined her in a bit. Sam appeared overwhelmed by the whole thing. Alex didn't blame him, it was very full on. But slowly, slowly, as Sam watched, mouth agape and standing very closely to Sylvie, he began to throw himself into the party atmosphere; his initial fear turning to shrieks of joy the scarier things got. It wasn't long until he too was racing door to door with Ellie, knocking and rawring and comparing the treasures they received. Every now and again he would jump up and down with excitement and grin at his mum. Sylvie's face was so flooded with pride and love it made Alex go a bit swooshy inside as well.

One house even had an apple-bobbing competition in its front garden. With Ellie and Sam struggling a little bit, they pulled Sylvie down on the ground next to them so she could show them how to do it. Alex watched as she knelt over the big barrel and with her hands stretched out behind her back – for balance, she said – managed to get an apple first time.

'Wow, Mum, and you don't even have vampire fangs.'

'Oh, but she does,' piped up the lady whose garden they were in. 'Don't you, dear? We'll be watching again tonight. We checked the listings and were so pleased to see it was on again.'

Sylvie removed the apple from her mouth as she smiled up at them.

'That's ever so sweet of you.'

'You don't really have fangs, do you, Mum? Does she?' Sam's new-found fearlessness took a knock as he worried that his mum might be an actual real-life vampire.

'You are both very pale, you could both be!' Ellie said, nodding seriously in her witch's hat, helpful as ever.

'No, no, of course I don't have real fangs.' Sylvie leant across, still on her knees, and plopped a kiss on his head, which he immediately shook off. 'Mrs Murray is talking about a ballet I was in – it had vampires, but we were only pretending. Now, are you two going to have a go? I bet both of you could get one with a bit of practice. Whoa, no, Ellie, don't just bash the water with your head, you'll hurt yourself... Ooh, and drown the rest of us with your splashing!'

'It's always such a treat. Your mother, God rest her, used to let us know whenever they were showing one of your productions, and they're all so beautiful. You have such poise, dear.'

Sylvie scrambled to her feet. 'Not so much any more, Mrs Murray, my life is all scraped knees and a hundred and one ways with pasta these days. But it was good fun, that production.'

'What production?' Alex was desperate to know.

'Oh, don't worry about it.' Sylvie waved her hand at him dismissively. 'Well done, Ellie. You now, Sam.'

'*Dracula*. They like to run it every other year at Halloween, now what channel is it, Roy? Is it Sky Arts or BBC Four? One of them. Nine p.m. tonight. Roy and I will be watching again, won't we?' Mrs Murray, round and smiley with a husband to match, was more than happy to fill Alex in.

'We will.' Roy nodded his head enthusiastically. Alex decided there and then that he would be too. A chance to see Sylvie dance, properly dance, not just take a class of young children – there was no way he was going to miss that.

–

After every door had been knocked on, every apple bobbed and marked with little teeth prints, and satsuma peel and lollipop sticks scattered recklessly upon the pavements, Sylvie and he led the children back home; both of whom were so hyped up on sugar that they insisted on acting out *Room on the Broom* before going into the kitchen to divide up their haul and do some more colouring.

Alex and Sylvie left them to it and headed back to their spots on the sofa, the habit now ingrained, and as she pulled up the blanket and reached for the remote he stopped her.

'Tonight was ace. I'm so glad I moved to Penmenna.'

'Do they not have Halloween in London?' Sylvie teased.

'You know what I mean, Penmenna's pretty idyllic and the community spirit down here is insane. I love it and I know Ellie does. Plus there's the fact that apart from tonight, obviously, which was terrifying, the most aggressive thing in the village is probably Marion. Oh, although there is a battle of the bands in the local pub by the way, Matt invited me on Sunday. Do you fancy coming?'

'For sure. I haven't been in for Sunday lunch for as long as I can remember. I went in with Mum last year but not since. I hibernated after her death until I met you, and your pernicious bad influence keeps dragging me out of the house and helping me find work and stuff!'

'Ha! You found work by yourself, that had nothing to do with me. But talking of getting you out of the house, I do have some news. I'm excited about this but also a bit scared you'll feel I'm micro-managing your life but...' Alex paused and looked at her.

'Well... come on!'

'But I heard a rumour and thought I'd follow it up to see if it was even a possibility before I said anything.'

'Oh, go on! Stop pausing and looking at me funny.'

'OK. I heard that Matt and Rosy might be moving in together, but didn't know who was going where or even if it had been agreed, but he rang me this afternoon and followed up on a conversation we had a couple of weeks ago. Matt is moving in with Rosy. Something about how she loves her tree. Anyway, he's moving in with her and was looking to sublet his cottage on a long-term basis to someone he knows he can trust. Now he took some persuading because he'd heard that despite looking all fragile and ballerina bird-like that you have a shocking temper and a tendency to dance on tables but...'

'I have never danced on a table outside of a theatre!'

'I can live in hope. Maybe on Sunday. Anyway, Matt's cottage. It's available and he would quite like you and Sam as tenants. Provided your employer will give you a reference, obviously! The rent is fairly peppercorn because he's more concerned about having the right person than turning a profit. What do you... whoa... let me breathe, I take it that's a yes!'

Sylvie had launched herself across the sofa and thrown her arms around his neck, crossing them so that her hands were clenching his shoulders with excitement. Rather like he had seen Sam clench his fists open and closed when he was excited.

She drew back and looked him straight in the eye.

'That is a huge yes. It's a yes, yes, yes! Is it really peppercorn? I can afford it? Is this actually going to happen? Sam and I can live in the village and let Tom move Julie into Lovage Farm? He can stop fretting about me making him homeless and Sam and I can have our own fresh start, somewhere light and airy? Really?' Her words tumbled out over themselves as she held eye contact and he felt the grin slowly creeping across his face to match hers. He was overwhelmed with the desire to just lean forward and briefly touch his lips to hers. Their eyes locked and then, from nowhere, he heard his own voice in his head, *Don't you dare spoil a good thing.* And he broke eye contact, forced his shoulders back and flashed her a smile.

'I think that you can probably afford it, and yes, I see no reason why Tom can't have his love nest. Matt said tonight that they've moved most of his stuff out over half-term but he wants to give it a quick freshen-up, and then you can start moving your stuff in next weekend from Saturday lunchtime. I said you were starting your lessons in Penmenna on the Saturday and he said any time from then on was fine. Sunday works brilliantly too. He's quite happy not to begin the tenancy until you're fully moved in. You're to let him know if you want it fully furnished and I'm to pass on his phone number for all the questions you're bound to have.'

Sylvie rocked on her heels and sat back at her end of the sofa.

'I don't know how to thank you, but thank you. Life is going to be so much easier being in the village. Sam will have all his friends within walking distance, and it doesn't matter how many times the crappy car dies on me, or at least not so much, Thank you.'

'Absolute pleasure. It'll be nice to have you in walking distance. We can spend more time together. Ells will love that.' Alex knew the statement was true but felt a bit of a coward hiding behind his daughter. Couldn't he just say *I would love that*? No, because he could not afford to scare her away and rock the boat. Her presence in their lives was making his and Ellie's so much better, and there was no way he was introducing any kind of drama that could upset the delicate, the perfect, balance they currently had. She had never indicated she wanted more than friend-ship and she had enough to deal with right now. Sure, having Matt's cottage would help her out considerably and a secure tenancy in the village where she could live independently from her uncle was a great thing, but she would still have the stress of moving house, and her job was also still relatively new, as was setting up the ballet classes in the school. Now was not the time to throw more change at her; now, as her friend, he needed to put his own wishes to one side, support her with what she needed and accept that she just wasn't interested in him as a potential partner. And that was fine. If he wasn't her cup of tea then that was that. He just rather wished he was.

'So, tell me how I can pay the favour back? How can I help you? You seem to have life so completely together I can't think of anything you need help with.'

'Ha! You have met my daughter, right? I need *all* the help there, all of it. Seriously, you don't need to do anything. It was just a happy coincidence that Matt told me he was considering asking Rosy if they could live together. Right place right time.'

'I can't believe it's this simple, that you've completely sorted a house out for me. A house!'

'Strictly a cottage and it turns out it was an itty-bitty thing that literally landed in my lap, and like I say, your presence in this village is keeping me sane – you tether me, and Ellie. Being able to give something back to you, it means I'll sleep better at night.'

'I'm keeping you awake at night?' Her eyebrows shot through to the roots of her hair and she smiled the naughtiest little smile he had possibly ever seen.

# Chapter Twenty Four

Sylvie had scooped Sam up and driven him home, and Ellie had had her story read – speed-read because it was late and Alex was aware that nine o'clock was fast approaching and he had no intention of missing a second of *Dracula*. Not a second.

He raced back down the stairs, grabbed the last glass of red wine left in the bottle and settled himself on the sofa. Tonight had been so perfect; Ellie had curled up in her bed, warts and all (she had point-blank refused to take them off) and with such a satisfied smile on her face, that he had to declare their first ever Cornish Halloween a complete success. Although he had a horrid feeling she might never eat another apple unless it was presented to her in a bowl of water first.

He looked across at the blanket Sylvie had left on her end of the sofa. It wasn't very manly, but it was practically November. He grabbed it, and the remote, turned on the TV and found *Dracula* just in time.

As he covered himself in the blanket, he could smell the very scent of her. He scrunched it up, lifted to his face and breathed deep. This was ridiculous. What had happened to Alex McKenzie, man's man? A couple of months in Cornwall and he was watching ballet and sniffing blankets.

The music started and before he knew it he was hypnotized. He had always imagined ballet to be pink and white tutus and gentle romance. This was not that. This was black and red and smoke and suspense. The dancers were incredible the way they flung themselves across the stage. How they managed to do what they were doing with their toes, let alone their entire bodies, was beyond him. Surely no one with normal joints could possibly do that?

The story was dark, compelling, and he was pulled right in when there, and with no warning, his Sylvie was dancing across the screen, red hair loose, eyes fixed and convoluting her body with such a sensuality he didn't know what to do with himself. He couldn't pull his eyes away, entranced by her movement, her fluidity. She was like nothing he had ever seen. How could someone flow like that? Contort her body into such extreme positions, practically fly through the air as if she were on wires? Not to mention that every movement was so goddamn sensual. And then be doing the walk to school as if she was just like everyone else?

The power behind her body was phenomenal and as Dracula came up on the stage, all ebony and scarlet, power and threat, Alex wanted to be able to jump in, rescue her from what was inevitable. His glass remained in his hand, untouched as he just stared at the screen, forcing himself to remember this was a well-known story and that she was playing a part.

As Dracula seized her and the two danced a battle of wills, he found himself both enchanted and wildly jealous. He wasn't used to jealousy, hadn't really experienced it since school. But right now, he could imagine her twined around him like that, twisting her curves across his body. Not in opposition but in tandem, meshed together, moving in rhythm…

He realized how tightly he was gripping the stem of the glass and knocked back the remaining liquid whilst reminding himself that her performance was exactly that, and jealousy or lust were not emotions he could afford to feel right now. Yet still he couldn't take his eyes off the screen.

## Chapter Twenty Five

Summer had fought a good fight but the sea had turned from blue to grey, and the leaves were now rich orangey browns and were providing the most delicious scrunch underfoot as Sylvie walked Sam into school, his little ears and neck encased in wool and wrapped up warm.

She was loving this new stage of their lives. Her job was so much fun, it wasn't like work at all; the kids were adorable and although each teacher had their quirks she had a sneaking fondness for them all. She woke every morning feeling so damned lucky to have been welcomed into the bosom of this school so quickly, and as she returned through the great granite doorway after half-term she was itching to get back to it.

A couple of weeks ago the governors had approved her use of the hall on Saturdays so half-term had been largely spent with Alex and Ells, and on the very first weekend littering so many flyers for her new classes around the village that her mobile had been on fire all week. In a slightly less tangible fashion, having a best friend again was pretty special. Even though that best friend was the most gorgeous and most off-limits man she had ever met.

For the sake of her sanity and all the support he provided in her, and Sam's, life she needed to firmly keep him in the friendzone. Indulging only in daydreams and never in real life, increasingly hard the more time they spent together and not helped by the fact he was now the first thing she thought about in the morning and the last thing at night. The way he laughed when they were together and the way she occasionally caught him looking at her and...

'Hello, miss! Are we getting the bars out today?'

'Oh, hello, Alfie, Harry. Not today, I'm not with your class until tomorrow morning, but I will get them out then. You can see if you can get all the way to the top using those circles – you were so close last week, weren't you?'

'Oh, it's going to be easy, miss. I know I can do it this week. See you later then. Sam, are you coming?'

'Yeah, bye, Mum. See you later!' and Sam sped off with his classmates, all three of them clattering as they went, bags, so big for their little frames, wobbling on their backs as they ran.

She headed up to the staffroom to make herself a coffee before she started work. On Mondays she had Amanda's class after morning assembly, and Sarah's after breaktime. Both were going to have a first go at hockey today and she couldn't help but smile at the irony of her teaching it, her least favourite sport when she was at school. She would definitely be keeping a very firm hand on anyone who got a bit too happy with their sticks; she could remember the battered ankles as if it were yesterday.

'Oh, hello.' Marion burst into the staffroom, and seeing that it was empty apart from Sylvie, she knew there was no chance she was addressing anyone else. Marion had been even more stand-offish since the evening at Alex's, brushing past her haughtily as she made her way through school, her minions trailing behind and never feeling the need to say hello up until this point. She had notably *not* taken up Sylvie's offer of help with the PTA.

'Hello,' Sylvie answered, wondering what was in store.

'How are things going?'

'Well, thank you. Um, would you like a coffee?'

'Oh no, don't worry about that. Sarah will be in in a minute – she can be a little tardy, but she'll sort all that out.'

'It's no problem, I'm happy to.'

'Honestly, don't worry. Now tell me all about you. I understand you're running ballet lessons here. I knew you were a dancer in London but I…' she tinkled a very scary sounding laugh, '…I think I must have misunderstood, I thought you were more on the exotic side of things. But actually you were a *ballet* dancer for quite a reputable company?'

'Yes, I was. I loved it. We got to travel the world.' Sylvie didn't know why she felt she needed to add that bit, but she had.

'Quite, very glamorous. So, tell me, dear, why did you leave, and come back home? I understand your mother, dear woman, recently passed away, but you seem to have settled here. Put down roots?'

'Um… yes. Did you know my mum?'

*Scary tinkle.* 'No. But I knew *of* her, of course. Everyone said she was a lovely lady, lovely.'

'She was.'

'So, future plans? Reason for leaving?'

Wow! Sylvie was beginning to get antsy and could feel her red hair starting to kick in but somehow she was still answering this woman's questions.

'Recurring injury. The ballet world does seem terribly glamorous, and it can be. It can also be cruel and I knew that I wasn't going to progress much further with recurring shin splints. Each time I was having to take more and more time off to recover, so when I found I was pregnant I wanted to come home, and soon afterwards Mum had her diagnosis and that's it really. I love Penmenna and can't ever see me leaving, or certainly not whilst Sam is still a child.'

'Good, good.' The woman was virtually rubbing her hands together. What had brought on this turn of events?

'And you're running classes here in the school. My husband is chair of the governors and I take on his role in his absence – I was so pleased to approve your request on his behalf. It was my idea to waive the hire cost – after all, having a prima ballerina offering lessons in the school does rather increase our cachet. I've been meaning to hunt you down for a chat but life, well, you know, and then half-term. I've just got a new puppy which is taking far more of my time than I imagined possible. A Weimaraner, very now. My Richard knows I like to stay on trend...' *tinkle tinkle*, '...but I'm getting side-tracked. I wanted to say how very lucky we are to have you, dear. I was thinking of enrolling my boys.'

Sylvie prayed her gulp wasn't visible. She decided not to correct Marion's misuse of the terminology regarding her position in the company. And as to Marion's boys, she liked them all. They were sparky, quirky and smart – individually. Together, despite all of Sylvie's skills, they had the potential to turn the entire class feral.

'Oh, that would be wonderful, but you wouldn't believe how quickly places have filled up. I'd be more than happy to pop them on the waiting list and let you know as soon as there are vacancies.' Luckily this was entirely true, she had already filled every class for the Saturday.

'Ah, I see. That's a shame.' Marion smiled and cocked her head to one side, and Sylvie's spider senses tingled. She guessed what was coming and decided to head it off.

'Obviously, Mrs Marksharp, I would love to be able to bump you up the list, but I know how seriously you take fairness and I would hate to cause any ripples. Caesar's wife and all.'

'Absolutely, dear, I couldn't possibly ask for any special favours, that would set tongues wagging in the playground.' She managed to mask the vinegary look that had flitted across her face and replace it with concerned interest again. 'Especially as I know we're going to become such dear friends, with you being… ahem… so close to Alex McKenzie.'

Aha, Marion was up to mischief and it wasn't so her boys could perfect an arabesque. Presumably the revelation that Sylvie was a ballet dancer and not a stripper suddenly catapulted her into Marion's 'acceptable' category, and hence Sylvie was now part of her plan to keep Alex local. Sylvie was not sure she liked the turn that might take. She had not been working extremely hard to keep her crush at bay, in the name of not rocking the boat and maintaining the friendship, to have Marion come in and explode it now. For goodness' sake! This woman should come with a health warning. She'd have to get in first and reassure Alex that she really wasn't after anything other than friendship before Marion scared him off completely! She realized she hadn't answered and

Marion was still standing waiting for a response as Sarah hurtled into the staffroom and breathlessly apologized.

'Marion, I'm so sorry. Dear Jonny has come down with mumps and the childminder was being most unreasonable. I've left him with a neighbour but I will have to get back… if that's OK… after assembly. The neighbour is a little absent-minded. I'll have your coffee ready in an instant and then I'll go and set up for assembly.'

'Of course, dear, no hurry. I'll see you in the hall shortly.' Marion addressed her friend with more than a hint of steel before beaming again at Sylvie. 'See you later, dear, so glad we're chums.' And swished out of the staffroom towards the hall.

# Chapter Twenty Six

Sylvie headed to class before the kids came streaming through, but was still a bit shell-shocked by the staffroom. Marion had thought she was a stripper? Although actually, so what if she was? It would be her choice how she earned her money and bugger all to do with anyone else. Presumably a possible career in exotic dancing meant she wasn't 'good enough' for Alex in Marion's book.

She didn't know why she was getting so riled up over such a stupid conversation. Marion was obviously Marion, there were lots of things Sylvie wasn't too keen on about her as well. Why was she letting this particular interaction get to her?

As she crossed the hall she had heard Alice, Class Four's teaching assistant, discussing the upcoming Bonfire Night assembly with Pippa from Class One and how she didn't understand why Rosy didn't just outright ban *her* as well after last year. Sylvie was itching to join in and get the details; she could only guess at the *her* but it was a fairly secure one, plus she knew Pippa didn't have any problem holding back and was great fun to get into conversation with, especially when she was riled. But Sylvie *did* hold back and knew her own barely simmering fury with Marion this morning could mean she would be way too venomous, and venomous was never a great look in a new workplace.

After the register was taken and the children had marched into the hall, Sylvie plopped herself on the floor with Jade. She felt sorry for the girl and had noticed she often tended to fidget badly in assembly, leading to Mrs Adams dragging her out and the whole day spiralling downward from there. With Sylvie next to her she managed to hold it together for a little bit longer, thus avoiding the wrath of her class teacher and having a much better day overall.

The eldest sat down first and watched as the young ones trooped through. The school held a Bonfire Night celebration and fireworks display every year and today's assembly was the last one before the event later that night. Rosy stood at the front smiling her gentle head teacher's smile as the children filtered through and took their places. As soon as all were settled she raised her hands for silence and began to talk about how exciting it was to have Fireworks Night come around again, as Marion jigged around from one foot to another, hair perfectly set, beaming out at the children and waiting for her bit.

Oh God! Watching her there, all jittery in her mustard dress with magpies on it and matching espadrilles, was making Sylvie's temperature soar. With all of this '… so close to Alex' nonsense, Marion was going to screw everything up. As soon as Sylvie had got herself some measure of happiness and security outside of Lovage Farm, Marion bloody-mustard-magpie Marksharp was going to screw it all up!

'Now, Mrs Marksharp – and I know you all know her and have seen her around the school – is going to quickly talk to you about her plans for tonight. Marion.'

Sylvie watched as Rosy shot the head of the PTA a Very Stern Look.

'Right, my darlings. It's a very exciting day today and I have asked all the teachers to collect the best work you have done to celebrate Fireworks Day and the fifth of November, whether that be the beautiful paintings from Class One, or the interesting historical discourse from you older ones.'

'The what?' Jade turned to Sylvie.

'Your history work,' Sylvie whispered back.

'Well, why doesn't she say that then?' Jade muttered under her breath. Oh, she normally has no problem saying what she means, flitted through Sylvie's head and the panic set in again. She would make sure she was out on time today and get to Alex first. Surely if she had a whole firework display to micro-manage and parent helpers to terrorize, she wouldn't have time to put a grenade in Sylvie's first decent adult friendship in years? Not until teatime at least.

'So, I'll be coming around your classrooms to choose the best of the work on offer. No scribbles and I want lovely joined-up writing from you older ones. We will be showcasing Penmenna at its best. We want winners at Penmenna, none of this taking-part-is-all-that-counts nonsense, eh?'

Sylvie's eyebrows went through the roof and she felt vindicated as Rosy glowered at Marion and interrupted, 'As you know, Mrs Marksharp, we celebrate everyone who tries their hardest here.'

'Well, of course we do.' Marion beamed at Rosy and then, where the head teacher couldn't see, turned around and mouthed, 'Joined up,' at the children and gave them a jolly thumbs-up as she nodded to reinforce her point.

'Now, Mrs Adams used to deliver the safety advice for Fireworks Night but I think we all remember last year,' Rosy said as she avoided making eye contact with the rest of the staff, who all suddenly became very interested in their shoes.

'She was terrifying,' Jade whispered. 'Three of the little ones cried. She told us all we'd burn our fingers off and not be able to hold a pen or use a computer ever again if we didn't all wear gloves. Lara only had mittens so she refused to come and said her mum got really cross and rang the school to complain.'

'Jade James!' Mrs Adams barked.

'Sorry,' Sylvie whispered across to the teacher. 'That was my fault. She was answering a question I asked.'

'Miss, did you just fib?'

'Oh, um, well, yes. Now shush,' Sylvie hissed, and then as an afterthought, 'Doesn't mean you ever should!'

As Rosy started to outline the main points of the fireworks code, getting the older children to join in and pulling up volunteers to act out what to do, Sylvie felt herself zoning out as she put the finishing touches to her plan. She would just get to Alex and make it really, really clear that she wasn't interested in him before Marion could get there with her tuppence-worth. Alex would be relieved; after all, she was fairly sure he valued the friendship as much as she did and all should be OK as long as she didn't get distracted by his arms, shoulders, hands, eyes, smile, legs, upper thighs…

Oh, for goodness' sake, she'd have to speak to him with her eyes closed at this rate. She would need to remain focused, hope he didn't give her that look that he had started giving her when he saw her, the one that melted her tummy and made her feel she was going to disintegrate into a puddle of lust. Yes, as long as he didn't do any of that, she'd be fine.

# Chapter Twenty Seven

Alex strolled up to school to meet Ellie. He had spoken to her yesterday about how Penmenna were going to help raise funds for her old orphanage and be part of a campaign which coordinated donations of books, stationery, e-readers and laptops from schools all across the country to schools and orphanages in South Sudan. The remit for his foundation was expanding and was now made up of these two prongs – raising funds for orphanages and helping them coordinate the reuniting of children separated from their families, alongside the resourcing and mentoring of schools attached to said orphanage in an attempt to give these displaced children as good a start as they could.

He had asked Ellie if she would mind Penmenna School being involved in such a project and was so proud of the way her eyes had lit up, excited at the thought of being able to help the friends she had left behind. As she pointed out, Penmenna had an awful lot of books, it only made sense to share. His heart filled.

And now he was hoping to catch Sylvie. As committed as he was to the foundation he found his mind wandering a lot recently. Starting with the boys teasing a few weeks before and culminating in the time they had spent together at Halloween, it was increasingly apparent that not only did he seem to make Sylvie the topic of conversation whenever he could, but she was constantly on his mind. He was making great strides in trying to control this, but it really was quite hard.

She was his best friend in the village. Well, not best friend, that had to be Chase – after all they had gone to school together – but certainly the one who he spent the most time with, wanted to see even more and the one he felt truly connected to. And as respectful as he was, he would be lying to himself if he didn't admit that the curves of her body, the graceful manner of every movement made, and the way her smile lit up her face didn't cross his mind as his head hit the pillow at night. And stayed there until morning.

Maybe he needed to stop arsing about with this, fretting that they would jeopardize their friendship and that of the children's. Both were adults, highly reasonable ones with enough life experience under their belts to accept that sometimes you had to put your head over the parapet. You had to take the leap, or you stayed stuck, never moving on and missing out on all the might-have-beens.

He promised himself that if he tried to take things out of the friendzone then he wouldn't allow it to mess things up with the kids. He didn't think it would, to be honest. If anything, he had convinced himself that he and Sylvie in a successful relationship would help create an even more stable environment for Ellie. A traditional family unit.

If she said yes, that was. And he really hoped she would. He saw the way she looked at him whenever she thought he wasn't looking, and the way she practically melted into him when he put an arm around her or squidged her up on the sofa. Surely he had a chance? And if she said no, and he had read this all wrong, well, he was man enough to cope with rejection. That would be that. At least he would have tried, and with any luck the daydreaming would end.

He had come pretty close on Halloween, but stopped himself because he didn't want to add to the pressure she was already under, but there came a time when one had to be honest, and that time was fast approaching. In fact, he had spent all of the last week thrashing it out in his mind. If nothing else he needed clarity, absolute clarity, with regards to where his future was going with Sylvie, so he could get his head back into the game. Closure on the massive crush he now recognized he had, would mean he could get on with the other aspects of his life.

Things were going from strength to strength within the foundation. Penmenna was his first school on board with the educational side of things and Rosy was spreading the word amongst other heads. There were already contractors out in South Sudan beginning to improve the existing site and planning the building of another orphanage with reunion facilities attached. Not an easy job whilst the area was still so unstable.

Now as he approached the outside of Class One he saw Sylvie race across the quad, red curls flying, her urgency out of character. Had something happened to Sam? Surely not? She reached where the parents stood, nodding at some but not engaging in conversation – no emergency or she would have flown through the door.

He saw her face light up, as it always did when she caught sight of him, and then she scurried towards him, looking as if she was trying to compose her features into a slightly sterner look. OK, this should be amusing. He was particularly fond of stern Sylvie, she always utterly failed and he wondered how Sam fell for it every single time.

'Hey, how's you? That's a very stern face for Fireworks Night. Do you want me to come pick you up later? Then you can have a drink. I think they're serving mulled cider or something.'

'Yes they are, but no, that's fine, I'll drive in. But I do need to talk to you.'

'Or you could come for supper. And then you can tell me what it is. Is it about classes tomorrow? You know you're going to smash it, right?'

Sylvie started scrunching her mouth up and looking at him funnily, then she cocked her head to one side and started to speak. Then stopped herself, paused and let out a sigh and started to speak again.

'OK, none of that then. Come on, what's wrong? Just say it.' He had seen her do this before; it had been an awfully big build-up to being told he had spinach in his teeth.

'Um… oh…' More head cocking and sighing.

'Coo-ee… you two!' The high-pitched call came from across the playground. It was amazing how that woman's voice travelled.

'Oh my God, um…' Marion's frantic waving seemed to speed Sylvie up, her eyes darting from Marion to Alex and back again, '…look, Alex, I really like you and everything, I love spending time with you, but as a friend, OK? *Only* as a friend. I'm sure… um… that you'll find someone soon, but I promise that someone is not me. OK? Do you understand what I'm trying to say? Quickly, do you understand? You and me, great friends but I'm not interested in anything else. Really not interested. It doesn't matter what anyone else has to say. I'm telling you, I'm happy with how things are and that's it.'

'Whoa, OK. Um, I hadn't suggested…'

'I know you hadn't, and that's why I'm trying to say I'm agreeing. Oh, hi, Sam. Hi, Ellie. Good day?' She didn't pause to listen to their answer but just carried on babbling at speed. 'Marion looks like she wants to talk to you, Alex. Sam and I are going to race off, but we'll see you tonight at school, OK? I really have to go. We are all good, aren't we?'

Alex felt his head nod up and down but the truth was he wasn't entirely sure what was going on. Had she suddenly developed some kind of super-psychic mind-reading power and decided to head him off before he embarrassed himself later this evening? In which case he supposed he should be grateful, if he could just shut off that sharp pang of rejection currently coursing through his body.

'Brilliant, laters. Ooh, sorry, Marion, can't stop. See you all tonight.' And with that Sylvie practically sprinted out of the playground, cheeks red as cherries, having grasped an indignant Sam's hand and dragging him behind her.

Alex turned and there was Marion by his elbow in the place Sylvie had been just seconds ago, an odd look in her eye as she gazed after the rapidly disappearing redhead. '*Such* a lovely girl, so talented, and such a dedicated mother. We really are lucky to have her in the village, don't you think?'

## Chapter Twenty Eight

Bing. *Marion has roped me in for safety duty, having to go in earlier. See you there?* Sylvie scanned the text from Alex and grinned. Now she had headed Marion off at the pass she was much more relaxed again. He did make her laugh. She could only imagine how delighted he was to be forced into a volunteer role.

Bing. *What's worse is she's roped my friend Hector in as well, now it's a sure thing that the school will burn down and you'll be out of a job tomorrow.*

Bing. *Oh my God. She's making me wear a tabard! Hector's doesn't fit – the advantages of a diet based on port and grouse – so she's let him off. Do you know anything about the Equality Act?*

It would seem that her somewhat embarrassing explanation to Alex hadn't dimmed their friendship, nor anything Marion might have said in her absence, so she had definitely done the right thing by getting in and letting him know she wasn't some crazy lust-filled stalker. She certainly wasn't stalking him, he just kept popping up. The lust bit, hmm, that might be a thing but she would dwell on that later. Privately. And without him ever knowing.

She grinned a big grin and hurried Sam along. She hadn't been to a Bonfire Night celebration in years and was possibly more excited than her boy. If she could get down to the school early she could see if they needed any help with the final touches to either the marquee where Marion's minions would be serving food or the bonfire itself. Although after today she'd have to restrain the urge to Rohypnol Marion, dress her up in old clothes and pretend she was the Guy. That comment about her dancing being for a reputable company and its implication that Marion had previously assumed her dancing was something not quite as respectable was still annoying the bejesus out of her!

As they pulled up to the school, dusk had fully turned to dark and Sam was sitting in his booster chair talking nineteen to the dozen.

'We didn't come last year, did we, Mum? But I have seen fireworks before, haven't I, Mum? Ellie says she's seen them a million times. I don't know if she's telling the truth because she had a funny look on her face and sometimes Ellie lies. Did you know that? I've told her she shouldn't but she still does but I can always tell because of the funny look. She says Angelina says something called white lies are being kind and that everyone tells fibs but I said that lies don't have colours and all lies are bad, aren't they, Mum?'

'Sometimes people do tell a little lie, but you're quite right, it's important to always tell the truth.'

Sylvie squealed into a parking spot, hardly able to believe her luck that there was still one left close to the school, and she and Sam wandered over to join the queue to get into the school field for the bonfire extravaganza. So much for being early – the queue was snaking around the large fence and all down the pavement. She had just got chatting to some of the other mums when a silence descended. It could only mean one thing.

'Yoo-hooo! What are you doing in the queue? Come on now, come this way.' Marion's voice rang across the heads as everyone either looked around to see who Monster Marksharp was talking to or started examining the ground in the hope that her glance didn't fall upon them. Sylvie saw that her buckle was looking a little tarnished, she really did need a new pair of boots.

'Mum, I think that lady that did the assembly is looking at you.' No. Had she not had enough Marion for one day?

'I'm sure she's not,' Sylvie whispered to Sam, as she touched his hand to stop him yanking her sleeve off.

'She's a prima ballerina, you know? She shouldn't be in the queue, for goodness' sake!'

How did that woman manage to make her voice quite so loud? She must deserve a place in the *Guinness Book of Records*.

There was hardly likely to be another ex-ballerina in amongst the parents tonight. Plus, she needed Marion to stop repeating this nonsense. There was a massive difference between the leading light in a ballet company and Sylvie's old role. She felt the fire come back.

'Marion...' she heard the bark in her own voice, '...I wasn't a...'

'Come on now, don't be modest, dear, that doesn't help anyone. Sarah! Why did you not pop Sylvie straight to the front? She *is* staff and invaluable to the PTA as well. You really do need to shape up! Come on through.' She felt Marion's hand grip her arm with even more force than Sam usually used. Did this count as assault? She dallied with a ten-second daydream about getting Marion arrested and carted off in front of all the parents. Although knowing her luck, the policeman would probably roll up his trouser leg, perform some kind of weird hand gesture and take Sylvie away instead. Best keep her protest verbal.

'Marion, really. Please let go of me.'

'The *Royal* Ballet, you know, *and* she's teaching lessons here at Penmenna. Such a waiting list, even my own dear boys haven't been able to get in.' Marion bustled her through the crowds of parents and public, most of whom gave Sylvie looks of sympathy as opposed to the anger she'd expected for such outrageous queue-jumping. Marion's grip was like that of a boarding-school matron. 'Penmenna really is the darling of the famous at the moment, what with Sylvie here and of course our very own Alex McKenzie. We are ablaze with celebrity.'

'I'm not in any way a…'

'And…' Marion continued to anyone who would listen, and it appeared that was the whole school, '…such a good pairing. Take my word for it and watch this space, the sizzle between those two is quite something.' They cleared the queue, which was now silent and agog, and stood in the school field, looking across at it all lit up and sparkling with an enticing Bonfire Night welcome. The smell of sausages and jacket potatoes flitted across the field and Sylvie could see Sam's nose twitching. However, first she needed to deal with this bloody woman and her vice-like grip.

'Marion!' Sylvie had had enough and forcibly shook her off. 'I was not a prima ballerina and there is no sizzle between Alex and myself. None at all.'

'Hohoho, I have a knack for these things, dear. I can spot romance a mile off, Rosy will tell you. There she is…' Rosy was walking across the field, in deep conversation with a man with the curliest hair and a naughty-looking dog bouncing along by their feet. '…Rosy! Cooo-eee, just me and Sylvie.' Marion waved across at the head teacher before turning back to Sylvie, Sam and the three henchwomen who had trailed alongside them. 'And what's more I know about sex, trust me. I know about good sex, and you two are going to have a lot of it. Mark my words.' Sylvie's mouth dropped open as she brought her hands upwards by her side and waved them in horror whilst shooting desperate looks at Sam.

'Who's going to have lots of good sex?'

Oh, wow. If the ground could just open up now and swallow her whole.

'Oh, look, why don't you run along and play with Ellie, Sam.' It was intended as a request rather than a question.

'No.' Sam had a mutinous look on his face whilst Ellie, who had appeared with her father out of nowhere, was dissolving into giggles. Sylvie psychically willed her to pop on the ear-defenders she was carrying with her, or at the very least give them to Sam.

'Hello, Alex darling, mwah, mwah. I was just talking about you and Sylvie. I know all about these things.'

'Yes, Chase has mentioned that you might.' Alex smiled a familiar smile at her and Marion giggled, *giggled*, back. 'But I'm afraid you're wrong in this instance. Sylvie has made it quite clear that that sort of thing won't be happening.'

'Please. The children are right here.' Was anyone other than her thinking this was not an appropriate conversation to have? Ever? Let alone in front of their children. Sylvie had never thought of herself as a prude but for goodness' sake!

'Hoho, Sylvie, life is life, they do need to learn…'

'Not at four and five years old! Sam, here, I think they're selling drinks over there, would you like to…'

'No.'

'Ellie?'

'No, we're OK here.' She managed to squeeze the words out between giggles. 'Are you going to be my daddy's girlfriend after all? Like I said to Angelina.'

'No, I am not! Mrs Marksharp here has made a mistake.' Sylvie sent Marion another very pointed look to reinforce what she was saying and rubbed her arm just to show how unimpressed she was with being manhandled to the front of the queue.

'You'll see, I'm always right. Now, Alex darling, where's Hector? You haven't left him unattended, have you?'

'He is a grown adult, perfectly capable of taking care of himself.'

'I know exactly what he is capable of, that's the problem. Now I'll leave you two lovebirds alone but I will need you Alex, in ooh…' she glanced at her watch, '…half an hour, for fire-safety duty. See you in a bit.' Marion scurried off, mustard dress and minions, leaving an amused Alex, a furious Sam, a smirking Ellie (neither of the children should have understood any of that but seemed to have done) and a mortified and enraged Sylvie.

'Honestly, that woman…!'

'…is an absolute hoot, no one takes her seriously. Now, let's go get ourselves some burgers, hey, kids? Hmm? Come on.'

Alex carelessly threw his arm around Sylvie's shoulder as if they had known each other for ever, and gave her a reassuring squeeze, before leading them all towards the tempting waft of the barbecue.

Marion and the PTA had decorated the marquee beautifully, it was as if *Homes Beautiful* had stepped in and designed the perfect setting for a Bonfire Night party. Red, orange and yellow bunting fluttered in the light breeze, all lit with subtle orange fairy lights and with strings attached to the roof of the marquee, floating down and across, featuring some of the children's work on Guy Fawkes, and firework pictures in paint, chalk and pastel demonstrating the range of age across the school. As well as long queues at the barbecue stall there were even longer ones near the mulled cider where the spices and smells, and alcohol content, were putting warm smiles on parents with every sip. In the corner of the marquee was a human-sized Guy, seated in a wheelbarrow, a jam jar on string hanging off its hand and pictures of an orphanage in Africa scattered discreetly about, informing parents that this was the charity the PTA was collecting for this year alongside raising funds for the school.

'Look, Daddy! It's the Healing Hearts Orphanage. Like you said. Now we can get the Penmenna children to help too. We can give them loads of books. This is awesome.' Sylvie watched Ellie's face turn to her father's, pride flitting across it.

'We can indeed. Miss Winter thought this could be a start tonight, and then we could tell the rest of the children much more about it next week. You up for that?'

'Damn straight!' Ellie jumped up and high-fived her dad with her free hand.

'Ellie! That's another bad word.'

'Sam says it.' Both Sylvie and Alex's heads shot around to look at Sam, who merely shrugged *à la* Ellie. She exchanged a look with Alex, both parents more amused than cross. It would appear their children were sharing their skills.

'Can we put some money in as well, Dad? Look, Sam, look, that's where I used to live before I came here with Daddy.'

Sylvie looked at Sam's face and was so grateful she had had the chat with him before about Ellie's adoptive status and she wasn't going to have to do it again in front of the girl in question or her father and make some hideous faux pas by not choosing the right word and unintentionally offending the both of them.

'Cool. I'll put my pocket money in. Mum, can I?'

'Of course. Here you are, you can have it now.'

'Thanks, come on, Ellie.' Sam looked at Ellie and waited for her to start walking with him towards the Guy.

'That's kind of him. Thank you, Sylvie.'

Alex smiled at her, that smile he had that made the whole marquee melt away and Sylvie gulp and have to think really hard to ground herself and remember what they were talking about. That smile. The dangerous one. The one that didn't make her think of children and responsibility but of crumpled duvets and tumbled bodies, piles of clothing and blissed-out morning smiles.

'I didn't know that you had involved the school with your foundation. That's a brilliant idea. I presume this is to do with that.'

'Yes, this is the orphanage Ells was put in after... well, when she lost her family, and they were amazing. I'm using them as a blueprint for another that we're building and sending funds to them so they can continue to grow. And help lead the way for the others. Matt told Rosy about the foundation and she suggested this as a tiny start and is apparently going to tie in a lot more in the build-up to Christmas. She's booked me in to do an assembly in a couple of weeks! I'm a bit scared.'

'You're so awesome, it'll be fine. You really are the best man I've ever met. You don't need to do any of this, and yet you do.'

'I kind of do though, that's the point. I've spent so long covering war, trauma and death and making a living from it, I need to give back. Something that doesn't just raise awareness of what's happening in the world but something to redress the balance.'

'I stand by my statement.' Without thinking twice Sylvie raised herself up and planted a light kiss on his cheek. It wasn't until she had both feet on the floor and saw his face that she realized what she had just done. Talk about mixed messages. Shit, she'd have to talk to him again later, a bit less frenetically maybe. He smiled at her but it wasn't too hard to read the confusion in his eyes, even in the dark November night. She was an idiot! Why had she done that? A bing from his phone sounded.

'Right, that'll be my call to action. Best go sort out these fireworks.'

'OK, go do your bonfire duty, and come track us down when you're done.'

'Will do.' Alex leant forward for a millisecond as if he were about to return the kiss. Then he pulled himself back, and they stood looking at each other, a pause as the world carried on bustling around them. Then he gave her a great big beam and headed off.

Sylvie watched him go and turned to see Ellie and Sam had pulled in a large gaggle of children to listen to her talk about the orphanage, showing them pictures of her old home and waving her arms about furiously. She really was quite something, Sylvie wouldn't be surprised if she was ruling the world by thirty. Her audience were rapt before going to get their mothers and put money into the jar. It soon filled up and one of Marion's minions, dressed in exactly the same magpie dress but in a slightly more subtle shade, emptied the jar twice over simply in the time that Ellie held court by it.

Eventually the children were ready to leave the marquee and go and stand as the bonfire appeared to kick into life. They crossed the field together, with Sylvie stopping to talk to other parents who wanted to congratulate her on her new ballet school venture or, in some cases, tell her how she was the talk of the dinner table after her PE lessons, with the children loving what they were doing. It was these moments that made her heart swell and her face glow, unable to believe how quickly she had slotted in to this marvellous school community.

A gaggle of children from Class One, who had all donated their money earlier, were now swaggering around the field, parents loosely behind, letting the children revel in their new-found independence now they went to big school. Ellie rushed to join them, dragging Sam behind her as they shouted over their shoulders for permission.

'Mum, can we join the others, please?' Sam called as he was helter-skeltered across the field by his best friend.

'Yes, can we, Sylvie?' Ellie called and then after a millisecond's pause, 'Pleeease.' Sylvie shouted yes back, noting how Ellie might still be the confident young girl she had met on the beach but now had slightly improved manners and a clear skill for fundraising.

Sylvie was desperate for the loo, and had been since arrival, so as the flames of the bonfire licked the sky and the children reached it, pausing to stare in awe as the orange and yellow leapt and danced and filled the inky black, she asked one of the other mothers to keep her eyes peeled whilst she jogged to the staff loos inside. As she headed in that direction she caught a glimpse of Alex, his frame outlined by one of the orange strings of light, casting his shadow long and tall. He really was something else. It felt like every time she saw him the breath was knocked from her body. She needed to get a grip on that.

Right now, he was standing with Rosy and her partner, the three were laughing and she could see even from here, with his face illuminated, that Alex was looking very pleased with himself. She stood and watched as he shook the curly-haired man's hand and clasped him on the shoulder and then bent and gave their head teacher a peck on the cheek before, presumably, moving off to fulfil more of his bonfire duties. She jerked herself away from the scene and entered the building; with so many parents and children milling about the field the silence of the school in comparison to the buzz outside was notable.

The minute her mind felt the silence it decided to fill the gap by suddenly working itself into a frenzy with regards to Alex and his remark to Marion – *Sylvie has made it quite clear.* What did he mean by that? He hadn't said, *Neither of us feel that way, Marion.* Nor had he said,

*I like her as a friend but she doesn't do anything for me in any other way.* He had laid it at her door, as if the only reason was her objection. Could that mean that he wouldn't be averse should she have said something different, had she let Marion continue in her matchmaking plans? No, of course not, that was stupid. She had good reasons for keeping Alex at arm's length when it came to sex and nothing had happened to change that. The children were still the children and the absolute priority here. Sam was the one she had to put above all else. And Sam needed security, not her marching 'daddies' through the door. Not even one. Lust-filled hope was not going to be of practical help to anybody.

# Chapter Twenty Nine

Sylvie wove through the hall, the bright light of the school a sudden shock after the dark outside. She smiled as she walked past the primary colours of the gym bars folded against the wall – they did love those bars – her feet clacking loudly across the wood of the floor when she heard voices.

'I couldn't believe it when I saw you the other day. You're still a damn fine woman, despite all the years passing. Rather like a fine wine.'

'Why could you not believe it? Did you not think Richard and I would last? That he wouldn't be willing to marry me?' The language, although combative, had a distinct coquettish tone.

'I had hoped you wouldn't be willing to marry him. He always had very good taste – there's nothing as attractive as a capable woman, Marion, and you are very capable. I suppose had he not, someone else would have snapped you up, so I should be grateful that he kept you in our circle.'

'Well, exactly. Had I not married him, I wouldn't be here having this conversation with you, would I?' Marion's giggle, her most simpering one, bounced off the walls of the small cloakroom, the echo making it even louder, and more irritating than usual. 'Although hardly in your circle, I haven't seen you for years and we're not exactly a regular feature on your Christmas-card list.'

'Well, I would love to make *you* a regular feature.'

Oh, gross. Sylvie hurried past. She had heard that Marion was a little predatory but from the second-hand snippets Alex had gleefully shared with her she had thought she adored her husband and was faithful. However, seeing as she had spent all day bitching about Marion's snap judgements maybe she shouldn't make them either. Just because someone was having some kind of assignation amongst the children's coat pegs, didn't mean she was automatically unfaithful. Anything could be happening.

As she came back she could still hear them, and it appeared from the change in tone of Marion and her friend, that anything actually was.

'So where is your husband, leaving you alone at the mercy of all the wolves?'

'You're hardly a wolf, Hector, and he's working very hard at the moment. If you must know he'll be back Friday night. We're thinking of having a weekend break, Venice maybe.'

'Venice, can he not do better? I would whisk you off for more than a couple of days, you only have to say the word.'

'As flattering as that is, I think not. I really must get back – these sorts of events don't run themselves.'

'I'm not stopping you.'

Marion tinkled her laugh, but this time Sylvie wondered if she could detect a more nervous element than flirtatious this time. 'Actually, you are. If you just moved your arm then I could get past. If I didn't run off with you at the age of nineteen I'm hardly likely to now.' Sylvie really wanted to carry on walking, and whilst there was no sound of real panic in Marion's tone, girl code dictated that she step in and make sure.

Bracing herself and taking a deep breath she walked through into the cloakroom to see Marion hemmed in against the pegs and Hector grinning with his arm outstretched against the wall, slightly blocking her in. There wasn't a feel of menace, and Marion didn't look particularly relieved to see her, so Sylvie wondered if she had misread the situation and there was all manner of subtext that she was not privy to or able to interpret.

'Hi, Marion, thought I heard you. I was wondering if you needed any help with anything whilst I've got a minute?'

'No, no. I think it's…' She didn't get to finish her sentence before Hector interrupted her.

'Ah, you must be the flexible redhead Alex has got the hots for. Haha, I can see why.' Hector looked her up and down thoroughly and practically rubbed his hands together. Marion's face lit up as she turned to the man that Sylvie had mistakenly thought was pestering her with far too much glee for a woman being subjected to unwanted advances; indeed, she looked like that cat who got the cream.

'I was trying to tell her the exact same thing today, but she wouldn't listen. You should see the sparks fly between them.'

'Why? Is she pretending not to be interested? Oldest trick in the book when a woman wants to snare a man. Ha!'

'Ha! Ha? I'm sorry, but you've never met me. How can you decide what's true for me or not?' It wasn't in Sylvie's nature to be so aggressive before an introduction had been made, but she had had it with all these assumptions about her friendship. And the use of the word *flexible* was just downright sleazy. Who the hell did this overweight, pink-faced buffoon think he was? Friend of Alex or not, no one was speaking to her like that!

'Oh, OK darling. You're one of *those*. You want to take a page out of Marion's book, she knows how to be a woman. Alex never said you had a temper to match your hair. I assume from your outburst that has to be your natural colour.'

'Wow. You are really rude.'

'And you're a liar.' The words were sudden, forceful, dripping with white, male, upper-class privilege as they were drawled by the man in front of her.

'What, how dare…'

'You're a liar because you're a woman and all women are liars. Known fact.'

'Now, come on, Hector, surely you've grown out of that attitude by now. It was outdated in the nineties.'

'A truth is a truth regardless of fashion, Marion love, and all women are liars.'

'I don't even know where to start with that. Alex said that you were slightly old-school in your views but he didn't say you were positively Neanderthal. Come on, Marion, let's get back to the field before the fireworks start.'

'Oh, they seem to be starting now, and right here.' Marion clapped her hands.

'So, Alex told you about me, did he? He certainly told us all about you. Absolutely besotted, and you, madam, may think you feel the same at the moment when everything is lovely, fresh and new, but trust me, when he gets bored of playing happy bloody families – and he will – when he gets bored and heads back to Africa to do what it is he does, then that's your relationship down the tubes. No woman wants a man who's putting himself in danger all the time. Every woman says she wants a hero, but as I made my point earlier, women lie and to themselves more than anyone else. The realities of living with a hero, well, that doesn't tie in with the suburban dream, that involves roughing it, going without the feather-bloody-duvet and the Egyptian cotton, eating whatever you can find, locusts, rats if you're lucky, not having a meltdown because Deliveroo won't be here for another half an hour...'

'We don't have Deliveroo in Cornwall, darling...'

'Not the point, Marion, as well you know. You, young lady, need to leave Alex alone or accept that he will ultimately break your heart and leave you. If you tell yourself any different, you're a liar, and if you think he's going to stay because you've got some kind of magical redhead power between the sheets then guess what, you're a fool as well as a liar!'

'I don't how many times I have to say this, but I am not in the slightest bit interested in Alex. And even less interested in your opinions. Marion, I'm heading back to the field. Hector, I'd like to say it was a pleasure to meet you, but then I *would* very definitely be a liar.'

Sylvie turned on her heel and stalked out of the cloakroom, furious that she had got drawn into this, hating everything that odious entitled man had brayed and knowing that when it came to her response – that she wasn't at all interested in anything other than friendship with Alex McKenzie – in that instance and that instance only, Hector wasn't too far from the mark.

## Chapter Thirty

The fireworks had been spectacular, blues, greens, reds, pinks lighting up and cascading down in the sky. Oohs and aahs from children and parents alike reverberating around the field, each one barely having time to finish before the next crackle and pop of colour rioted across the night. The bonfire had fizzled out, the Guy (not burnt because Rosy had very firm views on the burning of humans, fake or otherwise) sitting in his chair observing the night's festivities in his honour had collected a small fortune for the orphanage, and as Alex walked home with the others he felt all was right in his world.

He had realized that as they had stood watching the fireworks together (and they were dim compared to the heat with which Sylvie had delivered her opinion about her first meeting with Hector) he had slid his arm around her shoulder again. That had been the second time that evening and he realized only afterwards that he had done it. But it wasn't meant as a sexual come-on – Sylvie had been quite clear about how she would respond to those – it was an instinctive thing. Because as they all stood together and did these things – Halloween, Bonfire Night, school – they felt like family and he just didn't seem able to stop doing it. But his emotions were beginning to helter-skelter out of control as well.

In the moment he had realized that his arm had snaked around her shoulders, he had been embarrassed for a second or two. He noted that she hadn't jumped away, or even stood there stiff as a board and uncomfortable, but had nestled into his arms, the oohs and aahs over the fireworks pouring from her mouth, as both children stood in front of them. And so he kept it there, resting on her shoulders, the warmth of her making him feel stronger somehow, as if he was contributing something positive to their world.

Alex had been worried about bringing Ellie tonight, concerned that the whizz, bangs and explosions might trigger memories from *that* day. He had spoken to Natalie, the counsellor who had been with them through the whole adoption process, and it was she who encouraged him to take her, to let her fully participate in school life, just with a pair of ear defenders to reduce the noise to less alarming levels.

And as he looked at his daughter standing next to her best friend he was glad that he had listened. Ellie was loving it even though it was Sam who was jumping up and down with the energy of a little fireball, whereas Ellie spent most of the evening standing stock-still and staring in awe, the excited squeals largely coming from Sam's lips for a change.

At one point Sam had jumped up so high and squeaked so loud that Sylvie had turned her face up to his, and looked at Alex with that collaborative smile that he assumed parents shared in moments of pride. He had felt himself grin back at her, knowing with no need for words how happy she was made by the leaps and bounds in confidence her boy had made over the course of this term.

Afterwards they were all walking back to his, as they seemed to most days, for a debrief after their evening, rather than the cold hard break of going straight home once the fireworks were over. Hector had decided to stay on and help Marion organize the clear-up and then was heading back to Chase's, so Alex didn't have to worry too much about managing any discord between him and Sylvie this evening. It was going to be a late night for the children but with the weekend beginning tomorrow it was so worth it; he was never quite ready to say goodnight to Sylvie and wanted some time with her that wasn't punctuated by bangs and whizzes.

His initial plans, the plans where he laid out his heart, might have been changed by her outburst in the play-ground, but still he wanted every minute with her that he could have.

'And then that green one went bam! And it all trickled down like rain and then the red one, they were awe-soooome.'

'They were the best fireworks I'd ever seen. They were amazing. Were they the best you had ever seen, Ells?'

'Definitely. Definitely the best ever, probably in the whole wide of the world.' Ellie turned from the in-depth conversation she was having with Sam and grinned at her dad, hope in her eyes. 'Can we go again next time, Dad? Can we?'

'Yes, I think we should go every year.'

'Every year, for ever?'

'I think so.' Alex noticed that as ecstatic as his daughter and Sam looked at that, Sylvie appeared to flinch, not in a body-jerk obvious way but in some kind of minuscule, almost intangible, manner that he felt rather than saw.

What could that have meant? He would ask her once the children were settled.

When they were in, the children decided they were going to have a midnight picnic. The fact that it was just past eight rather than twelve didn't faze them at all, as they tried to sneak half the fruit bowl under their jumpers and up to Ellie's room.

'I'm sorry you were subjected to the worst of Hector. He is a complete arse, but when you get past the outdated opinions and his compulsion to vocalize them loudly to anyone in the vicinity, he really is a decent guy. Things are never black and white and I can assure you, Hector has *all* the shades of grey. For all his apparent privilege he has not had the easiest life and really has the most generous heart. He just doesn't seem to have learnt when to shut up. I'm not suggesting the two of you will ever be friends, but you should know he is not all evil. I wouldn't jump to his defence if he were, especially as I know his behaviour can at times be indefensible. But he is a good man at his core. He's loyal to the very end. I really think he would die to protect Chase and myself if it were necessary. Although obviously I'd rather he didn't. It was hard to hear the exact nature of what you were saying over the noise of the fireworks, though. Do you want to tell me the worst elements again and I can see if I can make any sense of it?'

The two of them sat at opposite ends of the sofa. Sylvie had grabbed his blanket, and snuggled underneath it, as if it was now hers. Which he supposed it was. He would never look at it and not think of her, he knew that, no matter where life took them.

'No, not really.' She scrunched her nose up at him. God, she was so cute. 'But he was pretty bloody rude.

Really hating on women. I'm not going to be his best friend any time soon, but as he's an old mate of yours I promise not to tear his head off with my bare hands should I ever see him again. But only as a favour to you. Obviously.'

'OK, deal. No tearing his head off, but I'd love to see you flip him over your shoulder – that might sort out his misogyny. I can only begin to imagine what he had to say, so I'm not going to defend him.'

'Good, because he's pretty indefensible. Anyway, I don't want to talk about Hector tonight. I want to talk about you.'

Was this the bit where she admitted that she wanted more than friendship? That when she had tiptoed to kiss his cheek earlier she had meant to aim for his mouth? That she wanted what he wanted? Should he lean in and make this easier? Alex heard her words from earlier replay in his head. *Only as a friend. Really not interested. I'm happy with how things are.* What on earth was wrong with him? Of course, that was not what she was about to say. She couldn't have made it clearer had she worn a placard.

*Great friends.* That was all she wanted, and he could do that. He might not want to particularly but he could. What he couldn't do was change their dynamic, ignore her actual words and replace them with his own wishes and make any sort of move on her now, especially not in his house as they were relaxing with the kids upstairs. He was just going to have to be grateful that he had found his best friend. And try not to look at her mouth.

'I wanted to say…' Sylvie continued talking, seemingly unaware of the inner turmoil of the man next to her, '…and I know it's not my place, but I'm so proud of you.

Of all that you're doing. Not just for Ellie but for all those other kids as well. It was lovely to watch your daughter tell everyone about her story and how she ended up in Penmenna tonight. I think you've done a grand job of helping her reconcile her two worlds, and having her see what you are doing for the children that have remained in South Sudan, children born into the same situation as she was. You're teaching her such great lessons, and I think she's going to grow into a real force for good.'

'I hope so. I'll be happy if she can just grow up as normally as anyone possibly could, given what she has been through. She doesn't need to do anything, she can just be her.'

'Of course she can, and she was so matter of fact about things tonight when she was talking to the other kids, but I worry about you. I get that you don't want to talk about any of it, and I respect that. Really, I do. But I need you to know that if you do need to talk, sob because it's raw and it's painful, I am always here. Always.' And she looked at him with such force behind her intent and such love shining out of those grey-green eyes that he felt himself take a deep breath, gulp, breathe out heavily and change the direction of the conversation.

'No one likes someone who bangs on about themselves all the time, forcing their opinions down the throats of others… you found that out tonight.'

'Whoa. You think you talking about what you've witnessed and been through is on a par with Hector and his unwavering belief that women are all evil liars with a high-dependency duvet habit?'

'Is that what he said? Hahahaha! He has serious mother issues, tars all women with the same brush and then wonders why he can't sustain a relationship.'

'Well, he was trying very hard to sustain something with Marion amongst the PE bags.'

'Really? Marion's not his type at all. He likes young girls that are easily influenced by money and multiple houses and spend all their time plugged into their phones so he doesn't have to talk to them. Marion? Are you sure?'

'"You are a very capable woman. I like capable women."' Sylvie imitated Hector's voice and Alex struggled not to fall off the sofa, he was laughing so much. 'When you've stopped laughing can we discuss an action plan about how *I* can help with your fundraising? Can I get any of my high-falutin' ballet contacts to pad out your glittering media contacts in the quest to save the children?'

'OK, that might work. We're doing pretty well. Chase is willing to pop in money and promote us in the States – he has an address book that the Queen would envy. And then Hector also has a pretty impressive old-boy network. Matt says *Green-Fingered and Gorgeous* aren't happy for him to promote the charity on the show but he will do so on social media and is up to be part of the first major fundraiser event – you know the sort of thing, a big gala dinner, celebs and chequebooks. I'm toying with auctioning him off for a dinner date but will have to OK it with Rosy. Chase reckons he can get Angelina on board. Since her outburst on Graham Norton last week where she scratched Mary Berry she is in serious need of redefining her image again so is going to have to undertake quite a lot of charity work whilst looking properly repentant.'

'You want a woman known for attacking Mary Berry on your list?'

'I want Chase, and Angelina's not all bad, Ellie adores her. Before you she was Ellie's primary female role model.'

'That explains why you're so keen on me.'

'There's slightly more to it than that!'

'Sorry?'

'Don't know why I said that. Ignore me. But I figure the more people involved the greater reach we have, and yes, Angelina can be a veritable demon but she has over a million followers on Instagram and unfortunately the world we live in today, that sort of thing has some heft.'

'So what can I do? When is this event?'

'No dates yet, have only just started looking into setting up some kind of gala, but any glamour you can provide from the dance world is great. But even more valuable than that is you just being you, you're kinda my rock. Everything seems a lot more doable when you're around.'

She flashed her eyes up at him as he felt this truth drop from his lips so freely and he couldn't quite determine what her reaction was. It was the very epitome of inscrutable. He wished, not for the first time, that he could read minds. Although usually that was in a warlord kind of situation and not a chance to work out what on earth his current crush was thinking.

'Be there for you, that's what you want.'

'Yeah, I know it's a big ask, but…'

'Huge ask. Huge. How dare you suggest I spend my spare time with the person whose company I enjoy most in the world? Except Sam's, of course.'

'You enjoy my company more than anyone else's in the world?'

'Oh, hush, man. Why do you always pick up on the unimportant stuff?'

And as he looked at her and saw how true she was, he was suddenly overwhelmed with the urge to do as she suggested and tell his side of the story. Tell her about the day they were filming a group of rebel fighters in the jungle when they heard an attack on the nearest village. How they ran to help, shocked not to be running into people fleeing as they did so. How when they got there, the heat, the smell, was overwhelming. How that smell woke him up in the night as often, if not more, than it woke his daughter. How he and his cameraman dashed from burning house to burning house but there was nobody left to save. Nobody until he heard a baby scream and ran and found a woman fallen to the floor on the edge of the village, her body slumped over unnaturally, and he realized the cries were coming from a baby underneath her. As he opened his mouth to tell his best friend, the woman he loved, how he had found Elechi, the tears streamed hot and fast down his face.

# Chapter Thirty One

Sylvie approached Penmenna School tingling with nervous excitement. The morning had dawned clear with a nip in the air. The seagulls, no respecters of weekend lie-ins, were circling overhead, their cries noisy but reassuring. This was just another day for them, nothing momentous happening here.

But Sylvie wasn't a seagull and today was the first day of her dreams becoming a possibility. She kept trying to downplay it in her mind, just another class, nothing special, but her heart hammered out the rhythm dream-come-true-don't-mess-it-up-dream-come-true-don't-mess-it-up as she marched up the granite steps and turned the key in the heavy iron lock.

It was scary enough being responsible for the opening of the school, let alone anything else. She had never had to do that before and the huge bunch of keys that Rosy gave her jangled with burdensome responsibility. The key jarred in the lock, the door heavy, and Sylvie felt the rush of panic as she struggled to get the clunky metal key to turn.

As she jostled it in the lock and muttered up a little prayer she felt it shift a little and then turn. The other, slightly more modern, locks undid easily and her shoulders relaxed back down into a normal human position.

They had practically been as high as her ears as she imagined not being able to get into the building on the first day that the Sylvie Williams School of Ballet came into being. She would have had to transport everyone to Lovage Farm and watch Tom drop dead on the spot as a class of ten preschoolers started trying to twirl and spin all over the hay shed.

The door lumbered open, creaking like an ancient beast arising from sleep. Sylvie put her bags down on the step and raced inside the door; she had thirty seconds to get to the alarm and enter the code correctly before it started alerting the whole of the village that someone was breaking into the school. This was the bit Sylvie was dreading the most. She dashed to the box and managed to put the code in, then stood, breath held, as the box flashed a sequence of lights before settling down. Phew, she was in.

Grabbing her bag she wandered through the school, putting the lights on as she went. There was something very surreal about being here when it was completely empty, lifeless. She might be an adult, a one-time professional ballet dancer, mother to a budding genius and niece to the grumpiest man on the planet, but she was still freaked out by silence. Inside the building she couldn't even hear the screech of the gulls. Nothing.

She started to hum to herself as she pulled the weighty door to the hall open and put her things down. Then the first thing she did was put some music on. As the opening chords of *Romeo and Juliet* crashed through, the building suddenly felt more alive.

She took a deep breath. This place was Penmenna School, there was no more fitting place for her to trial this.

She had been teaching for years, and the only difference was that today she was working entirely for herself, not some faceless leisure corporation. She could do this. She had faith in herself. In her ability. This was going to be fine. Another deep breath.

She started to sing. It was hard to be anything but optimistic with the powerful music filling the hall. If nothing else it reminded her she was a fighter. Now she just had to fight her way through the PE equipment cupboard and pull out the mats before the children came filing in.

She had six classes planned for Saturdays, and felt a little guilty that so many of her children from the leisure centre had switched allegiance and signed up with her. She had the pre-school class first, then her primary class for beginners, followed by her Grade One ballet class, then a Grade Two, Grade Three and a Grade Four class. It was going to be a long old day and she had scheduled breaks between all of them, but still it would be a marathon with each class lasting forty-five minutes.

Sylvie started to do some stretches when she heard a voice join in with her humming; it was a little off-key but knew the music. Hmm. Interesting. Although she rather hoped it wasn't a new parent who was super-ballet-obsessed; they liked to try and run the class themselves, explain how she was doing it all wrong and that little Annabel had come out of the womb humming Tchaikovsky and the whole family knew she was a star in the making.

She stopped and watched the door to see who the humming belonged to.

'Hello, dear, I do love this. Prokofiev? I thought I'd come along and watch.'

'Ah, hello, Sheila. That's kind of you. I'm not sure that watching…'

'No, of course not. That wouldn't be right. I meant support, I came to support.' She started to rustle in her bag but, not appearing to have any success, she took her glasses from the top of her head. 'Such a useful thing, this chain thingy, should have got one years ago. Anyway, in here somewhere…' She rifled through again, but looking as she did so this time.

'Aha!' Her triumphant sound pierced the air and she pulled out a large Tupperware container. 'Here, oranges, for half-time.'

'Ohhh…'

'I was watching a programme, my dear, only the other night and do you know what? They say that ballet dancers are a lot stronger than football players, stronger than many athletes, so I was thinking if it's harder than football and they get oranges at half-time then I should cut some up for your little ones. So I did. Here.' Sheila proffered the very large Tupperware container filled to the brim with little orange segments.

'That is so kind. I've never dished out oranges before. I think they're going to love them…'

But before she could finish her sentence, Sheila was back to rummaging through her bag.

'And look dear, while I was doing it I had an idea and I thought, oh, go on, why not? So here, have this as well.' Sylvie had to take a step back as the school secretary brandished a cheese-and-pineapple hedgehog at her. A hedgehog with a little bit of tissue and some bag fluff stuck to it.

'Thought a bit of protein wouldn't go amiss, and look, I've given him sultanas for eyes.'

'So you have. This is great, thank you. Um… the thing is, though, I don't think I'm supposed to let people wander in and watch…'

Sheila's face fell. It would appear this was how she planned to spend her Saturday.

'…but I could really do with an assistant. Just for today, the first day. What do you say?'

'Oh yes, yes, that would be grand. I'm very good at assisting. *Very* good. And I wouldn't want any payment. I can hand out the oranges – what else should I do?'

'This first class will just be the little ones, so nothing very tough or formal, just playing some music, getting them to respond to it, playing with some props, practising First and Second Position, some toe work, that sort of thing, that's all we'll be doing for today. You can just keep your eyes peeled and make sure everyone is OK. How does that sound?'

Sheila's face broke into a huge grin but before Sylvie could continue the children started to pile in. Sylvie switched straight into professional mode and soon all the money was collected and ten very little children were standing in front of her. None of them particularly still bar one; the Annabel of the class, Sylvie guessed. She stood in front of them and smiled a welcome at them all – she loved this – then she looked up. Up at the parents who all stood along the back wall of the hall waiting for her to do something.

Her heart sped up again. In the leisure centre parents had to view lessons from behind the glass; now they were in here with her, watching, listening, waiting. Boom,

boom, boom. Her heart was bound to explode out of her chest at any minute now, splattering the class and ending the Sylvie Williams School of Ballet before it even began. Surely it wasn't meant to beat this fast? Another deep breath and with any luck the parents would just think she was a leading example of Zen calm. Not frozen with fear at all.

The parents might have been fooled but the line of four-year-olds in front of her was beginning to shift and fidget. One little girl with the cutest plaits was picking her nose and another one suddenly dropped to the floor on her bottom and started to try and take her ballet pumps off.

Boom boom boom. She needed to do something.

Der… der… der… der… Suddenly the introduction from *Swan Lake* was playing, the calming notes gliding through the hall, all the children suddenly still and transfixed and waiting to see what would happen next. Before she knew it, she was in full swing, the music having picked her up and popped her right within her comfort zone.

The children were soon caught up in the exercises, lying on the mats, kicking their legs up as elegantly as four-year-olds can. Making their toes as pointy as can be and then having a go at First Position and Second before finishing it off by taking turns at being butterflies.

The session flew by. As she showed the children out, each clutching an orange segment, she couldn't stop the grin crossing her face.

'Sheila, that music saved my life. I could kiss you.'

'Ooh, OK then.' The school secretary stood on her tiptoes and closed her eyes as Sylvie gave her a great big kiss on her cheek.

'No kissing in class.'

'Ah, hello, Alex, come on in. Hi, Ellie, just in time for your class. Are you excited?'

'Yes, and so is everyone who has been waiting. I've told them all that you're the best dancer in the world and they are really looking forward to it. I said I wouldn't be surprised if you did a giant leap and flew out of that window.' She pointed up to the skylights in the ceiling of the school hall. 'Do you think you could? I sort of promised.'

'Ellie, Sylvie may be the best dancer in the world, definitely the best vampire dancer by the way, but I don't think she's going to make it out that window today. And you need to not tell people things like that. In fact, you need to tell them all that Sylvie will not be leaping through that window, and you need to do it now.'

'Da-ad.'

'Hi, come in, everybody, come and find yourself a mat. Mums and dads, Shelia is happy to take the fees.'

'Oh yes, and look, a ledger, a proper ledger. This takes me back.' Sheila sat at a table in the corner and waved Sylvie's membership fees book at them all.

'Everyone, Sylvie won't be flying through the window. Dad says I have to say that. OK?'

A dissatisfied murmur arose from the group of children.

'But what we will be doing is teaching you guys how to get so good at ballet you'll be able to leap through the air all by yourselves one day, which has to be more fun than just watching me do it. So, if you all grab a mat.'

This time the parents didn't faze her quite so much. Having Alex standing there gave her a focal point. It reminded her a little bit of when she was onstage, getting a flash of stage fright; she would look out to the seat her mother always chose, slap bang in the middle of the theatre, and be calmed by her presence, or in her absence the knowledge of her pride was enough to puff her up again and get back to doing the best job she could. Having Alex there was like that. And she never thought she'd experience that security, that surety again.

She tried to express her gratitude, and her respect, to him in a look. Although how one said all of that in just a look she wasn't sure.

As he cocked his head to one side in response and smiled back at her, she knew she had managed. He understood.

## Chapter Thirty Two

Sylvie returned to the farm that evening absolutely shattered. The rest of the classes had raced by, all old pupils who were working towards their gradings and knew what they were doing. She might be exhausted, her whole body aching with fatigue and her mind feeling like it was made of trifle, but she was also on a high. She had done it! There had been no major accidents or upsets, and she knew that she was going to be able to build on this, expand and turn it into a proper professional specialist school, one that catered for all levels; it was just a matter of time.

What made it even more special was the fact that not only was she bringing home money but she was also building her dream, a future to support her and Sam.

However as well as her high, she couldn't help her mind repeatedly getting pulled back to the night before, all that Alex had told her, and the very fact that he had opened up to her at all when she knew what a private man he was.

It had altered her opinion of him a little. Made him more human. She had always accepted that on a superficial level he was drop-dead gorgeous, and even more so on a deeper level – the way he was with the children, the work he was throwing himself into right now, and the way in which he was a constant support to her.

Now she saw his vulnerability as well, the burden he carried through no fault of his own. The things he had witnessed and the life he had lived before now informed her picture and she wanted more than ever to be the woman who supported him, helped him heal and raise the daughter he had chosen. The same way he had taken on the role of support to her. His presence in class today filling her with confidence, letting her know that he had faith in her and so should she. That was worth more than anything. He really was beyond special.

On a more complex level she also realized that the people who knew him best of all might be speaking truth, in this case, the loathsome Hector who thankfully had sodded off to wherever he came from. For now Alex was revealed; she understood his need to heal somewhere peaceful and secure. His jokes about Marion being the scariest thing took on more meaning than she had realized at the time.

She also knew that there was a strong truth that he would be compelled to return to this life at some point, Hector had not been joking. Alex's whole adult life had been dedicated to adrenaline-fuelled reporting, and at some point when that siren call began again he would be unable to resist. Whilst she would understand the need to answer it, could accept that he would only be in her life temporarily, she couldn't impose that upon Sam. It would be hard enough letting him go as friends but if she made a family with him, there was no way she would stand by and see Sam left behind.

Sam might have developed so much in the last month, his confidence soared to heights she hadn't believed, but she could not impose on him the pretence of security in a family unit that she knew couldn't be sustained. She just couldn't. As friends she could prepare Sam for their departure, protect him.

If she took things on from mere friendship with Alex, it would be wonderful; she knew they wouldn't be a wham-bang-ma'am scenario. It would develop into a relationship that would bring them both joy, and that she imagined they would both flourish within, but it wouldn't last. It *couldn't* last. Not with Alex being the man he was. A man with that itch for travel, a man who could never be happy contained in a small Cornish village. And she would not present Sam with a perfect family, knowing it was on a temporary basis only. Family was for ever. Alex couldn't be.

Talking of family, was that Tom hovering at the gate, dog by his heels? What was he doing up here near the house?

'All right, maid?'

'Yes.' Sylvie got out of the car and eyed him with suspicion.

'Why are you looking at me like that?'

'Like what?'

'Like you're a sheep just minding its own business and I'm a wolf that's broken into the pen.'

'I didn't know I was. Are you a wolf?'

'Fairly sure I'm just another sheep.'

'Yeah, a sheep that thought I was the most evil wolf in the village up until a few days ago.' Sylvie shocked herself as the words came out in a petulant whisper. That was childish. She should have forgiven him by now. She knew what it was like to feel insecure with your living

266

arrangements, so she shouldn't have been surprised that Tom had felt the same.

Tom quirked an eyebrow. 'Fancy a cup of tea? The boy is feeding the chickens.'

'On his own?'

'Aye, he told me he wasn't a baby and could do it hisself. I've been saying that for at least a year, so aye. Now, cup of tea or not?'

'Go on then, I could do with one. Do I get the comfy chair? 'Tis my last night.'

'Don't push it!' Tom's smile let her know that for tonight his favourite chair was very much hers.

'Race ya!'

He brought her a mug of tea and placed a large, really large, pasty on a plate in front of her. He had even dug out a paper serviette with holly printed on it from the drawer and laid it next to the pasty for her.

'Long day.'

'Yes, certainly was, but worth every minute. I think I'm going to make it work, Tom.'

'Aye. Eat your pasty.'

'Oh, I will. I'm ravenous. Cheese and pineapple isn't as filling as it was when I was six.'

'Eh?'

'Never mind.'

'I wanted to talk to you, maid.'

Sylvie saw a bit of pasty fly out of her mouth and across the room. Had she been transported to some kind of alternate universe?

'I'm not one for speeches…' Sylvie managed to rein in the millions of sarcastic replies that flew into her mind, '…but I wanted to speak to you before you went.'

'OK.' She put her mug down carefully. She didn't want her tea going the same way as the pasty.

'I want you to know that this will always be your home. Always. And if you need it again, in an emergency, then you just come on back.'

'Tom…'

'I ain't finished.'

'Oh, OK.'

'I've been waiting to make an honest woman of Julie for some time now, but women shouldn't have to share a kitchen. My poor old ma did and I tell you, your great-grandmother Sylvie, she were not a kind woman. Steely eye and harder heart they used to say about her and she was forever tutting any time my mum tried to do summat. So I promised Mum I wouldn't ever do that to my woman. And now, now I can move Julie in and she'll have the kitchen to hersel'.'

'I'm glad. Julie is a good woman.'

'I know. She made that pasty. I'm not finished yet. I also want to thank you. I thought you'd be bound to sell the farm, move back upcountry, up London, so the fact that you haven't, that you're staying here where you was born and meant to be, and keeping the farm in the family – well, that's some special. I'm sorry I misjudged you. I thought with your mam gone, you'd have nothing to keep you here and I'm sorry for that. You're a country girl at heart after all, a good girl, Sylvie.'

Sylvie tried to respond but words wouldn't come. She gulped, looked across at Tom sitting in her chair and gulped again.

Tom gave a gruff smile, stood up out of the chair and then as he made a move to leave, leant forward and ruffled her hair, giving her a nod, then hotfooted it back outside before she could form an adequate response. Ruffled her hair! That was as strange as if he had put on a tutu and suddenly pirouetted all the way to the milking shed.

Sylvie took a minute or two, gulped down the last of her tea and headed to the chicken house to get her son, pretty chuffed to be labelled a country girl by her uncle (that was his highest praise), and glad in her heart that with Julie and Tom, Lovage Farm once again could have some romance at its core.

# Chapter Thirty Three

Sunday morning arrived. It had been such a crazy weekend so far, and now was the last hurdle before she could properly relax. With Sam and all their possessions squashed in her car (there wasn't much to take, Matt was leaving the cottage furnished and the furniture at the farm belonged there) she drove away, noting how happy she was to be doing so. She had said her goodbyes to her mum so long ago now that she didn't feel any guilt at moving on; she was more than ready to embrace her future. A future with her and Sam sharing their little house and it just being the two of them – her dream since his conception had been this, she just hadn't expected it to take so long.

She drove down the hill and through the lanes from Lovage Farm into Penmenna as she and Sam sang loudly to the radio. Thankfully he no longer insisted on having 'The Wheels on the Bus' on a constant loop. A couple of months in school and he was a much more sophisticated being.

The village felt like it was singing to her as she drove through… 'You're coming home…' to the tune of the old football song, which was ridiculous because Lovage Farm had always been her home, rather than the village itself. She swung around the corner past the old granite school, empty on a Sunday, and then past the church where the last of the congregation were heading out into the graveyard, the vicar shaking everyone's hand. Alice was there and spotted their car as it dawdled past – with the narrow streets you were limited as to how fast you could go – and Sylvie saw her wave her hand and mouth something at her. She assumed it was, 'See you in a bit.'

Alice from school, the teaching assistant for the terrifying Mrs Adams, was one of a whole army who had offered to help move Sylvie's stuff, but despite Sylvie's insistence that it was unnecessary they had all stuck firm and planned to meet her at the cottage later because they claimed it was still a huge job and many hands make light work.

They passed the butcher's, also shut on Sundays, and the village shop that seemed to always be open these days. Not like when Sylvie had been a child and it only opened in the mornings and the queue was around the block as everyone stopped to chat as much as pick up groceries.

The beach still had people meandering down across the sands; it was a sunny day and ridiculously warm for November. Locals were locals, and as such would head to the beach at all times of the year. With two cars in front of her stopped at the intersection and having a chat she was able to see all across Penmenna Sands. Dogs were allowed on once the summer season had passed and not only could she see numerous dog owners and their pets, she could also see that Marion was one of them and being pulled along by her puppy, clearly as headstrong as the entire family. They looked rather like a comedic before shot for a before-and-after dog-training class.

'Is that Mrs Marksharp from school?'

'Yes, looks like.'

'For someone who is so bossy, her dog isn't being very good.'

In fact the Weimaraner was now haring after a smaller dog and dragging Marion across the sands at speed. Sylvie wondered if she should help, but how she wasn't entirely sure. At that point, and only because of some frantic beeping from a car behind her, presumably an out-of-towner, the cars ahead went their separate ways and she could drive on.

Around the corner, over a little bridge, past some fisherman's cottages and there was her own new home. The two cottages sat in front of her. Rosy's she assumed was the one with a car on the drive and a little walled garden all around and Matt's, the one soon to be hers, was the one without the wall and an empty driveway. She drove up onto it and got out of the car. Should she go next door and ask for the key, or would they be in the house waiting for her? Maybe she should just try the door first.

Sam had no such qualms and jumped out of the car, raced to the door and wrenched it open, upon which there came a great big shout of, 'Surprise!' and there were Rosy and Matt, Alex and Ellie, Pippa from Class One and two tall blonds who she didn't know, one male with a huge welcoming smile on his face and a woman who was yawning whilst staring at her phone at the same time. She was dripping silk and effortless glamour and had the most complicated hair of anyone Sylvie had ever met – and that included the swans from *Swan Lake*. How on earth did she manage that on a daily basis? Oh my goodness, could this be the woman who had attacked Mary Berry? And she was in her house. That was hilarious.

'Hello. We know you didn't need any help but we wanted to support you anyway.'

'Yep,' said Matt as his dog raced out of the hallway and bounced so high up Sam's legs that the look on the small boy's face was priceless. 'Plus, we figured you'd need the keys, so here you go, and then you can choose whether to chuck us all out while you unpack and we would sod off next door *or* we could help you and then crack open a bottle or two to celebrate.'

'Let's do that then. I didn't agree to unpacking, for Christ's sake.' The glamorous blonde spoke, already halfway out the door and still staring at her phone.

'Angelina!' the tall, very clean, Viking-looking man said, in tandem with Ellie who was looking at the blonde in dismay. Ellie continued, 'Sylvie is nice and we should help her. I think that was rude. It *was* rude, wasn't it, Sam?'

Sam nodded sagely and gave her a broad beam which Sylvie noticed made Alex look very pleased indeed. Pippa gave Ellie a thumbs-up.

'Wow, really!' Angelina looked at her little friend with surprise tinged with disappointment but she did turn around again and come back to the others, although very dramatically yawning once more as she did so.

'Yep, you've just been called out by a five-year-old.' Matt went to high-five Ellie, who leapt up, cornrows and all, to tap his hand. 'Well done, that girl. I've been trying to teach my sister some manners her whole life and failed.'

'You're such a drama queen.' Angelina smiled back at her brother. 'Right, watch this. Hello, I'm Angelina.' She came in and double air-kissed Sylvie's cheek. 'I'm Matt's sister and I used to live here too. Welcome to the neighbourhood. I'm sure you'll love it.' The words were drawled out with such boredom at their mundanity that Sylvie couldn't help but smile. 'Is that the sort of thing I'm supposed to say? That's what *she* said when we moved in and we all know she's the patron saint of all that's good and holy.' Angelina gestured in Rosy's direction.

'Actually, Ange, you never lived here, you just visited and didn't leave until you met Chase if I remember correctly and even then you didn't say anything, just disappeared. Although I'm ever thankful.' Matt nodded at Chase. 'And stop having a go, no one thinks you're funny, just rude, and you're supposed to be trying extra hard at the moment, if I remember correctly.'

'Hello, you two, I've made you a welcome cake, it's on the side. I went for carrot cake, I think it was just because I assumed ballerinas didn't eat chocolate, but now I realize that's a bit daft. I'm happy to make a chocolate one if you prefer.' Rosy motioned to the most delicious-looking cake on the side topped with little carrots that looked like they had been made out of marzipan, whilst Angelina made a gagging noise until both Sam and Ellie gave her very hard stares *à la* Paddington Bear. Pippa, upon seeing the children, started to laugh.

'No, that's OK, we love carrot cake,' Ellie stepped in. 'This is going to be my home-home now. Our house is home. Chase's used to be home-home but this is now, which means Chase and Angelina's will be home-home-home.'

'Oh, OK.' Sylvie was a bit blown away by this welcome. There seemed a lot of people and they were all being so nice. 'I don't know how to thank you for such a welcome. Let's get the stuff out of the car and popped in the rooms and then I guess we can open a bottle or two and have some cake. Ooh, here's Tom with the last of the stuff, ooh and Alice behind him – has she brought the vicar?'

# Chapter Thirty Four

It took no time at all for the wardrobes and cupboards to be filled, the beds to be made and Sam's curtains to be hung. Rosy and Matt had stocked the fridge with basics like milk, cheese, bread and pasta and they were sitting out in Matt's garden, although she supposed it was hers now, all sharing a glass of wine. Sylvie was aware as she took another sip of wine that she seemed to spend far too much time these days watching everything the man sitting next to her did.

It was almost as bad as that pride you have when the children are babies – *oh, look, isn't it cute how he holds his spoon; look how sweet he is when he stares out of the window* – that sort of thing but very definitely not maternal and the sentences that popped into her head contained words like *rippling, naked* and *breathless*.

It felt a bit surreal to be sitting here like this; in fact, the pace at which her life was moving at the moment also had a sense of the dreamlike. From the moment she had left London, suddenly jobless, pregnant but optimistic for the future, and had moved into Lovage Farm, time had passed so slowly. Having Sam was joyful but the pace of life since she had moved back down was *very* slow, so different to London. Then before she knew it she had to care for her mother through the heartbreaking inevitability of her illness. She had become used to the pace of life, doing what she could to brighten it for Sam, but nonetheless it had all been very grey.

And then somehow this summer had changed things; she had been able to get to the beach every day with Sam and it was as if the sunshine and sand and sheer yellowness of summer had infused their being. Meaning that when they went back to the farm every evening they returned with a bit more colour in their souls and it tingled out of their fingertips, affecting the rest of their life. Then at summer's end they had met Alex and Ellie, and Sam had started school. Despite the two being separate events they seemed entwined for her and the truth was that since Sam had started going to school her life had changed beyond measure.

She looked around her, full of love and gratitude towards her small community, all these people making sure that she and Sam had the easiest house move ever. Pippa had proved hilarious today, had taken against Angelina and been quite vocal about it. At one point the two blonde women looked like they might fall to the floor and wrestle each other, but Angelina had the good sense to beat a hasty retreat when Pippa put her hair in a ponytail and rolled her sleeves up.

In two short months she now felt involved in the heart of the community as opposed to rotting alive on a farm that still seemed entrenched in the 1940s. She wouldn't be surprised to learn that Tom had whipped out a secret stash of dripping and dried eggs the minute she had gone. Whilst she and Sam were now sitting in the garden of their own cottage, with a whole group of new colleagues. Colleagues who felt like friends.

Having been able to leave the leisure centre and find a job she loved close to home, and having taken the first step to setting up the Sylvie Williams School of Ballet, meant she had a little more money to play with than when she had been her mum's carer, and a whole lot more self-esteem to boot.

She knew she hadn't been a passive player in this; she had been offered the job at the school and the chance to use the hall on Saturdays based on her own merit. Yet somehow it felt like Alex was involved, consistently there as a cheerleader, helping her find her way and cheering her on. And right now, as they sat side by side in her new garden, their children playing and giggling at their feet and surrounded by their friends, she had never felt more like reaching out and holding someone's hand.

## Chapter Thirty Five

Sylvie was having a fabulous morning going through dance moves to *The Nutcracker* with Class One, although her hangover from too much celebration last night was distracting her a little from the Sugar Plum Fairies dance. She wondered if Sheila might have a stash of paracetamol.

However, first she needed to concentrate on the part where the Mouse King comes to do battle – the children always got a little bit too into that. She had learnt the hard way the week before not to give them all ribbon wands, put the music on and then shout, 'Fight!'

She was making sure they did it properly this time when Marion – who appeared to have complete free run of the entire school – wandered into the hall and stood watching her and the children for a bit.

'Marvellous stuff, marvellous.' Somehow Marion's voice managed to overpower even Tchaikovsky.

'Hiya.' Ellie waved at Marion. 'Hiya, fireworks lady. Come and join us.'

Sylvie forced a smile to her face. It was probably harder taking Sam and Ellie's class than any of the others simply because it was so difficult striking a fair balance. She was so desperate not to play favourites that she worried that both children might often get the harsher side of her tongue. However it didn't seem to bother Ellie in the slightest who still struggled to call her Miss Williams, which was remarkable seeing that Sam managed it, and tried to give her kisses when she saw her around the school.

'Oho, no, I won't, but lovely to see you doing something so highbrow, no reason small children shouldn't be cultured. This is marvellous. If you all hold still I'll just take a photo for Instagram.'

'Something so what? We just like the Mouse King and the Fairy.' Ellie put on a gruff voice and then a high-pitched one to suit the characters as Sylvie bowled through the children, forcing herself in front of Marion's lens.

'Um, no, sorry, Marion. No! You know school policy on taking photos.'

'Of course I do, dear. I helped make sure everyone knew. We can't just have anybody taking photos of our children. Not in today's world.'

'Right, so could you put your phone away.'

'But it's only me, dear. We all know I can be trusted.'

Sylvie could feel her eyes roll. Why were there so many people in the world who thought the rules were only for others?

'I'm afraid Miss Winter was quite clear when she took me through the safeguarding policy. I'm sure if you nip and see her then she can tell me that it's OK and all will be good but I just can't let you, I'm afraid.'

'Oh well, I certainly don't want to upset our prima ballerina. I shall put it away just this once but it's best you have another chat with Rosy, dear.'

'I wasn't a…'

'Yes, yes, I know. So modest. Anyway, pleased to have caught you, dear, you're doing a wonderful job. Now I must dash. Should that child be climbing the wall bars in just her knickers?'

Sylvie turned speedily. Marion was right. The wall bars weren't supposed to be out today and Ashleigh was busy scaling them whilst they were attached to the wall, naked apart from her knickers whilst Mouse Kings and Sugar Plum Fairies watched, unusually silent and mouths agape.

'Ashleigh, come down at once and get dressed. You know the rules in school. The rest of you, it is almost lunchtime, so let's get ourselves changed instead of watching Ashleigh and then we can have a quick chat about what we've learnt today.'

As she helped the small, practically naked, girl get down she glimpsed across the hall to see Sam and Ellie deep in conversation with Marion. She dreaded to think what that was about, but as she caught Sam shooting her a quick, guilty look and saw Marion actually rubbing her hands as Ellie bounced up and down on the spot, she decided that one headache was more than enough to deal with today.

## Chapter Thirty Six

Alex had spent the morning on the phone, and the fundraiser he was organizing in London, planned for New Year's Eve, was taking shape nicely. He had been blown away with the response from those he had reached out to. The upcoming celebrity auction had such a varied list of celebs, from renowned academics to television personalities like Matt and Angelina, that there really was something to cater for everyone's tastes. Although he suspected that Chase's prize package offering a special one-to-one with him and a weeklong stay at his premier retreat in the Napa Valley was going to be the lot that blew the fundraising to stratospheric levels.

It still made him smile to think that the gangly young boy he had befriended that very first week in school, the one who had already been picked out as victim by the arseholes in the year above, had gone on to carve such a name for himself. Chase might call himself a motivational speaker and healing facilitator, but it all smacked a little bit of cult leadership to Alex.

If he didn't know for sure that Chase was a truly good guy and utterly lacking in malice he would steer well clear of such quackery. The fact that it was the man he knew him to be doling it out forced him to accept that there might be some validity in the way his best friend earned his living. It was a shame that so far he had had zero impact on Hector.

It wasn't just prizes for the auction that they had offered; once Matt had headed home after their boys' night both Hector and Chase had promised substantial donations, and they had been good for them too. Alex had known his old school friends were wealthy but the donations that had turned up for the foundation from the both of them had made his eyes boggle.

The knock-on effect was that he could start his expansion plans for the Healing Hearts Orphanage before he had anticipated. And to this end he had been able to track down his old fixer from Juba and offer him work overseeing this project. He wasn't sure that Kene would take it, but hoped that the man would not only appreciate a regular income, a little less danger (hopefully) and a chance to contribute to the act of nation-building that was so important for shaping any chance of a future. The other big positive was that Alex knew there was no way anyone would be getting shoddy supplies and corrupt practices past his old friend. Kene's eagle eye and refusals to take any nonsense would mean the whole process stood a much better chance of success in a newborn country built on constantly shifting sands.

The whole thing was snowballing but in a good way. He had had a meeting with Rosy who had suggested that she not only make Penmenna School a twin to the school that he was going to attach to the new extended Healing Hearts Orphanage, but also that she promote his work amongst her fellow head teachers. She had already arranged for all the schools within her Cornish Network to donate five books per school, which would lead to a huge new library for the children that Alex's foundation was designed to help.

Rosy had also appointed Pippa, her teaching assistant from Class One, to oversee a citizenship project that would continue to raise funds and teach the children at Penmenna about how things were different for others, namely those in South Sudan.

He was planning to fly out and oversee the building work in January after the fundraiser and talk to some other NGOs on the ground about the best and most effective way to take forward any plans for reuniting children separated from their families during the fighting. With tens of thousands of children displaced this was probably the issue closest to his heart and he was so excited to see how he could go on and make a difference.

On top of all his work he had been developing a plan for Sylvie. She had had such a crazy few months and he knew from experience that when all the trauma was over was when you needed support too. When everything was good and right, that was when the emotion hit, and whilst that needed to be processed it was nice to have something else to look forward to. He had been toying with doing something lovely for her, something to help her relax, and had had a brilliant idea based on one of their very first conversations.

He was just beginning to put it into play (thank you, Hector) when Marion had approached him with reports of the children developing a plan of their own. And most alarmingly they had taken it to her. He wasn't sure which of them decided Marion was the best person to bring onto their side but he had to admire their nerve and judgement. She was scary enough to approach when you were an adult, let alone a five-year-old child. Recognizing that she was a woman who got things done, though, showed pretty effective judgement. He couldn't do anything but bring them on board. It had to be a better decision than allowing them to carry on as a splinter group with a very clear, and very different, agenda to his.

The last thing he wanted was to put pressure on Sylvie; he wanted to make it clear that he had heard, processed and accepted that Sylvie didn't want anything other than a platonic relationship. He might be receiving mixed messages, but he had to listen to her words, or risk being one of *those* men, the ones who thought they knew what everyone wanted, what was for the best, regardless of what they might have been told. It was just that trying to get the children, and Marion, to listen was proving tricky.

It had been quite cute the way the children had plotted behind his back. He had been aware that Ellie had been pushing for a mummy since the time she met Sylvie on the beach but what he hadn't known was that Sam had been colluding willingly too.

Sam had told Ells that he was sure his mummy was in love with Alex, quite a sophisticated concept for a four-year-old, but he was learning every day how much wisdom and insight small children could have. Once Alex had been admitted into their inner circle, Ellie had glee-fully relayed that according to Sam, Sylvie had never smiled at anyone other than Sam the way she did Alex, and that she was always happy these days and that Sam really wanted her to carry on being happy and thought Alex being his new daddy might be a very good idea indeed. Sam had nodded vigorously and then high-fived Ellie.

Sam had been so animated when Sylvie had been teaching last weekend and Alex had offered to babysit him so they could hatch their plan. The only difficulty was keeping the other three on task. All were convinced that he and Sylvie should be married tout de suite and as much as their agenda might be reflective of what he really wanted, what his heart wanted – and his mind and body were pretty keen on too – he had to keep reminding them this was not a romantic operation, this was about friendship only. It had taken all of Alex's persuasive skills to convince them that forced marriage had been frowned upon for several hundred years. He wasn't sure they were listening.

He was also increasingly worried that what he was going to have to try and achieve next week for Sylvie was going to be far more difficult than anything the foundation might throw at him.

## Chapter Thirty Seven

Despite all the lovely changes in Sylvie's life, the world did not stop spinning on its axis, or explode into a hundred happy unicorns; instead it carried on its unrelenting trudge. Luckily Sylvie's unrelenting trudge was one she enjoyed immensely. Getting Sam up in their cottage in the dark mornings and walking into school on days when the rain held off, stopping to pick up Ellie and Alex on the way, was her idea of heaven.

This morning had been crisp with its cold, the temperature having dipped drastically in the night. As Sylvie and Sam marched stoically up the road, Sylvie wondered if perhaps she should have driven this morning. It had been terribly tempting, but she and Alex had made a deal when she moved into the village that they would make the children walk every morning unless there was Flood (seriously heavy rain), Fire (unlikely) or Famine (impossible with the way Alex insisted on feeding them all at every turn).

She was just wondering if she could convince Alex somehow that extreme cold made her very cross so surely hit the criteria for Fury when she saw Ellie jumping about on her front step, fluffy ear muffs on and ladybird gloves, joined with a long piece of yarn and threaded through her coat – Alex had learnt the hard way.

'They're here!' Her excited shriek resounded down the street and Sam speeded up. Instead of running to meet him as she usually did, Ellie raced inside and popped out again with two travel mugs, Alex behind her, also with two mugs and a pair of woolly gloves.

'Morning.' He leant in and gave Sylvie his usual morning kiss on the side of her cheek, and like every morning she wished she could angle her face (or her resolve) just a little so he hit her lips instead, and then she could open her mouth just a little and… Anyway, she never did – the children were here and she had established that giving in to her feelings was not a good long-term plan. She had her life on an even keel for the first time in years; she was waking up happy now, and feeling complete. She assumed that's what it was – that made the most sense, and it wasn't really something she had felt before. There was no way she was going to topple it, not even for… Alex handed her a mug and she found herself glancing at his hands, well-worn and sinewy. For goodness' sake!

'Hot chocolate.' His words broke her reverie and she realized she had been staring at the mug, or the hands offering it, probably with that lost lust-filled look she seemed to adopt a lot recently. 'It's blooming freezing so I thought we could walk to school with these and then I'll bring them all home with me later.'

'You are a marvel.'

'I know, I'm an absolute keeper.' His whole face lit up and there was a teasing lilt to his voice.

'Damn straight. You're going to make someone very happy.'

Although, selfishly, she rather hoped it wouldn't be for a while yet. She smiled up as he shut the door and they walked along to school companionably with the two kids chattering away in front of them, Sam explaining fun facts he had learnt about crows from Matt the day before. The two had taken to talking through the fence, Sam standing on the patio furniture, and they'd chatter for ages about plants, animals, birds and so forth. Two old men putting the world to rights.

She could feel Alex keep glancing over at her; there was clearly something on his mind and she couldn't quite work out what it was. He might not be hers but they had become so close over the last few months, she couldn't, didn't want to, imagine her life without him in it. She figured she had a couple of years at least before action and adventure called him back.

They reached the school and walked through the gates towards the quad and the entrance to the Reception Class. Everyone they saw greeted them by name and yet again, she was filled with a sense of community. And the niggling comprehension that 'Alex and Sylvie' and 'Sylvie and Alex' was such natural phrasing for everyone these days.

As they reached the classroom the two children handed Alex their empty mugs and Sylvie reached over to wipe Sam's chocolate moustache, but seeing her intention he stepped back and did it himself. Then both kids said goodbye and Sylvie waved them in and handed Alex her mug as she prepared to go to the PE cupboard to get the resources she needed for later. But instead of walking her most of the way there as he left, he took the mug and stayed where he was. That seemed a little odd.

Not having time to question it too deeply, she headed off. As she reached the other side of the quad she remembered that she had forgotten to ask Alex whether he and Ells would like to come to the cinema at the weekend. Looking over her shoulder to see if he was still there, she saw both the children had come back out of the classroom and were huddled with him, outside in the cold, and most scarily of all, Marion Marksharp was with the three of them.

OK, she wasn't delusional, something *was* up. She turned on her heel and prepared to find out exactly what was causing them all to be together and looking so conspiratorial.

'Ooh, Sylvie. Perfect, I'm so glad I've found you. Could you come with me? I really need you.' Harmony had appeared from nowhere and looked like she wanted to physically grab hold of her.

'OK, I'll be there in a minute, I just need to...'

Harmony's voice crescendoed. 'No, no, no! I'm afraid it's an absolute emergency. You must come now! Rafe Marksharp has locked Alice in the stationery cupboard and I was supposed to be keeping an eye on Amanda's class as they came in whilst she was doing an early-morning parent meeting. You're the only one he'll listen to.'

'Marion's over there,' Sylvie gestured across the tarmac. 'She'll sort it out.'

Harmony paled in front of her. 'Oh, please, no! That's even worse than getting Amanda. With Mr Marksharp away so much she's practically the chair of governors now, and she's been trying to get rid of me for years. She says I lack the gravitas needed to teach, and she tried to introduce a staff dress code because she said Penmenna

School was not a Native American encampment. She doesn't have a compassionate bone in her body which is why she doesn't recognize that some of us have soft skills that are far more important than her bullying style. You have really good soft skills, Sylvie. Please.' Harmony's words were delivered at such speed and with such genuine terror that Sylvie didn't have a choice. That stationery cupboard within that classroom was tiny – how Rafe had managed to squash Alice in was beyond comprehension – and she couldn't have Alice running out of air. Goodness knows how long Harmony had battled with Rafe before giving up and coming to search for help.

With a deep sigh, Sylvie accepted defeat, but she needed to find out what was being discussed on the other side of the playground, so she'd be hunting that man down later!

# Chapter Thirty Eight

Alex grinned as the children came tumbling back out of the classroom door and Marion appeared at the exact same second. Organizing this was so much fun, and the others were treating it as if it were some kind of spy operation. It was as if the *Mission Impossible* theme tune played every time they met.

'Right, so today is D-Day, tonight is the night. How is everything going?'

'Good. I've spoken to Chase and he has a tent we can borrow.'

'Chase has a tent? I wouldn't have thought he and Angelina were the camping type!' Marion's eyebrows went up.

'No, I think they're firm believers in the power of hotels, but it's more a marquee kinda thing – he's got a couple and I've bagsied the smaller one. If we can attach lots of billowy things then it'll work perfectly.'

'She's seen us, she's coming over.' Marion delivered this information in what he could only assume was her spy voice. It sounded as if she were addressing her words into a walkie-talkie.

'Are you sure, OK… um…' Alex briefly debated the karma attached to teaching Sam to lie to his mother;

he was fairly sure Marion and Ellie's was already pretty buggered.

'Oh, it's OK, that stupid hippy woman has her.'

'Mrs Marksharp, you shouldn't say stupid!' Ellie was outraged.

'And you shouldn't lecture your elders.' Marion flicked a look across to Alex, and then he saw her gaze land upon Sam who had crossed his arms tightly and was giving her his most intense brow furrow. 'But you are quite right, and Mrs Rivers is a… well, um… I'm sure there are lots of things she's very good at. Ooh and look, distracting your mother seems to be one of them. Goody! Now that's the tent done and the scene set. I've been a whizz with the costumes, I have one for us girls, now did you say yours was ready?'

'Oh, Marion, there really is no need. Just the children…'

'Where is your gumption? We've talked about this. Commit to the cause, for goodness' sake, we're trying to make a statement. I know that you've made one for Sam and I'm sure you'll look very dashing in yours as well. If that doesn't turn her head, I don't know what will. I already have one from a class I took a few years ago, and I modelled Ellie's on mine so we shall all be matching. Isn't that cute? Are we all secure on the routine? We can practise again tonight.'

Alex felt his masculinity evaporating in front of his eyes. He was not a natural dancer. He would rather wrestle a very hungry, very big crocodile. And now he had to dance – and in costume. Ellie would never ever forgive him if he didn't.

'Hello, could I have the children back please?' Rosy popped her head around the door.

'Oh yes, of course, sorry,' Alex said but he was drowned out by Marion.

'Two ticks, Rosy dear. And then we'll be with you. But I'd quite like your help with this as well. I'll come and find you at breaktime before I head off to Alex's.'

'Hmm, if this is what I think it is, and I don't know for sure, I think it's best for me not to get involved. Sorry, Alex, but I'm sure you know what I mean.'

'Rosy Winter! You know I'm Cornwall's best match-maker. These dear sweet children…' Marion turned them to face Rosy, '…just want one teeny thing and you want to deny them? When your help could be so instrumental? I'll find you at breaktime.'

Rosy's shoulders sagged with the inevitable.

'There is no matchmaking, Rosy, promise,' said Alex. 'This is just about doing a nice thing for a friend.' All four of the people standing there looked at him as if he had started talking in tongues. When were they going to believe him? 'Right, kids. Back to class now. We'll find a way to make sure Sylvie is distracted after the staff meeting and as planned I'll pick you both up tonight and we'll go do the last-minute things. OK?'

'OK.' They both gave him a big cuddle around his waist, Ellie's head on his tummy and Sam's head resting on hers, before they headed back in with Rosy. Alex thought he might melt.

'Rosy will keep Sylvie, won't you, dear?' Marion piped up.

Rosy gave Marion a look, one Alex suspected would quell the most unruly child as she took Sam and Ellie back in.

'How are you doing with the food, and the other thing?'

'Yep, all done. Hector is a go-go.'

'He always is.'

Alex smiled; he certainly was. 'And the air miles, although they call them Avios now, have been gifted to Sylvie's name so she has complete control. Music also sorted and downloaded to the laptop. It's going to be perfect. Thank you, Marion. She's going to love it.'

'Of course she is. When I set my mind to something, well, you know. I'll have you married yet.'

Alex rolled his eyes *and* arched his eyebrows at her, but it didn't stop the huge grin spreading across his face as, clutching his four travel mugs and turning to leave the playground, he really hoped she was right.

# Chapter Thirty Nine

Alex couldn't believe the day had come around so fast, but tonight was almost upon them and he was going to have to dance, and make a complete fool of himself, in front of the most breathtaking, passionate dancer he had ever seen.

That aside though, things had been going quite well. Marion had turned up at the cottage at eleven and confirmed that she had arranged some additional way for Sylvie to be detained at school after the staff meeting. Alex didn't dare ask.

But now, as he was leaving the house to go and pick up Ellie and Sam, he was proud of what they had achieved. The tent looked fabulous, really conjured up the air that Alex had wanted. Marion was an absolute bloody marvel; what that woman could do with a few metres of voile and some ribbon was nobody's business. He found it a little disconcerting that she brought a couple of minions with her, all very similar, one in a dress with synchro- nized swimmers on and the other wearing clothing dotted with giraffes. He was more than a little uneasy with her methods; they smacked slightly of Egypt's ancient era of slaves, although on a much smaller scale. He was half expecting her to whisk out a bullwhip at any moment. In fact, had Marion been alive then, it would have been quite possible that pyramids would have dotted the entire globe.

Watching her in full-on Marion mode this afternoon had made him consider starting a revolution in the PTA; he had never seen himself as particularly rebellious in nature but watching this made him feel very uncomfortable. Why these women never snapped back at her he did not know. He couldn't help but think if Chase and Marion ever joined forces then world domination would be but a step away.

Now though, the food was all laid out and covered ready for this evening. Couscous jewelled with roast peppers and olives; lamb marinated with ginger, turmeric and cinnamon; a myriad of salads, one peppered with feta and pomegranate and mint, another a traditional zaalouk made with tomatoes and aubergine. He had even imported a special flour to make the flatbreads to accompany the home-made hummus. The whole kitchen was filled with the most delicious smells, with preserved lemon, rosewater and ras-el-hanout all competing for primacy.

All that was left to be done was assemble and bake the baklava, weave some lights through the gauzy voile and prod some of the super-sized bamboo candles into the garden to create a lit pathway to the tent entrance. Oh, and practise the bloody dance one more time.

He returned to his cottage with both children, accompanied by Marion and her brood. He left them in charge of organizing the lighting. Marion was to weave the lights through the top of the tent and the children were given the responsibility of banging the bamboo torches into the ground. He was fairly sure Marion's boys were strong enough to do so and hoped that with her eagle eye they could be trusted to behave. He had pistachio-and-filo pastry to perfect.

He heard the sounds of children laughing and relaxed as he daubed his pastry with the syrup he had made from honey, water and lemon juice. He was loving this life. If you had told him years ago that he would have found his happy place in a small village in Cornwall, constructing sweet pastries for an ex-ballerina, listening to the sounds of children playing just as dusk descended, he would have laughed his leg off, yet here he was, happier and more relaxed than he had ever been, looking forward to every new day.

Just as he placed the tray on the side ready to pop in the Aga, he heard a child's scream rend the air and felt a chill clutch at his very core.

As he raced outside he saw Ellie's back, her shoulders shaking and her sobs loud, and he took a deep breath of relief – thank God for that, she was fine – only for his heart to still again as Rafe, Rufus and Rupert moved a fraction and he saw, just by the entrance to the tent, Sam's little body splayed out, still and seemingly lifeless, upon the ground.

# Chapter Forty

The staff meeting was dragging this evening, and Sylvie was feeling a little odd. She wasn't sure what was wrong, there was no identifiable symptom as such, but there was definitely something that wasn't right somewhere, like that feeling her mother used to describe as someone walking over your grave. A shiver for no reason. A frisson of unexplained anxiety. All she knew for sure was that she was desperate to get to Alex's, grab Sam and head home. She had never felt this way before about the school, but this evening she really didn't want to be here.

It didn't help that the school phone had been ringing off the hook in the office but with Sheila gone home there was no one to transfer the calls through. Whatever was making Sylvie antsy this afternoon, the constant shrill *bring-bring* of the telephone wasn't helping.

'Right, I think that's us all done, and I'm sorry it's dragged this evening. But you know what this term is like with the run-up to December, there are a hundred and one things to organize, which is why I appreciate all the teaching assistants joining us this evening, thank you. But I reckon we've done enough for now, so let's get home.' Rosy smiled around the table at her staff, shuffled her papers back into a tidy pile and Sylvie felt a breath of relief whoosh out of her mouth.

'Oh, apart from Sylvie. Sylvie, do you mind if we have a quick word before you go?'

'Of course, no problem.' Sylvie smiled, using up every last professional bit of her.

Suddenly they heard a door bang and the huffing of someone running along the corridor, the staff's low-level mumbles paused as they heard the *thud-thud-thud* pound urgently along the corridor.

The door swung open and there was Marion Marksharp, slightly dishevelled, panting heavily and looking as if she'd been crying.

'I'm so... so...' She seemed unable to formulate words into a coherent sentence. 'I've been... been...'

'Marion, for goodness' sake, sit down, breathe. Now what on earth has happened?' Rosy took immediate control of the situation but Sylvie felt an awful sense of foreboding creeping up her neck, crawling into her head and making her brain fuzzy.

'Marion, what is it? Just tell us what on earth has happened,' she barked sharply, the words staccato, and the head of every member of staff turned around in response to the unflappable Sylvie being so curt. 'Marion? I'm serious.'

'Sylvie, I'm sorry, all my fault...'

Marion's boys burst into the staffroom.

'Don't be cross with her. It wasn't Mum's fault, honest, it wasn't. It was just an accident.'

'Rafe, *what* has happened?'

'It's Sam, Miss Winter. I'm sorry, Miss Williams, it was an accident, Mum's been trying to get hold of you for ages. But your mobile kept going to voicemail and no one was answering the school phone.'

Sylvie gulped, trying to get some air into her lungs as the room began to spin. An accident, Sam? Breathe in and out. Calm, she tried to tell herself, calm, you need to get to Sam, you need to be calm and get to Sam. She felt her legs wobble and the next thing she knew she was grabbing the side of the table. Grasping so hard that the wood almost felt soft in her hand.

'What hospital, Marion?'

'Roscarrock, minor injuries. We called the ambulance but by the time...'

Sylvie didn't hear the rest of what was being said as she grabbed her bag and raced out of the school. Her car was at home. OK, someone would have a car. Who would have a car?

'Sylvie, Sylvie.' Rosy came running down the granite steps in front of the school. 'Wait, let me drive you, it's not sensible for you to drive.'

'OK, where...'

'It's just here, come on, we'll be there in a flash.' The two women zoomed away from Penmenna School watched by the staff, each and every one of them praying that everything would be all right.

# Chapter Forty One

Alex raced to Sam and hurled himself onto the ground next to him. He knew not to move the boy and shouted at Marion who was standing paralysed to the spot, phone in her hand and mouth wide open.

'Ambulance, Marion, now!'

'Of course, of course.'

'Ellie, go get me some cold water.'

He didn't know why he said it but it felt right, plus he needed to examine Sam and he didn't want Ellie getting distressed and distracting his focus. He tentatively laid his hand on the boy's cheek before preparing to check his pulse.

As his hand touched Sam, the boy batted his eyelids a little and emitted a small groan.

'Sam, Sam, it's Alex. Sam!'

'Umhmmm.'

'OK, good boy, don't move. Don't try to speak. Brilliant, well done.' Phew, he didn't think his heart could have gone any faster. Sam was conscious, that was huge. He tried talking to himself, stating the facts, keeping himself calm so he could be effective. When he had seen Sam lying there, so still, he had immediately thought the worst had happened. 'OK, I think you're going to be OK, but we've got an ambulance coming just in case.'

'An ambulance? Awesome.' The boy managed to form words but they were a little slurred. His usually pale face so white it was almost green.

'Don't try and talk, don't move your head, just rest for a bit. I'm going to have a look at you, check for injuries. I don't want you to move but do let me know if anything hurts.'

'I flew.'

'Yes, you did. You certainly did.' Alex found himself laughing, if slightly hysterically, at Sam's words.

'Now is this sore?' Alex asked.

Sam's wrist looked remarkably swollen and he was amazed that the boy wasn't showing any other signs of pain.

'Everything's sore, Alex. But I flew.' And a beatific smile spread slowly over the small boy's face as he lay otherwise stone-still on the ground.

# Chapter Forty Two

Rosy sped to the hospital, paying no regard to speed limits and reassuring Sylvie all the way. Sylvie had been silent since they got into the car, and her silence was far louder than all of Rosy's reassurances.

'Marion said he's OK, they think he's OK. It's going to be all right. I chased after you as soon as I had got all the details from Marion. They were planning some kind of surprise and Sam took it upon himself to climb up the tree in Alex's garden...'

Rosy flicked a look across at Sylvie, still nothing.

'I don't know where Alex was but Marion was outside with them. That's why she feels responsible, I think. She took a call from Richard – between us she's not been having an easy time of it and was distracted. She is beside herself with guilt but I really think Rafe was right, it was an accident. No one expected Sam to climb up there. His confidence has grown so much over the past few months but even I wouldn't have expected him to try and scale a tree. Apparently, one minute the boys and Ellie were all talking about threading some lights somewhere, that bit's a bit patchy, and then apparently – and this all comes from Rafe, although the other boys agreed – Sam was racing up the tree like a monkey, and missed his footing. But he's OK. Sylvie, they said he's OK.'

'They said he was taken to hospital in an ambulance.'

Rosy let out a sigh of relief as Sylvie spoke, before responding to her.

'Yes, which they called the second it happened. Apparently by the time the ambulance got there he was asking for chocolate. Alex had some job stopping him from sitting up. But the ambulance took him in anyway, just to run checks. Now, I know you won't rest until you see him, but it sounds like things are going to be OK. I expect Alex will have turned his phone off, but have you tried to call him?'

The word *chocolate* seemed to crack Sylvie's mask; previously she'd been sitting there pale and still, but now she appeared to come back into her body. She took a deep breath before answering.

'Straight to voicemail, but to be fair to him when I turned my ringer on, I saw he had tried to call me a heap of times. I imagine he'll call back when he gets a chance. What else did Marion say? Did she hear Sam talk? She's absolutely sure?'

'From what I understand, absolutely sure. Alex went in the ambulance and they let Ellie too. They wouldn't have done that if he was considered an emergency situation. They must have assessed and decided he was in no danger. They couldn't have a small child riding along if there was any chance of a possible intervention being needed. I'm kind of surprised they did, so I think it's a strong indicator that you've nothing to worry about.'

'Do you think?'

'Yes, I do.'

'I couldn't bear it, I… well, I don't know what I'd do.'

'Of course you don't, no one would. But I think you're going to get there and he'll be fine. Happy to see you and cross it's spoilt whatever surprise they had going on.'

'Oh, I really hope so. I can cope with cross. Life's been throwing me a lot of lessons this year, especially to do with family. And knowing that lives can change for ever in a split second is not the lesson I want to learn through my son, not today, not any day.'

'Yes, you've had an incredibly tough time, but we love having you at the school and hopefully life will start getting a bit easier now. And I know your mum's gone and that is an irreplaceable loss…'

'It is, but we knew that was coming. If I were… I couldn't… when I thought something had happened to S… wow, we're here already. How on earth?'

'Matt says I could always have a career as a rally driver if I get fed up with teaching. Now, I've been in Marion's car and that is terrifying. Believe me. But me, I'm super-fast and super-smooth.'

'And the super-best boss. Thank you so much for this.'

'Don't be daft. Go on, hop out. I'll park up and come and find you.'

'Oh no, no need. I'll be fine from here on.'

'But if Alex came in the ambulance…'

'We'll work it out. I don't know how long I'm going to have to stay. You get on with your evening. And I'll text you and let you know what's happening. Thank you so much.'

Then Sylvie planted a kiss on Rosy's cheek, and with the grace of a woodland sprite, albeit it one with a catch in her throat and nerves threatening to overtake her, slid out of the car to go and fetch her boy.

# Chapter Forty Three

As Sylvie strode swiftly through the open doors of the minor injuries unit her heart was in her mouth again. She meant what she had said; life could turn on a sixpence and she promised a prayer that if Sam was all right, then she would stop taking things for granted and be a lot more grateful for the good she had in her life.

If Sam was all right she would make sure she was always kind to everyone, properly kind, not just slapdash like she was now. She didn't want to promise to be a saint because that would be an out-and-out fail but she was going to be the best person she could be and she was going to take every opportunity to tell the people she cared about how much she loved them. She'd ring Tom for a start in the morning and tell him how she appreciated him having her at the farm for so long. And that he should hurry up and get a ring on Julie's finger. And then she would stop being scared and...

'Hello, hi, I'm Sylvie Williams and I believe you've got my son, Sam Williams, here. Can you tell me anything? Is he OK? Can I see him?' Reaching the desk meant her promises for the future got overtaken by the need to know now about her son.

'Oh yes, hello, Sam's mum. We knew you'd be coming. Although your friend who rang ahead to let us know was a little… um… unusual. However, the important thing is that Sam is here, he's all good, ready to go home almost, sprained wrist but otherwise looking all OK. We're just waiting for a couple of things to come back and then the doctor will come find you, but it shouldn't be long. He's a real daredevil, your boy, from all accounts.'

Sylvie heard herself laugh. It sounded slightly hysterical but then she figured she probably was, and that was fine. For here, in front of her, was a medical professional reassuring her that all was as Rosy had said. Everything was OK. Sam was OK. Now she was going to have to make good on those promises. She just needed to see him with her own eyes, hold him in her arms and possibly never let him go.

'Can I see him? Is he just around there?'

She indicated past the nurse to the bays behind her that stretched down the corridor. She had been to this hospital more than once over the past few years.

'Yes, love, just follow the giggles. Your boy hasn't stopped laughing since he arrived, a real breath of fresh air, and your husband, I know I shouldn't say but – phew. He's caused a flutter or two, I can tell you! Not often you get drop-dead gorgeous, attentive and good with kids. You've hit the jackpot there!'

'Oh no, he's…' Sylvie didn't get a chance to finish her sentence as the doors swung open and a trolley was wheeled in, a paramedic astride a patient doing CPR, and the nurse rushed from the desk shouting emergency medical codes that Sylvie didn't understand but was truly grateful for an NHS staffed by people who did.

She wandered down the corridor, fears about having to pull back curtains and disturb people dissipating as she realized the nurse was right – she could hear the giggles of Sam and Ellie and Alex from here.

She rounded the corner and her heart smiled as she saw her boy, all curled up in the crook of Alex's arm and chuckling away as Ellie did some kind of dance in front of him, shimmying her hips whilst shouting, 'I say, Rufus darling, that's really not how people like us behave.'

Alex was wiping tears from his face whilst holding on to her son as tight as tight could be and Sylvie realized, in that moment, that her family wasn't just Sam. Or indeed Sam with Tom on the periphery. But her family, her core family, was this – Sam, this man and his daughter. These three people here in front of her right now, these were the people she wanted to be her family for ever. All she had to do was put her head above the parapet, find the courage and tell them.

## Chapter Forty Four

'Mum!' Sam wriggled himself off the bed and gingerly out of Alex's arms. Alex gulped as he watched Sylvie scoop Sam up and cover his head, neck and shoulders with kisses, being careful not to bang his arm. Sam, for once, didn't squirm but nestled in for a second, only bringing his head back so he could look at her face as he told her his super-exciting news.

'I flew, Mum, I flew. And then the doctors said I was very brave, which I was but Alex says I'm never to do it again. It wasn't Alex's fault, he was making the… oh, never mind. But I flew like a bird.'

Alex got off the bed and moved forward towards Sylvie. He wanted this bit done as quickly as possible. He knew she was, rightfully, going to be livid at him and was surprised that her face didn't match her hair yet. But then she was the perfect mother and would keep it together in front of Sam and Ellie, and probably just flay him alive and feed him to bees when there were no children around to witness it.

He couldn't even begin to imagine the depth of rage she must feel; if it had been Ellie who nearly died he wouldn't be as composed as she seemed now. Yet she hadn't flicked him an angry look, not once – and she normally did that pretty speedily for even the smallest offence. Last time he put too much sugar in her coffee she looked as if he had stamped on kittens.

'He's OK, Sylvie.' Alex looked her directly in the eye as he spoke. 'The doctors have given him the all-clear, and we're just waiting on a final check before discharge. They wanted to monitor him for concussion but he's shown no signs so far and obviously I've said we'll – you'll – monitor him this evening. It's quite remarkable that he hasn't broken anything although they say he'll probably ache for a few days, but just keep him topped up on basic painkillers.' He glanced at her as she checked Sam over herself, gently touching and patting him down. Still no apparent killer fury. 'I cannot begin to tell you how sorry I am. I can't believe this happened. You have no idea… Never mind, that's not important. The main thing is he's OK and you're here. I'm going to chop that tree down as soon as we get home. I did try and call but…'

'I know, my phone was switched off. I shall never be doing that again, I promise. You must have been beside yourself when you couldn't get hold of me. Please don't chop the tree down…'

'No, don't. We love the tree,' Ellie pitched in as Sam added, 'It wasn't the tree's fault.' Both of them giving Alex their very biggest pleading eyes.

'Look, from what I can understand you have nothing to be sorry for. He's fine. Look at him, he's fine. He thinks he's a hero so that's going to need to be addressed…' at this point she shot Sam a faux-angry brow furrow that looked identical to his real-angry one, 'and you did your best to get hold of me and then chose to not leave his side until I got here. I'd much rather that than you keep leaving him here alone to try and get hold of me. And besides, you put Marion on the case. You knew she'd get to me. I have nothing to be cross at you for. Accidents happen. And now that this one has, Sam is going to promise me no more tree climbing unless we say it's OK first.'

This couldn't be right. She was still smiling at him. Not an I'm-smiling-now-but-I'm-going-to-kill-you-later smile but a real I'm-smiling-with-my-mouth-and-my-eyes-because-I-mean-it smile.

He smiled back and she smiled wider, with Sam still tucked under her arm.

'I'm glad you're not cross with Daddy. He thought you might be. He didn't say that but I think he thought it. I know my daddy and I have never seen him scared of anything before. But today he turned green.'

'Did he?' Sam said. 'Green like the Hulk? I didn't see – can you turn green again? Mum, scare him, go on, see if he can do it again.'

'No, silly,' Ellie giggled, 'he didn't turn green 'cause he was scared of your mum, he turned green 'cause he was scared when you didn't move.'

'But I did move, I flew.'

'You fell and then you were very still. Like, very still. I cried and I never cry. Do I, Dad? I never cry. We were all scared but look, Sylvie, he's OK now. And it wasn't Daddy's fault, it was Mrs Marksharp's. She was meant to be looking after us whilst Daddy made the… um… Anyway, it was her fault.'

'No, it wasn't. That's not fair, Ellie,' Alex responded quickly.

'I flew!' Sam stuck his chin out.

'Look, all of you. Come here.' Sylvie opened her arms and smiled at each of them individually. Alex advanced towards her arms, not unaware of the irony that he had waited months to hear those two words from her lips; he just hadn't pictured it occurring in a hospital with the children around. And he thought he had covered practically every scenario in his daydreams. It would appear he was wrong.

As they stood closer together, Sylvie reached her arms around all four of them and pulled them tight in to her. 'We're all OK, we're all here and we're all all right. I reckon that means life is going pretty well. I love you all so much, and of course I'm not cross with anyone. Although no more flying, mister.' She looked at Sam, the love pouring out of her eyes into puddles. 'And you, my dear, clever, confident Ellie, I love you too. You were the one that taught my Sam to fly, and I don't mean that in a bad way. You have shown him how to reach out and grab life with both hands, wake it, shake it and take it to the fullest, and I will love you for ever for that. And you...' she transferred her attention to Alex but this time the puddles of love contrasted with very pink cheeks, '...you are the most incredible man I have ever met, you have transformed me and my life in so many ways, both obvious and intangible, and I don't think I shall ever meet another adult who gives me what you do. Everyone else can only ever be a poor second.'

Alex looked at her, her elfin face, shining eyes and crazy blushing, and he wanted to answer in as eloquent a way. He wanted to tell her that she and Sam were the world to him, that together the four of them made his perfect family and that he could never see himself loving, respecting and wanting another woman as much as he did her. That she was the first thing he thought about as he opened his eyes and deliberately the last thing he thought about as he fell asleep at night. That she guaranteed his dreams were full of life and hope and vigour and that translated into his every day too. That with her at his side they really could make an indestructible team, go on and change the world, and that without her he wasn't capable of being half the man he hoped to be. He wanted to say all of that and then he wanted to turn the children so they were facing the wall, take her in his arms and kiss her so long and so deep that they would be arrested for public indecency. That they could lead him away in handcuffs, imprison him, burn him at the bloody stake but for her he would do anything. For ever.

However, he didn't say that.

Instead he just held her eyes, long and hard. The journalist, the man who made his living through words and action, rendered incapable of either.

'So, you're not cross then?' Luckily he had his daughter, never likely to be short of words, who stepped in.

Sylvie let out a huge laugh, a deep whole-body laugh that carried on until tears, of what Alex couldn't tell, flowed down her cheeks.

'In which case can we still do the surprise?' Ellie continued.

'Oh, please, Mum, please. Pleeeeaaase!'

'I don't think so, I think Sylvie has had enough for one day.'

'But she's not cross, the doctor says Sam is OK, and we have worked so hard. Please. Plus, it will stop Mrs Marksharp feeling so bad.'

'I think I should get Sam home. It's been a big day.'

'Grab the moment, Mum.'

Alex watched Sam squeeze his mother's hand and smile, her face crinkling in return and them all knowing that he had won. He immediately gave Ellie a double thumbs-up and nodded.

'You'd better ring that woman then, Dad.' Ellie side-nodded at her father as she spoke.

'Whoa, I'm not that easily swayed.'

'But you kinda are.' Alex couldn't help himself.

She nodded back at him and shrugged her shoulders.

'Mr and Mrs Williams…' A doctor came bustling through the curtain, yellow stethoscope around her neck, and dark hair in twin plaits resting on her shoulders.

'We're not married. We're not together. Just friends.' Sylvie was quick to reassure her and Alex felt a pang – he quite liked being Mr Williams. *Alex Williams* kind of rolled off the tongue rather nicely. Just friends definitely did not have the same ring.

'Apologies. In that case, Ms Williams, looking at everything it seems that Sam is absolutely fine to go. He's a very lucky boy. Keep an eye on him overnight – the discharge nurse will give you a leaflet about concussion but we've seen no evidence of any harm done. And you, young man, no more jumping out of trees. Not even a bush, you hear!'

'Yes, doctor.' Sam put on a contrite face and Alex couldn't help but grin. This boy was getting good!

'So I should take him home and have a quiet night?'

'Yes, that sounds sensible.'

'Does he have to have a quiet night? We've got an important thing to do. We could do it quietly.'

'Ellie!' Alex put his hand lightly on his daughter's shoulder, ready to remind her that they were standing in a hospital so their previous plans were hardly a priority.

'Yes, if it's important and you can do it quietly and your parents are happy to, then I can see no major problem. Like I say, Sam is fine.' The doctor punctuated her words with a laugh.

'Oh, for goodness' sake,' Sylvie said after the doctor left. 'It appears that I am outnumbered. I don't know what is going on here but you all seem to be up to something. And whilst it really was an accident, you've all been very coy about what Alex was actually doing when Sam fell, why Marion was there, and one wonders what prompted you, young man, to climb the tree? None of you have actually told me anything about that. So, the way I see it, if I want answers I'm going to have to say yes to this surprise. But *only* if you can do it very calmly, Samuel Williams.'

'Are you sure? Don't let the naughty little toads pressure you. It was just a fun little thing.'

'I love fun little things.' As she took her focus off the children and concentrated it all on him, he felt his heart beat faster and he tried to take a deep breath while at the same time hiding the fact that he was doing so. But she just fixed him with that all-knowing look and slightly smirk-smiled, blinking slowly as the smile crept across her face.

'I know you.'

Her words were slow and deliberate. Did they contain a hidden subtext? Or was he just so besotted that he hoped they did? He paused, unsure of himself, and therefore not knowing which words he was supposed to say in return. *I know you* carried so much weight. Was this a flippant *I know you*? A my-soul-sees-your-soul *know you*? An I'm-so-happy-our-kids-get-along-but-otherwise-I-wouldn't-want-to-know-you *know you*?

'I know you,' Sylvie repeated, 'and whatever you have cooked up between the lot of you, it's going to be pretty awesome, and if it's important to these two toe-rags that they do it, then so be it. As long as you all promise that it's gentle and not going to make Sam do loads of stuff. I still want him to take it easy tonight, no running about. If that's OK, then let's do this!'

'Sure? I'll have to ring Marion.'

'Yes, sure. Then you can tell her that Sam's OK. Actually, do either of us have a car here? Nope, we're going to have to ring Andy's Cabs.'

'Is there no bus service?'

'Seriously, you've been living here for months now and have you ever seen a bus past five o'clock other than the college bus?'

'Yeah, good point, but I also know Andy's Cabs seems to use the Smuggler's Curse as his base from six on in the evening, so he might not be a good idea?'

'Oh, bloody hell, I thought he had stopped that.'

'Marion?'

'Letting her come over to yours to do this surprise thing is enough. We've all been in the hospital once today as it is – have you seen the way she drives? Rosy claims to still be having nightmares.'

'Fair point. Right then, I guess you're going to have to ring Tom?'

'OK, on it.' She pulled out her phone to call her uncle, and grinned at the people in front of her, resolute in her determination to grab the moment.

# Chapter Forty Five

Sylvie sat in Tom's car once the others went in. Marion had already arrived and she and the boys had greeted Sam like he was some kind of miracle child. The boys were patting him on the back and Sylvie had to resist the urge to screech, 'Gentle!' from the car window as they all went in the house together. She had been instructed to stay in the car for five minutes so they could set up whatever had to be set up, although they all reassured her Sam would not be allowed to even look at a tree let alone go within three feet of one.

'Some day you 'ad today, maid.'

'Huh. Tell you, I've never been so scared in all my life, Tom.'

'Aye.'

'It hammered home the point that life is too short to not grasp it.'

'You've always known that, bird.'

'I know, but it's been reinforced. That family, be it blood or chosen, is the most important thing in the world. And that life is too short for miscommunications, for secrets, for misunderstandings, and that sometimes you just have to stand up and own the truth that you see.'

'Aye.'

'Like you did Julie.'

'Aye. I did.'

'So, I'm going to with Alex.'

'Aye. That you should.'

'Really?'

'Aye, of course. He's a good man and he's besotted with you, and I think that you need to hurry up and get on with it. He's been hanging round now for months and you treating him casually like he's just your friend when even the cows can see you two are meant to be together. So yep, stop this damn stupid shilly-shallying and gerron. Or he'll go elsewhere. There be women everywhere eager to get a man like him. That blonde bit he teetered into the house with, for example.'

'Yeah, I don't think Alex and Marion are going to sleep together, Tom. She's happily married.'

'That's not what I 'eard.'

How the hell had Tom heard anything? He didn't even leave the farm apart from emergencies like this. She bet it was Julie. Honestly, the WI here, all very modern, beautifully entwining proper Cornish old dears who'd been milking since they could toddle with trendy yoga-loving kefir-drinking yummy-mummies getting together for a weekly stitch and bitch. The stitching taking a very firm secondary position.

'That WI your Julie is part of is something else. Honestly, there's nothing they don't gossip about.'

'There is something.'

'What's that then? Are you getting married?'

'Course I'm getting married. I can't expect a woman like Julie to wait now you've gone. But that's not what I meant.'

'Are you going to tell me?'

'I'm trying. You don't make it easy. You haven't had a smooth time of it these last few years. You didn't have an easy time of it as a child, truth be told. When your father died, well that was awful for all of us but my heart went out to you. You were the apple of his eye. Your mum was in bits you know, couldn't go near that slurry pit for years after. And then you were sent up to London, I know you wanted to go but it seemed harsh. But then you did so well, and you know how proud your mum was of your dancing. So proud. But there's something else. I knew your mum inside out and I knew your dad pretty well and I want you to know that they would be so proud of *you*. For how you are as a person. For how you deal with things when they're not good, like today with your boy, for your determination to do the right thing. You're a fighter – you don't give up and you put others first. Your mum and dad would be so proud of the woman you've grown into and I am too. I think you're a credit to your parents and I know that they would be swelled up with pride for the person you've become. No, don't say another word. Get out of my car, remember what I've said and bleedy go get that man!'

Sylvie took a deep breath in as she processed the longest speech her uncle had ever made, gave him the sloppiest kiss on his cheek, ruffled his hair just as he had hers the other day, and tried not to get too choked up as she opened the Land Rover door and slid out. She took another deep breath as she stood at the kerb and then wove her way to Alex's front door where she could face the surprise they had planned and finally find the courage to speak out about the family she wanted, her heart gladdened by Tom's words about the family she had been born into.

## Chapter Forty Six

As she approached the front door she tentatively pushed it to see if it would open. It did, although the house was in darkness.

'Hello?'

Three little torchlights bobbed out from the kitchen and across the dining room to welcome her. Torchlight, it was revealed, held by Marion's boys bobbing their mobile phones in the darkness. OK, this was weird.

'Hello, Miss Williams. If you would follow us. Rufus, you lead the way, me and Rafe can walk next to her. Be careful not to trip, miss, it's still quite dark.' Rupert spoke from the darkness.

She could smell something beautifully sweet baking but that in itself provided no real clue.

They led the way around the corner into the kitchen which was all lit up one side and had a table groaning with what looked to be North African food, couscous and tagines, stuffed vine leaves and a gigantic bowl of hummus, triangular flatbreads next to it and bowls of salads peppered with the ruby-red of pomegranates.

'Wow, this is amazing. This huge feast, what's all this about?'

'You'll see, miss. You just have to wait.'

'If you'd come this way, miss.'

Rupert, who was leading their little posse and making a pretty good butler, fell into a huge sweeping bow as he reached the back door of the kitchen. His brother ran forward to open it and did so with a flourish.

Sylvie's mouth dropped open.

This sure as shit had taken a lot longer than five minutes to set up! There was still no sign of Alex or the children, or even Marion – but there in the middle of Alex's garden, to the side of the tree they had picnicked under so many times, was a marquee, draped with all manner of gauzy fabrics in reds and purples and blues, and lit up with big bamboo torches outside and fairy lights strewn through the tree and across the top. That was obviously where Marion came in – it was no secret that fairy lights taken to the next level was very much her domain. Oh my goodness, that must have been how Sam had fallen; it had been whilst trying to set this surprise up for her. Her tummy flipped a little bit. Surely she was the luckiest mum in the world?

Where on earth were they? As she stood there taking it all in, and there was a lot to take in, her curiosity was piqued even more than it had been seconds ago.

'Go on, go in!'

Rufus nudged her with his elbow and as he did so she heard Ellie's nervous titter. Not that that girl was ever really nervous! So, they must all be close and watching her.

She entered the tent and could see they had managed to drag out Alex's Turkish rug from his living room and on it had placed some kind of wooden banquette covered in cushions.

'My mum got her friend to make that,' Rufus whispered, still close to her and pointing at the seating. For all of the horrendous things about Marion, this boy's pride in his mum made Sylvie's heart swell again. Much more of this and it was likely to burst out of her chest and this beautiful moment would be ruined as she was carted right back to the hospital.

'That was very kind of her,' Sylvie whispered back.

'You need to sit on it,' Rufus stage-whispered back again.

'OK,' Sylvie mouthed and tentatively went to sit on the banquette, lowering her hands first; it certainly seemed steady. As she sat she saw there was a little Moroccan tea set next to her, full of a steaming liquid. She picked up the jug and could see and smell the mint stems through the glass. Lifting the lid she inhaled deeply and could pick up not just mint but the sweetness of sugar as well as the tang of green tea. This was heavenly. She reached out to lift one of the coloured glasses also on the tray but Rafe came bustling over and insisted on serving it for her. As she sat there, having been presented with the ornate glass adorned with gold patterning, and took a sip of the steaming liquid, she caught a jangle on the air. Hmm, OK. This could prove interesting. What on earth did they have planned? This was followed by the very light strains of music starting up. Her trained ear immediately picked up the lute-like sounds of the Gimbri, the strings of a rabab, with the unmistakable beat of bendir drums, several of them, and a riq, or maybe two, the North African and Arabic equivalent to the tambourine. What on earth were they going to do next? She took another sip of tea as the three Marksharp boys lined up in front of her and all made a deep bow before walking out backwards.

'Twit, you nearly knocked me over,' she heard Rafe hiss at Rupert as soon as they were around the corner. They were quite cute, those boys, once you got to know them. And made sure there were no matches nearby.

Then she heard a thwack, and another and another, which presumably meant they had started hitting each other.

The music suddenly got louder and from a dark corner of the garden she saw Ellie and Marion shimmer out to the front of the tent and start to perform a belly dance. Ellie, dressed in traditional belly-dancing costume with dark pink harem pants, top and matching veil, had a natural ease and didn't put a foot wrong. Marion, clad in an identical outfit, was slightly more awkward.

The very angular nature of her meant she lacked the grace of a natural dancer – she jutted where she should glide – but Sylvie had to give the woman credit for her sheer determination. Marion clearly assumed she had the grace of a gazelle as she flailed about looking distinctly unsteady on her feet. Although to be fair, hissing, 'Boys, stop it, stop it right now,' out of the corner of her mouth, as she kept her eyes determinedly to the front and her smile as fixed as she could, wasn't really helping her achieve the vision of elegance that she was aiming for.

It seemed almost unfair that Ellie next to her was achieving it effortlessly. The girl had a flair for dance that Sylvie had noticed in class but that now, with an audience present, and the contrast of the heavily made-up woman next to her, made her appear more graceful. The music faded and it was possible to hear the small silver bells attached to their outfits whispering through the air as they started to move gently to the side of the garden.

Sylvie started to clap; this was all too much. A whole Arabian tent erected for her, furniture made for it and a North African feast presumably for her to eat after the girls' dance. She could feel the emotion choking in her throat but before she could thank them, or say anything, the music changed and she realized that now Alex and Sam were moving towards her wearing… oh my goodness, they looked rather like old white sheets that had been cut up and sewn together, presumably to resemble the traditional dress that Berber men wore to dance.

They began to shuffle in unison, stomping and clapping. Sam's face lit up as he followed Alex's moves, throwing himself into the dance, exaggerating all the movements, a real joy on his face, his little eyes shining. He was clapping his torso to save his poorly wrist and it was hard to tear her eyes away from his face, so lit as it was by the moment. But then she caught sight of the expression on Alex's face and had to fight the urge not to laugh out loud.

For a man so good-looking, normally so completely at ease with himself that it was slightly irritating for everyone else, to look so hideously uncomfortable was the funniest thing she had seen in years. Finally, it would appear that there was something this man didn't excel at, and it was dancing.

Alex caught her eye and raised his brows, acknowledging that he recognized how much joy she was getting from his discomfort, and then he put a little bit more life into his stomping and clapping, bringing his feet down heavier and clapping with more force. However, even with the extra effort, her four-year-old still outshone him. As much as she tried to get her grin under control she just couldn't help herself; it must be spread across her face literally, as the cliché stated, from ear to ear. She could feel it.

Then, out of nowhere, and completely dominating the music, came the sound of a woman ululating. Alex looked completely startled and missed his footing, clambering to get back into step, whereas Sam just smiled even wider and got faster as the sound continued.

The noise instantly transported Sylvie to a world of sandstorms and bright blue robes. Was that Marion? How? When did the woman learn to do that? That took some power. She really was a constant surprise. Rufus, Rafe and Rupert, just on the edge of the shadows, were jumping up and down as she carried on, the younger two joining in with cockcrows as if they were all Peter Pan.

'Go, Mum, go!' Rafe shouted, pride writ large.

The music wound up and the boys shuffled back off and then Sam, Alex, Ellie and Marion came back into the light and took a bow.

'Right, now that hell is over let's eat.' Alex grinned

'No! Let's dance again!' Ellie squeaked. 'Do that thing again, Mrs Marksharp, that was so cool. I want to try.'

'That was pretty impressive, Marion. Was that really you?'

'Oh yes, I learnt to do it decades ago when we were all in uni and went to stay at...' Sylvie watched her flick a quick look at Alex. 'When we all went on holiday. Years ago.'

More secrets, but then seeing that the secrets from before were clearly about setting up this evening, an evening dedicated to her and making her feel like the most spoilt princess in the world, she could let it slide. As much as Sylvie had loved her parents, even they had never done anything this jaw-droppingly gorgeous just for her.

'And the costumes, they were so cute. You must have been up for hours at the sewing machine creating these, Marion. I really appreciate all of this.'

'Oh no! That wasn't me, that was Alex. He did everything really, just called me in for the finishing touches. That man can sew, not so good at draping.' Marion winked at Alex and he winked back.

'Trust me, there are places in the world where knowing how to sew is a must. If I want to keep myself intact, safe from scorpion stings and all other sorts of nasties, I need to be able to sew in a hurry.'

'You are the most masculine seamstress I have ever met.' Sylvie grinned at him and they shared another of those looks, the looks that since her resolution about grabbing life meant she no longer worried so much about what the children thought, just how quickly she could whisk her knickers off. Although not here and now, obviously. But a girl could daydream.

'Right, let's eat.'

'I want to dance again,' Ellie interrupted.

'Yes, let's do more dancing.' Sam nodded in agreement.

'I'd love to but I have to get back and take the dog for a walk, such a sweet thing. Only a puppy, you know! Richard bought him for me quite recently. He misses me desperately in the day. I really should get home.'

'A puppy! I want to see the puppy.' Ellie's loyalty to dancing was suddenly fickle.

'A puppy? It's huge!' Sam wasn't quite as convinced.

'You've worked so hard, stay and have some food, even if it's only quickly, and then shoot off and rescue Darcy. Please, stay and eat with us, Marion.' Alex was quick to invite her and there was no mistaking the genuine nature of his words.

Sylvie looked from Alex to Marion as she saw the woman puff up, just ever so slightly, and smile.

'That would be lovely. If you're sure.'

'We're sure.' Sylvie answered for them both. She wondered how often Marion was invited places just for pleasure and not for her organizational skills. With the exception of Rosy she had never seen anyone other than her children show her affection, just fear and blind obedience.

All of them, Marion's boys as well, sat on Alex's rugs, the Maghreb music still playing very quietly in the background as they gorged themselves on the mountains of food that Alex had prepared; Marion being very quick to give him all the credit for that as well.

When Sylvie felt she couldn't eat another thing, Marion gave her boys a nod and within seconds – OK, minutes, but it was still super-impressive – all the food was cleared away. Every time Sylvie stood up to try and help, someone – and they all took turns, even Rufus, Rafe and Rupert – would bark at her to sit down. As she mock got up and down five times in as many seconds all of them were laughing so much that Sylvie, Sam and Ellie were crying.

Clutching onto the side of the banquette she tried to compose herself when she heard Marion break the mood with one more quick ululation. As everyone's head spun around they saw Alex approaching with a tray full of warm, sweet-smelling, sticky-looking baklava.

'One final treat,' he said, putting it down by her.

'Does it have to be?' she heard someone whisper flirtatiously in his ear, before realizing the words had come from her own lips. He held her gaze again; it was a miracle their eyes were still fully functioning, there had been so many meaningful stares this evening.

Then he turned to her ear and whispered back, 'There is so much more to come. I promise.'

She felt all goosebumpy as he spoke, the tingle racing up her spine and back down to her toes, making her a bit gooey in the middle. Rather like the baklava.

She quickly looked around to see if anyone else had noticed but everyone was busy munching on the sweet layers of pastry. Sam was licking his fingers and Ellie was reaching for more. She was safe. She quickly double-checked – nope, not even the Marksharp boys had blinked. Phew. She supposed it was a good thing they were all here. Otherwise she would be peeling this man's clothes from his delicious frame right now. He cooks, sews, dances (badly) and does all the manly stuff as well – who could blame her? Personally, she thought she deserved some kind of medal for being so staunch about resisting him up until now.

'Right, up we jump.' Marion's tone, back to her usual Mary Poppins briskness, galvanized the room; up the three boys popped and Sam and Ellie with them.

'Oops, no, Sam and Ellie, you're staying here.'

'Oh, but Alex, they want to see the puppy,' Marion interjected, very firmly, as if there were to be no argument. Back to her old self.

But it appeared that Alex had finally learnt to be brave in the face of Marion.

'It's late, it's been a crazy day and you've spent most of it helping us. They can see the puppy another time. Sam has been to hospital.'

'Yes, that's true and they could, but it's a Friday, I'm only around the corner and a good brisk walk will have them fast asleep in no time. Let me take them.' Marion was doing weird stuff with her eyebrow, almost semaphore, just slightly harder to decode. 'In fact, I'm just going to take them. You two can stay here and we'll be back in an hour. Now, who wants to see the puppy?'

'I do, I do.' Ellie jumped up and down.

'I do too, but he's the size of a horse, Ellie, not so much a puppy. I saw him the other day.' Sam shot Marion his most suspicious look and Sylvie covered her mouth with her hand. Her boy might not be a natural climber but he was no fool.

'Is he a horse? Oh! Can I ride him? I'm going to get an elephant soon, you know, Mrs Marksharp, so this would be very good practice.'

'No riding their dog, Ellie, or you can't go. Do you understand? We've had enough falls for one day!' Alex used his sternest voice. 'Are you OK with this, Sylvie, it's been a long day for you and Sam. They can see the puppy another day?'

'Please, Mum, please. I'm OK, the doctor said I'm OK, and Mrs Marksharp is probably practically a doctor, aren't you, Mrs Marksharp?'

'I am fully first-aid certified, and we won't go far. I'm sure he'll be quite all right.'

Sylvie wondered if it would make her a bad mother for letting Sam go but as soon as the thought popped into her head so did her mother. *For goodness' sake, fussing makes a fool not a fighter.* Should she let him go and make the most of this hour or so with Alex? Come on, where was life's-too-short Sylvie of a couple of hours ago?

'He seems to be fine. The hospital wouldn't have released him if they had any worries. As long as you keep him in your line of sight, oh, I don't mean that as in, you know, but as long as you keep him close I think it should be fine.'

'Of course I will. You know I will, especially after earlier. Right then, gang, spit spot, let's get going. I'll text you ten minutes before I return them. I'll be about an hour but I'm sure I can entertain them longer if necessary.' She gave both Alex and Sylvie the most terrifying leer and marched all the children out of the garden.

As Sylvie and Alex heard the front door slam, they looked at each other again, and Sylvie gulped. He was so beautiful it took her breath away. She looked at the whole of him, studied him, the curve of his chin, the shape of his brow, those soul-deep brown eyes, the strong, strong lips. Here it was. Her moment to make her words meaningful, her moment to follow through on what she had promised herself. As she sat there, unable to peel her eyes from the most perfect man in front of her, she prayed for the strength to follow her heart.

# Chapter Forty Seven

As she was searching for strength, and letching ever so slightly in between times, Alex came and sat beside her on the rug.

'It seems Marion has strong-armed her way again and left us alone for the evening. Which kind of works for me because there was something I wanted to talk to you about.'

'And me. I wanted to talk to you too.'

'Did you? You can go first, but I kinda really want to too.'

'I tell you what, I'm a bit nervous…' Sylvie decided she might as well be honest and the truth was she was so anxious about messing this up that her tummy was flip-flopping all over the place and she thought she might be sick.

'Nervous? With me? That shouldn't be the case. I'm so sorry.'

'No, no, no, you misunderstand me. I adore you. I'm just nervous about what I have to say so please, you go first.'

Alex grinned. 'You adore me? I like it when you say that. Could you get it tattooed on your hand, do you think, so you're reminded all the time?'

'No, I couldn't. Are you going to speak or shall I?'

'OK, OK, I just wanted to say that I really like having you in my life and I know Ells adores you, like you adore me…'

'I really hope not,' Sylvie muttered.

'Sorry, I didn't catch that.'

'You weren't meant to. Carry on, what are you saying?'

'OK, we know you've had such a rocky time so I, we, wanted to do something to make it special and the kids thought your special Berber-themed party was it, but there is another element to the surprise that they don't know about.'

Oh, goody, was he about to whisk his trousers down and save her from having to make the first move?

'But before I tell you what it is…' Oh, hurry up! '…I want you to know I have heard everything you have said to me so this is purely a platonic gesture, no pressure – this isn't a gift with a hidden agenda, OK? Promise.'

Sylvie looked at him, her face falling slightly. She wasn't keen on platonic any more. She was, however, quite keen on exactly the opposite. Should she speak up now?

Right, she was going to give it a shot.

'Promise, *really*?' she asked. This was his chance. Please say, no, of course not, and then they would both laugh and she could fall onto his face and slide her hands under his T-shirt and all would be perfect.

'Promise. You know how I feel about you, but I made my peace with our relationship some time ago. This isn't me trying to jump your bones, this is me showing you how much I value you. It makes me happy to make you happy, and I'm no saint but for now I'll take that.'

Bugger. She was going to have to tell him she had very definitely changed her mind.

'What I'm trying to say is that I know you said you really wanted to go to Morocco and learn more about the Berbers on the ground there, follow up your passions. Now, I obviously can't wave a magic wand and make all your dreams come true…'

'You're doing pretty well so far,' Sylvie mumbled.

'I swear, for some reason you have the worst diction ever this evening. Are you OK?'

'Yep, yep. Go on.' She had decided to hear him out before forcing herself on him.

'But – and I know you have very firm views on him but I'm hoping this might change your mind – Hector has a house in Morocco. Actually, he has two, one in Marrakesh and another in Tangier. So in an attempt to make up for his rudeness on Bonfire Night and because I asked him and because he really isn't as big a knob as he appears, he has gifted us the keys to both to use at your convenience. And I have…'

Sylvie couldn't believe it! Alex had now managed to find her a place to stay in Morocco. Whether she liked Hector or not was irrelevant, she could take Sam and they could go and explore and do all the things she had always wanted. She launched herself at Alex, peppering his face in kisses, furiously, like a three-year-old with a new guinea pig.

'Oh gosh, sorry.' She pulled herself back again. She wanted to go for sophisticated and sexy when she made her move, not this, not this at all. But it was all just so exciting. This man was absolute perfection. She didn't know how the hell she was going to afford the flights, but they would walk and swim if they had to. It's just it would be even better if…

335

'How big are his houses?'

'Oh, bloody huge.'

'Would you and Ellie come with us?'

'Are you serious? We would love to. That would be awesome.'

'I can't believe you've done this, I don't… don't really know what to say.'

'You don't need to say anything. And the fact that your first comment was to ask if Ellie and I could come is more than enough. That in itself is pretty awesome. But you know, we don't have to – don't feel you have to take us.'

'Are you insane? It would be so much more fun with you two. We're like a proper little family.'

'We are. I like it.'

'So do I.'

There was a silence while they just stared at each other and the hairs rose up on Sylvie's arms as she considered that this could be her moment, this *should* be her moment. She smiled sheepishly at him; she didn't really know how to smile seductively and suspected she'd look a bit like she was having a fit if she tried, but sheepish she excelled at. And then just as she planned to move in he started to speak again. Gah!!

'And, sorry, but just this bit and then I'm done and you can say anything you like. Honest.'

'Go on.' If she couldn't kiss him, she was quite happy listening to him. Not quite as good but a close second. And she was definitely going to try the kiss thing as soon as she could.

'And, just so this is a happy thing, with no stresses, and I hope you're not cross, but I set up an Avios account in your name – that's the new name for air miles – I've accumulated so many, like so many, over the years that I thought if I could give you a chunk you could fly whenever suited you without having to worry about prices outside of term-time and all that stuff. Now...' he took a deep breath and leant against the banquette and Sylvie could feel his eyes warm every last bit of her, '...I'm sorry I monopolized all of that and I hope you forgive me, but I was a bit excited and I wanted to let you know what all this was about. So that's it. I'm done. It seems we're all going to Morocco. Now, your turn, and I promise not to interrupt. What was it you wanted to say to me?'

Sylvie looked at him and knew exactly what she wanted to do – it was just she had no idea how to translate it into words. She wasn't good at fancy statements; Alex was eloquent, she was just her. Oh God, he was waiting so patiently, how on earth could she say it? Should she say how much she respected him? No, that was dull.

Should she say that just glimpsing the tops of his arms poking out of his T-shirt sleeves was enough to make her want to rip his zip down? No, that was pervy.

Should she say she was an idiot and she should never have said he wasn't her type when he was exactly that? In fact, she had discovered Alex was now her only type. Just him. Only him.

Oh God, what could she say?

She drew a deep breath, opened her eyes wide, leant in, the smell of him making her dizzy, and chose her words.

'Alex.'

'Yes.'

'You are my best friend, and the best man I have ever known, and I'm afraid I may have mucked everything up but I have fallen so deeply in love with you I don't know

337

what to do. Other than grab the moment. So I'm grabbing the moment and I'm telling you how I feel. So please, kiss me now before I explode, and never ever use the word *platonic* about us again. Unless I've got this all wrong and I've just made a complete tit of myself in which case, pass me my coat and I'll slide out and we'll pretend I never said any of this. But I would much prefer the kiss. I'm really hoping you would too.' The words were measured and slow, despite her embarrassment and determination just to get them out. She felt like an idiot. That barely made sense. Except it seemed it did.

'Really? You're not just saying it because of this evening?'

'Oh, dear God, man. Yes, I mean it. Just bloody kiss me.'

And Alex, with bright eyes and a racing heart, leant in and did exactly what he was told.

# Acknowledgements

I'd like to thank my editor, sunshine girl and all-round superstar, Hannah Todd at Canelo, for all her hard work and support. I can't tell you all how much I enjoy working with her. And another big thank you to my agent, Hayley Steed, for putting up with my questions and always doing so with a smile, you are a joy.

I also have to mention how blown away I was with the huge support for the first book from the book blogging community. You have been amazing and have made writing this second book in the series so much easier. I really can't thank you enough. Then there's the romance writing community and the writers I have met through the RNA, you're all awesome.

My friends in teaching, and who shall remain anonymous, thank you for letting me badger you constantly with queries. You are remarkably patient.

Then there's the offspring, sharp-tongued little demons who make the best soup in the world. And another thank you to my parents, ever supportive.

Also a big shout out to the decking gang, I love you, miss you and shall be back!